UNDER THE
PAPER MOON

UNDER THE PAPER MOON

SHAINA STEINBERG

KENSINGTON
PUBLISHING CORP.

www.kensingtonbooks.com

KENSINGTON BOOKS are published by

Kensington Publishing Corp.
900 Third Avenue
New York, NY 10022

All Kensington titles, imprints, and distributed lines are available at special quantity discounts for bulk purchases for sales promotion, premiums, fund-raising, educational, or institutional use. Special book excerpts or customized printings can also be created to fit specific needs. For details, write or phone the office of the Kensington Special Sales Manager: Attn. Special Sales Department, Kensington Publishing Corp, 900 Third Avenue, New York, NY 10022. Phone: 1-800-221-2647.

Library of Congress Control Number: 2023951498

The K with book logo Reg. U.S. Pat. & TM. Off.

ISBN: 978-1-4967-4780-8
First Kensington Hardcover Edition: May 2024

ISBN: 978-1-4967-4781-5 (ebook)

10 9 8 7 6 5 4 3 2 1

Printed in the United States of America

For Akiva

Chapter 1

Los Angeles, 1948

Evelyn Bishop often thought the inside of Ciro's night-club looked like a courtesan's fever dream. All white, the décor managed to be both tacky and boring at the same time. It was not a place Evelyn would normally choose for a night out, though she could afford the over-priced cocktails and her natural beauty fit in among the celebrities. More than a few starstruck autograph seekers veered toward her table, before realizing they did not know her name. Evelyn wasn't sure whether to feel flattered, amused, or slightly saddened that fame carried such currency. Anonymity had always been her preference.

"What do you think, Evie?"

She turned to James Hughes, sitting across from her. Tall and handsome, with dark brown hair and hazel eyes, he was almost too attractive for Evelyn. She preferred men with imperfections. They were usually more interesting, having the burden of developing a personality, rather than relying upon their looks. James's one quirk was the way his hair curled at random, defying the gel he used to slick it down. She found it endearing and often longed to tuck it behind his ear.

"Think of what?" she asked.

"The house."

"What house?" she said. Then, seeing his bemused expression, she apologized. "My mind's wandering."

James followed her gaze to a large man in his midfifties. Cigar smoke curled from his mouth as he reached for his martini and drained it in a single swig. A fresh one arrived before he had the chance to ask. He thanked his waitress with a five-dollar bill and a question. Evelyn was too far away to hear what it was, but the girl leaned forward, deftly offering him a glimpse down her low-cut dress. She had a cute figure and a fresh-from-Tulsa expression that still carried dreams of stardom.

"George Palmer," James said, naming the man. "He supplied tank munitions and bombs. He was rich before the war. Now I can't even imagine."

"He keeps interesting company," Evelyn said, looking at his companion. A middle-aged man, his expensive, understated suit belied the fact that he was Mickey Cohen's bookkeeper, and one of the most dangerous people in Los Angeles.

"Norman Roth," James said. "I worked with him in London."

"Never pegged him as the type to enlist in the army."

"He's Jewish. Still had family in Germany."

"Oh," Evelyn said softly.

"He's a good man," James said. "Well, maybe not *good*, but we got along."

Evelyn returned to the subject at hand. "So, the house is in Benedict Canyon."

"Four bedrooms. Pool. View of the hills."

"Four bedrooms is a lot," Evelyn replied.

"Room for kids," James said.

"Whose kids?" Evelyn asked warily.

"Urchins we pick up from the street," James teased.

"We'll put them to work cleaning the grout on the Spanish tile."

"Or teach them to swim so they can scour the bottom of the pool."

"Send them out with a pair of scissors to trim the grass."

Evelyn laughed; then the smile slid from her face.

"I don't know if I want kids," Evelyn said.

"You'd make a great mother," James offered.

Evelyn was not convinced. She knew herself to be selfish in small, petty ways: the indulgence of reading the newspaper with her coffee, of sleeping late on the weekends, of settling down with a good book and not rising until she had finished. They were luxuries she did not take for granted. Plus, after all she had seen in the war, it was hard to imagine bringing a child into this world.

"Buying a house isn't meant to pressure you," James said. "I've been in love with you for longer than I can remember. Don't see that changing anytime soon."

"What if I can't give you what you want?" Evelyn asked.

"You're what I want," he replied with absolute confidence.

Evelyn leaned across the table and kissed him. It lingered with the promise of something more. Sitting back in her chair, she watched George Palmer drain the rest of his martini, setting the glass down with a heavy thud. The waitress handed off her tray and apron, then headed toward the ladies' room.

"I'm going to powder my nose," Evelyn said.

"Your nose isn't shiny," James replied.

"Gotta love a good euphemism."

James looked over his shoulder to where George Palmer was signing his check.

"We're not here for the dancing, are we?" he asked with a knowing smile.

"Don't ask questions you don't want the answers to."

"Fine, but if you're not back soon, I'm picking the next drink," James threatened.

Evelyn made her way toward the ladies' room, where she found the waitress sitting on a low ottoman in front of a mirror. She had changed from her uniform into a cotton dress, cinched tightly at the waist. Her golden hair held its perfect curl, not moving as she turned her head in each direction to check her makeup. Evelyn sat next to her and pulled out her lipstick. She removed the bottom to reveal a small lens. Twisting it, she took pictures of the girl in the mirror.

"You have an admirer out there," Evelyn said as she dabbed perfume on her wrists.

"That's a nice scent," the waitress said.

"Thanks."

"Like something my mother would have worn. Old-fashioned."

Though she said it with a bright, cheerful smile, Evelyn had no doubt the remark was meant to be cutting. At twenty-eight, Evelyn knew she was past the time when most of her contemporaries were married with children, but she also believed women grew more interesting as they aged.

"You're what? Twenty?" Evelyn asked.

"Nineteen."

"That seems like a lifetime ago," Evelyn replied. She had been to war and the experience aged her more than the years alone. "That must feel doubly so for George Palmer."

The girl's eyes darted to Evelyn's in the mirror.

"I didn't realize you knew him."

"Everyone knows him," Evelyn said noncommittally. "And his wife."

"I haven't met her . . . though I'm sure I will soon."

Snapping her clutch shut, the waitress headed for the door. After a moment, Evelyn picked up her bag and followed the girl into the alley behind the club. Evelyn crept through the shadows, moving silently on the balls of her feet. The girl rounded a corner to where a car idled on the street. George Palmer stepped out. Evelyn snapped a few pictures as Palmer kissed the girl's cheek and helped her slide into the back seat. He followed her in and closed the door. The car pulled away and disappeared down Sunset.

Evelyn dropped the camera into her purse, then turned back toward Ciro's. The alley was dark and empty, with a few dumpsters beside the building. As Evelyn walked, she heard footsteps fall in behind her. It was tempting to think this was nothing more than coincidence, but coincidence could get a person killed. The heavy tread of a man's shoes grew closer and Evelyn sped up, seeking the comfort of darkness. The man quickened his pace. It was still another hundred yards to the back door. She slipped behind a dumpster and waited. The man walked past, then stopped, realizing his quarry had disappeared. Evelyn pulled out her gun and stepped out of her shoes. On stocking feet, she tiptoed until she was behind the man and grabbed him around the neck. She placed the gun in the small of his back.

"Why are you following me?" she asked.

"Hello, Evie," he said.

Slowly she released him, recognizing the voice. He turned and pulled off his fedora.

"Nick Gallagher," she said, stunned.

Chapter 2

London, March 1942

Evelyn met Nick at the Office of Strategic Services, or OSS, located at 70 Grosvenor Street, in London. Officially the US clandestine organization, it was often a home for those, like Nick, who did not fit in the regular army. Self-taught and brilliant, he made up for his lack of formal education by reading every book he could find. Yet, he was also plagued by demons that came close to getting him court-martialed. His commanding officer, appreciating his fearlessness, and frustrated by his irreverence, sent him to a place where his talents would be put to good use.

When Evelyn first found him, he was in an office, draped over the arm of a couch, so hungover his hair hurt. From the bullpen outside, the sound of typewriters and telephones was cacophonous, and he struggled to keep the morning's dry toast in his belly. Evelyn stood in the open doorway, letting the sound assault his pain-addled brain.

"No," he said without looking up. "Whatever it is, the answer is no."

"So I'm not supposed to report to you?" she asked.

Her voice was clear and light. There was a laughing

quality about it, as if the sight of his distress was less pathetic and more an understood misery. She shut the door and he noticed her perfume for the first time. The scent of summer roses cut through the musty smell of last night's booze seeping from his pores. He opened his eyes to see a woman looking down at him, one brow cocked as she assessed this mess of a man. He sat up quickly, making his head spin. It took another minute before he found his feet and stood to face her. He smoothed down his wrinkled shirt, stained with sweat, and straightened his tie.

"I don't think that's going to help," she said. "There's lipstick on your collar."

He didn't remember a woman from the night before. Then again, he also had no idea when he last washed his clothes. In contrast, she was impeccable, dressed in a tailored navy suit. Its color set off her bright green eyes. Her dark hair shone in the dim light, and he realized he was standing in front of the most beautiful woman he had ever seen.

"What can I do for you?" Nick asked.

"General Gibson sent me to find Mr. Gallagher. Said I should look for a hungover puddle of a man. Seems like I found him."

"Sorry, are you a secretary?" Nick asked, his mind struggling to keep up with this conversation.

"Don't type," Evelyn said. "Don't make coffee."

"What do you do?"

"I speak five languages, I'm a crack shot with a rifle, and I excel at jumping out of perfectly good airplanes. Also, I make a mean vodka martini."

"You're a spy," Nick said.

"Will be, as soon as you accept me on your team."

The last thing Nick wanted on his team was a woman. In fact, he didn't want a team at all. He was faster at gathering information on his own and he rarely trusted others to be competent. General Henry Gibson, who ran the missions, tried to convince him there were times when he needed an extra hand. What Nick could not admit was that he hated being responsible for someone else's life. He had been alone since he was twelve when his parents abandoned him, and by now, he was good at it. Other people made things complicated. Especially a woman who looked like Evelyn Bishop.

"It's too dangerous," Nick said.

"For me or you?"

"Both of us."

"Are you afraid I'll be a distraction?" Evelyn asked.

He was, but damned if he would admit it.

"Why do you want to do this?"

"Women can get into places men can't," Evelyn said. "We're less suspicious and soldiers always try to impress us. Besides, I speak French like a Parisian and spent my summers outside Marseille."

"That's not the real reason," Nick said.

"My reasons are my own," Evelyn insisted.

"Not when they can get me killed."

Evelyn snapped open her purse and withdrew a photograph. It was of a handsome man in his midtwenties. She handed it to Nick.

"His name's Matthew."

"Your husband?" Nick asked.

"Brother. He was captured by the Nazis seven months ago."

Nick felt an unwelcome relief at the word "brother."

"Looking for revenge is a quick wat to get dead," Nick warned.

"I said he was captured. Not killed. There are two ways my brother is coming home. One is if we find him and put him on a plane to the States. The other is if we end this war as soon as humanly possible. The first is my reason for going into the field. The second is the reason I'm willing to follow orders. Any other questions?"

"I can't protect you out there. When it comes to a choice between you and the mission, I'll save the mission."

Though he didn't know it at the time, it was the first of many lies he told himself when it came to Evelyn Bishop.

"Make you a deal," she said. "If you can get me in a hold I can't break, I'll walk out of this office and you'll never see me again."

"I don't want to hurt you," Nick said.

"You won't."

Tentatively Nick stepped up behind her and wrapped his arm around her neck.

"That the best you got?"

He pulled her close until she was pressed against him.

"Better?" he asked.

She pulled his thumb back at the same time she brought her heel down on his instep. With her other arm, she rammed her elbow into his sternum and he bent over in pain, releasing her. There was a knock on the door and General Gibson entered. He glanced at Nick, catching his breath, and then at Evelyn, who still looked impeccable.

"Getting acquainted?" General Gibson asked.

"I think this'll work out just fine," Evelyn said brightly.

"What's the worst that can happen?" Nick asked, resigned.

The worst was that in their three years of working together, he fell in love. Heart and soul, body and mind. All of it was hers.

Chapter 3

Los Angeles, 1948

At first glance, Nick looked the same as when Evelyn last saw him. The frequently broken nose tilted at a familiar angle and his broad shoulders still made him seem taller than six feet. Upon closer inspection, his eyes were shadowed with exhaustion and the edges of his mouth were set in rigid lines. His clothes were shabby, as if the effort of laundry eluded him. This was closer to the man she found at 70 Grosvenor all those years ago than the one she remembered at the end of the war.

"I see you haven't lost a step," Nick said.

"It's been two and a half years."

"Two years, eight months, and seventeen days."

"I can't do this," she said, slipping back into her shoes.

Pushing past him, she threw open the door to Ciro's. Nick followed her.

"Evie, wait!"

"You should know better than to chase women down alleys at night."

"I didn't think you'd stop for me."

"I wouldn't have," she said.

Nick grabbed her arm and wheeled her around. The darkness of the hallway shielded them from the main room. Behind them, couples danced and the band played Louis Armstrong. It felt like forever since they danced together at the USO, him pressed against her, their breath in harmony. She remembered looking into his eyes and feeling like she could see the whole trajectory of her life.

Now the air between them was irrevocably changed.

"I didn't know you were back in Los Angeles," she said.

"Carl got me a job at the LAPD."

Evelyn raised her eyebrows in surprise. The three of them served together during the war, often behind enemy lines. Risking death on a regular basis meant trusting each other and being vulnerable in a way they had never been before, nor would ever likely be again. It made them family. When Evelyn came home to Los Angeles, feeling like an exposed nerve, Carl was the first person she looked up. Late at night, when neither could sleep, they went out for drinks and talked about the old times. It was too painful to ask about Nick, and Carl never volunteered information. Yet, somehow, she thought she would have known if Nick was here.

"How long until you washed out of the police?" Evelyn asked.

"Less than a year."

"Never could follow orders."

"You're one to talk."

He said it lightly. Once upon a time, she would have taken it as the joke he intended. Instead, his words stung, bringing up the memory of his betrayal.

"I have to get back to my table," she said.

He followed her gaze to where James sat.

"If it wasn't for that lipstick camera, I'd almost believe you were reformed," Nick said.

"The war taught me I do one thing very well."

"Oh," Nick said with a smile. "If memory serves, I can think of a few things you do very well."

It was the same smile that always gutted her. Secret, seductive, as if they were the only two people in the world. Once, it got her blood pumping just a little faster. Now it was salt in a wound that had never fully healed.

"What that sniper in Somme started, I'm happy to finish," she said, tapping his chest, where she knew a bullet tore his flesh.

Nick nodded toward James. At the table, a waitress set down two large rum cocktails. Adorning them were hunks of pineapple and maraschino cherries, held in place with paper umbrellas.

"That guy have any idea of your many talents?"

It was a question he no longer had the right to ask.

"Yes," Evelyn said.

The smile fell from Nick's face. He feared that answer, but never expected to receive it. Not that he should judge. Lord knows he had not lived as a monk these past few years. There was a difference, though, between women whose names he didn't remember and this man waiting for her at a brightly lit club. He probably woke to her smile and felt her breath on his chest as he fell asleep at night. The way Evelyn looked at him, it was clear he was more than just an evening's entertainment.

"You have changed," Nick said, nodding toward the fruity concoctions in front of James. "No one goes from liking good scotch to . . . whatever that is."

"That?" Evelyn replied. "That's my new life. The one you guaranteed when you betrayed me in London."

"I didn't betray you."

"Then what was it?"

Nick didn't answer.

"We're done here," Evelyn said.

Nick grabbed her arm and pulled her back.

"Let me go," she said. "Unless you're going to explain what the hell happened."

"Evie . . ." Nick started. "I'm gonna need those photos."

"What?" she asked, confused at the sudden turn of conversation.

He nodded toward her purse.

"The photos of George Palmer."

"You're working security."

"Among other things," he said. "And you're a private investigator."

"Not quite the same as fighting Nazis, but it beats the hell out of the Junior League."

Evelyn opened up her bag and fished out the lipstick camera. She turned it over in her hand, contemplating it.

"If it weren't for these, would I even know you were in LA?"

"You made it pretty clear you didn't want to see me."

"You didn't even try."

"Evie, please."

Evelyn looked toward the camera in her hand; then she dropped it back into her purse.

"No."

"You're impossible," he said.

"At least some things haven't changed."

With that, Evelyn stepped out of the darkness into the blinding light of the main room. The music seemed louder, the dancers faster, and everything contained a slightly frenetic energy. Making her way through the crowd, she sat down across from James.

"You all right?" he asked. "You look as if you've seen a ghost."

"I did."

"Want to talk about it?"

Evelyn shook her head no, then took a tentative sip of the drink in front of her.

"Sweet Baby Jesus. What the hell is this?"

"Punishment for taking so long," James laughed.

"You're never picking the drinks again."

"Then don't ever leave me."

He reached across the table and took her hand. It was a reassuring gesture. One he did a thousand times without thinking about it. She tried to match his smile, but her eyes drifted back to the hallway. Nick was gone.

Chapter 4

Kingsnorth Air Force Base, England, March 1944

Kingsnorth Air Force Base was located just outside London. B-17 bombers and P-51 Mustangs stood in perfect rows, waiting to fulfill their deadly promise. Stationed in nearby barracks, American and British soldiers anxiously awaited the order to cross the Channel. The upcoming battle would be brutal, with every inch measured in blood.

Even more than most, Evelyn and Nick anticipated D-Day. They had spent the last six months laying groundwork in the French countryside, so the Allied troops would find support from the Resistance. They gathered information about Nazi strongholds and which roads offered the safest path. During the two years they worked together, Nick and Evelyn reached a comfort level that was greater than words. The effort of keeping secrets and the danger they faced bonded them. In their missions, they developed a profound trust and learned to respect each other's skills. Initially they were wary of their growing attraction, each wanting to put the mission first. Yet, as the war progressed, and they realized how life could change in an instant, it seemed foolish to deny they were in love. Her smile warmed a place in his soul he had not known existed. Meanwhile, Evelyn felt truly seen and understood for the first time in her life. Nick did not want or need her to be anything other than she was at that moment. There was no future and no past. There was simply the immediacy of now.

Killing time before their next assignment, Evelyn and Nick found themselves dancing inside a crowded USO hall. Her dark curls threatened to escape their pins and he longed to run his fingers through them, like he had that morning. Reading his thoughts, she laughed, her eyes twinkling as the music switched to one of their favorites: "It's Only a Paper Moon."

" 'But it wouldn't be make-believe, if you believed in me,' " Nick echoed the chorus.

"Don't you know?" Evelyn said. "I'll always believe in you."

He looked into her eyes. Their green depths filled him with hope. She saw past his rough exterior to the parts of his soul he kept hidden from the rest of the world. With her, he no longer felt the need to be guarded and angry. Those qualities that kept him alive through a brutal childhood, and ensured his safety during the war, had no place when he was beside her. She still wore the same perfume as that first day and roses became his favorite scent. Nick rested his hand gently above her hip. The skin was newly knit together after she caught a bullet during a mission three months ago.

It was supposed to be a simple handoff in Saint-Malo, France. Evelyn stopped in a café for lunch with Theo, a member of their four-person team. When the check came, Theo borrowed the waitress's pen. Inside was a roll of microfilm. They did not know that the secretary stealing the information had been discovered and tortured. They also did not know that the five-year-old daughter of their contact in the French Resistance was being held by the local Gestapo. They left the café and continued on their way, intending to meet up with Nick that night. The Pont Louis Martin was a natural choke point. As they crossed the short bridge, a jeep filled with Nazi soldiers blocked off the far end. They turned to see another jeep behind them. For a moment, they stood like deer in headlights. Then Evelyn whispered, "Go!"

They broke toward the edge of the bridge. The first bullet hit Evelyn, entering two inches above her hip. She tumbled over the low railing, into the water. Looking back for Theo, she heard more gunfire. It was only later she learned that the second bullet caught him in the thigh and the third shattered his knee. Unable to flee, he was picked up by the Gestapo, and they took him back to their headquarters. Theo was tortured; then his broken body, alongside that of the secretary, the French Resistance fighter, and his child, were displayed in the center of town as a warning to others.

Despite losing a lot of blood, Evelyn managed to swim over a mile in the freezing water to a beach outside Dinard. When night fell, she crept into town, stole some fresh clothes, and broke into the town's small pharmacy. There was no penicillin, but Evelyn found a few sulfa packets and sprinkled them into the wound. Wrapping it tightly, she prayed the ocean's salt water had acted as a disinfectant. She took several more bandages, as well as a bottle of pills to keep her awake. It was two more days of walking at night and hiding during the day before she reached the rendezvous point outside Évran. There she found Nick frantic with worry. They didn't know how to mourn Theo. It was the first time they had lost someone that close to them. His death pierced their sense of invincibility. They missed his intrepid optimism and dark humor.

He was the only one who could find a silver lining while lying in a bomb crater. Instinctively, they still looked for him to have their backs, and when that space was empty, the pain hit them anew. Evelyn's sorrow came out at night, when she wept in her sleep. Nick's manifested as an almost-paranoid concern for his team, especially Evelyn.

"I'm fine," she said, gently touching Nick's face and bringing him back to the dance floor in the USO.

"It keeps getting worse."

"The missions?"

"The fear that I'll lose you. I wish you'd sit this one out," he said.

"Please. Your French will get everyone killed."

"Aren't I allowed to worry about you?" Nick asked.

"Of course, you are. But you're not allowed to stop me."

"You know, one day all this will be over," Nick said.

"You'll miss it."

"Sure. The barely eatable rations. The crappy cigarettes. The freezing nights spent hiding out in barns. What's not to miss?"

"The adventure," she said. "The excitement."

"I've had adventure enough for a lifetime," he said. "What I want is a small cottage on the beach back in California."

"You'd be bored senseless."

"With a room just for books."

"I give it two weeks," she said.

"And you."

"Oh, we'd kill each other in less time than that," she laughed.

Nick pulled her in for a kiss. In it, was all his longing and love.

"Well, maybe we'd make it two weeks," she conceded.

"You came to find your brother," Nick said.

"Matthew's still out there."

"Yes, but in a few months, the Allies will invade. It won't be long until they're in France. Then Germany. The war will be over and we'll be done."

"I wasn't meant for a 'white picket fence' kind of life," Evelyn replied. "I'm not the girl who's going to cook dinner every night."

"I've had your cooking," Nick said. "That's torture I wouldn't wish on the lowest German soldier."

Evelyn slugged him playfully.

"You know what I mean. I love this life."

"And I love you."

"I love you, too," she said.

All he had to do was look in her eyes to see the truth of that statement. Nick did not often speak of the future, fearing to jinx its possibility with words. Sometimes, though, in the small hours of the morning, in that space between dream and waking, when Evelyn was at his side, it felt safe enough to whisper his desires. It did not have to be a cottage on the beach. It could be a house in the suburbs or an apartment in the city, or anywhere with enough space to put down roots. He was desperate for a place to call home and a family of his own. Before meeting Evelyn, he had never believed himself a person capable of love. He used to think love was a weakness. Evelyn showed him it was his greatest strength.

From behind Nick, David, the newest member of their team, approached. His uniform was crisp and clean and his face carried the buoyant optimism of the recently deployed.

"It's time," he said.

As the song came to the end, Nick took Evelyn's hand and led her from the dance floor. France awaited.

Chapter 5

James drove up the long driveway to Evelyn's house in Bel-Air. The three-story brick mansion was hidden behind tall trees and a wrought-iron fence. The Tudor-style building looked more like it belonged in the English countryside than among the palm trees. Behind it, the lawn extended back toward the hills. During her childhood, Evelyn, Matthew, and James would get lost there for the better part of the day, chasing lizards and creating new worlds in their imaginations.

As they grew older, the deep azure of the pool held more promise. They enjoyed the lazy afternoons and a teenage Evelyn appreciated the chance to observe James without his or Matthew's notice. She lived for the moments when he pulled her into the pool beside him. The feeling of his arms around her waist was enough to fuel her daydreams for weeks. Even now, there were times when it surprised her to see her childhood crush sleeping beside her. Rarely did life fulfill the promise of youth.

During the war, Evelyn worked nonstop. After each mission, she returned to her small attic room in London that held little more than a few changes of clothes, some family pictures, and letters from her father. Though her team was often granted leave, it rarely amounted to more than a day or two to recuperate, before they were sent to the next place. Not that she minded. The constant motion focused her mind on something other than her responsibility for all the lives they tried, and sometimes failed, to save. It was only after the Allies declared victory in Europe that Evelyn had the chance to stop and consider everything she had endured and everyone she had lost. Her experiences swept over her and she was crushed like a tin soldier under the treads of a tank.

It took a full year before she was able to return to Los Angeles, not knowing how to pick up the mantle of her old life. She had wandered the broken countryside of Europe, before finally catching a ship across the Atlantic, then taking a train over the vast expanse of her native country. She needed the incremental steps to readjust to a place unscarred by war. It was still a shock when she stepped out of Union Station to see the clock tower, tall and white against the bright blue sky. She had gotten used to ruins.

Those first weeks home, Evelyn felt like she was underwater. Sometimes it felt like serenely sitting on the ocean floor with the weight of the water pressing down on her. Sometimes she was tossed about on rocky shoals, never knowing how to surface. She wandered aimlessly through her house, picking up objects and putting them back down again. In the mornings, she swam in the pool, and in the evenings, she sat outside, watching the sky grow dark. Though Evelyn told no one about her arrival, somehow the rumor spread. Invitations flooded in for various dinner parties, casual tennis games, and charity organizations, all looking to welcome the heiress to the Bishop fortune. Evelyn did not respond to a single one.

One night, her father, Logan, invited James to dinner.

Evelyn knew he had worked for Logan since his discharge from the army, but it was still a shock to see him. When they were growing up, James felt more Matthew's than hers. The few times they saw each other in London, they both belonged to the war. Now he was a man who belonged to no one but himself. He was both a stranger and one of her oldest friends. For the first time in a long while, she felt her heart beat. Initially, it was a faint sound and she was startled to realize she had been numb to it for longer than she could remember. It reminded her that she was alive.

Each time she saw James, she felt another breath enter her lungs. He was here and he was real. Their history meant she could skip the effort of getting to know him. All the unendurable small talk never arose, nor did he ask her questions she did not want to answer. Their comfortable familiarity was tinged with the excitement of realizing they were both different people than the last time they were together in Los Angeles. Though James instinctively understood Evelyn needed time, they did not hide their attraction. It came out in small touches, like the brush of his hand across the small of her back when he held the car door open, or her arm resting against his at the movies. Their relationship grew from dinners that turned to drinks that turned into long conversations that lasted until morning. They talked about the past, but almost never the war. It was still too raw. He encouraged her to build a new life and helped her to see it did not have to be the one everyone expected of her. Though he had not anticipated this would involve working as a private investigator, he supported anything that brought her happiness.

Being with James was easy in the way of all things that seem inevitable. The first time they slept together, it felt like coming home. Evelyn thought back to her childhood crush and knew this was deeper and better than she could have imagined. She felt safe, knowing James would handle her heart gently. Never once had she regretted her decision.

James stopped his car in front of her house. A few lights blazed from the windows.

"Your father's home."

"That's rare. He's been gone a lot recently."

"TWA and Pan Am are ramping up production. Before you know it, Bishop Aeronautics will be the largest airplane manufacturer in the world."

"That's always been Dad's goal."

"So, are you going to tell me what we were doing at Ciro's tonight?" James asked.

"Change of pace. A fun night out."

"Please. Ciro's is everything you hate about Los Angeles."

"I don't *hate* it."

James gave her a skeptical look.

" 'Hate' is a very strong word," she conceded with a smile.

She reached over and flipped on the radio. Edith Piaf sang "*La Vie en Rose.*"

"Dance with me."

"You know I have two left feet," James protested.

"Your only flaw."

"Glad to know I have just one."

"Maybe, given enough time, I'll find a second."

"You can have all the time in the world."

"Dance with me," she said again.

Unable to deny her anything, James got out of the car and opened her door. Helping her to her feet, he put his arms around her waist, pulling her close. He kissed her slow and deep.

"This song was everywhere in Paris after the war," Evelyn said. "It streamed nonstop from the radio. The cafés had musicians playing it day and night. Even the buskers couldn't get enough. For some reason, it made me irrepressibly sad. I didn't know how I'd ever see anything but shades of gray. Then I came home to you."

"One of the best days of my life."

"You brought me back from the dead," Evelyn said. "You gave me hope."

"Do you have any idea how happy you make me?"

This time, it was Evelyn who reached for James and pulled him in for a kiss. In that moment, the ghost of Nick Gallagher was almost vanquished. The brutal memory of war was relegated to the back of her mind. There was only the present as Evelyn swayed in the moonlight with the best man she had ever known.

Chapter 6

Leaning over the marble bar of the billiards parlor, Nick grabbed the bottle of Macallan 30 and sloshed more into his glass. Part of him felt bad for wasting good single malt, but hell, it wasn't his scotch. Wasn't even his home. He was currently staying in George Palmer's mansion.

Nick's plan during the war was always to return to Los Angeles. Like Evelyn, he grew up here, but his childhood revolved around the struggle to endure another day. His family had always been hungry and often cold. His older siblings tried to shield him from the worst of the beatings, but when his father showed up, his breath sour with gin, there was no sanctuary. One day, when Nick was twelve, he came home from school to find new people living in his apartment. His family had disappeared without leaving a note, never mind a forwarding address. Sometimes he wondered if his parents were so drunk they forgot they had a fourth child. Or maybe he was just one burden too many. Nick scrounged what he could from the streets, rummaging through garbage cans and picking pockets along Hollywood Boulevard. He made friends who taught him the art of survival and offered companionship when his loneliness threatened to overwhelm him. When Nick was fifteen, he lied about his age to get a job down on the docks. Every day he plotted his escape, longing to be anywhere else.

The war drained him of his wanderlust. He no longer believed there was a better place waiting for him at the end of a voyage. Now all he wanted was a somewhere to call home. Los Angeles wasn't it. Not without Evelyn. Seeing her tonight was unexpected, and yet he knew he had been waiting for that moment ever since she walked out of his life. There was something unfinished between them. A better man might have called it love. Nick just called it pain.

Breaking from his reverie, he turned at the sound of footsteps.

"That looks like the beginning of a bad morning," George Palmer said, nodding to the half-empty bottle of Macallan.

"Passed that stage a while ago," Nick said.

He held up the bottle and George nodded. Nick reached behind the bar and grabbed another glass. He poured them both scotch as George took the seat beside him.

"Had my share of hangovers during the war," Nick said. "But never when I was in the field."

"It's the adrenaline," George replied.

"Fear of death keeps you from feeling like death?" Nick asked.

"Something like that." George took a sip of his scotch. "My doctor says I drink too much."

"There are worse ways to go," Nick said.

"If you're not careful, you'll beat me there. Want to talk about it?"

"It?"

"Whatever has you down here in the middle of the night. General Gibson said you were a drinker, but right now, you look like a man trying to forget."

"Not forget," Nick said. "Just . . . not feel."

"You ever miss the war?"

Nick stared into his glass. It was a hard question.

"Never thought I would, but yeah. Sometimes," he said. "Things were simpler."

"You knew who your enemies were."

"And your friends."

"You lost people?" George asked.

Nick nodded.

"Me too."

Gently George chimed his glass against Nick's.

"To fallen brothers."

They both drained their glasses. George poured them another round and Nick stared into the amber liquid.

"Do you have any regrets?" Nick asked.

"Too many to mention," George said. "You?"

"Just one."

"Then you're a lucky man."

"Doesn't feel like it," Nick said. "Did the wrong thing for the right reason. Still don't know if I'd make a different decision."

"The things that haunt our dreams are questions of what might have been."

"Sometimes that feels more real."

"Trust me," George said. "If I could go back in time, armed with the knowledge I have now . . ."

"Mr. Palmer, I'm grateful for the work," Nick began. "And all your kindness."

"Please call me George."

"George," Nick amended. "Keeping you safe would be a lot easier if you told me more about the threats you received."

George hesitated.

"I have secrets enough to last a lifetime," Nick said. "But I'll keep your confidence. God knows, I'm the last person to judge anyone."

Carefully George set his glass down. He tapped the rim

a few times, thinking. Nick remained quiet. Sometimes a man needed time to ramp up to a confession. The worse it was, the longer it took to gather his courage.

"I met my wife just before the war," George began. "When I saw her, it was like I'd been hit over the head with a shovel. Everything just stopped. I never believed in love until that moment. And the fact that she seemed to like me, too? How does a person get so lucky? I was determined to bring her back to America, but the Nazis were in her hometown before I could get her out—"

"Sweetheart, what are you doing down here?"

Nick turned to see Colette Palmer standing in the doorway. Her beauty was ethereal. She was in her early thirties and her porcelain skin's unlined perfection spoke of rich creams, gentle care, and a sheltered existence. Her thick silver-blond hair hung down her back in waves, brightly reflecting the pale light. Dressed in a white satin robe, the lace from her nightgown peeked over her firm, round breasts. The fact that her words rang with a French accent only added to her allure. When poets spoke of angels, this was the woman they imagined. Only her eyes betrayed that impression. The color of the sea in a storm, there was a wariness that bore testament to her struggle during the war. Nick wondered how long she stood in the doorway listening to their conversation.

"Sorry, my love," George said with a warm smile. "Did we wake you?"

"I waited up," she purred, coming into his arms. "You were out late."

"Business," George said. "Couldn't be helped."

Colette leaned her head against George's shoulder. Nick looked at the discrepancy between them. This stunningly beautiful woman resting in the arms of an aging businessman whose large body slid into softness years ago. A cynic would guess that his money bought her beauty. Nick admired the fact that she played her part well. To an outsider, the affection between them seemed genuine.

"Come to bed," she said.

George looked to Nick.

"How do you turn down a request like that?"

His arm still around Colette, George headed upstairs. Nick reached for the bottle and poured himself another drink.

Chapter 7

"Quick in and out. You'll blow the German munitions dump outside Lille," General Gibson said to Nick and his team.

They were seated in a wooden building that looked as though it had been thrown up in a few hours. The night wind blew sharply across the fields, through the thin walls. Evelyn was cold, but her only acknowledgment was rubbing her hands together. Beside her, Nick had a restless energy, like he always did before a mission. She knew it was the tension that came from fear—not for himself, but for her, Carl, and now David. At the front of the room was a map of France showing Nazi strongholds. Nick and Evelyn had parachuted into their depths more times than they could count. While these trips were common, they never felt routine. General Gibson made sure of it.

Gibson graduated West Point a few years before World War I. With a uniform that was always crisply pressed, and shoes shined to a high gloss, he emanated the aura of a tried-and-true army man. Yet, his experience in the trenches made him believe all war was evil, though sometimes necessary. His morality and faith guided him at every turn. He was unafraid of standing up to his superiors, especially when it came to protecting those under his command. A brilliant strategist, he was also smart enough to appreciate people's unique strengths. The freedom and support Gibson gave Nick's team made them utterly devoted to him. They knew he would never send them on a suicide mission—at least not without a very good reason.

Carl Santos sat beside Evelyn. After she joined up, Nick handpicked Carl. He was a large man who spoke little, but with purpose. His silence, while appreciated by Nick, wasn't his only appeal. He spoke French fluently, having learned it from his Moroccan grandmother. His Spanish came from his Mexican father. He always kept a book in his back pocket and was not shy about retreating to another world when the present one bored him. Nick met Carl in a bar after he put down five soldiers who didn't know enough to keep their opinions to themselves. Carl never sought a fight, but thought it best to end them quickly. His strength was balanced out by a genuine tenderness. Those he loved, he protected fiercely.

David Bernstein was the newest member of the foursome. At twenty-one, his eyes still carried a light that was undimmed by the horrors of war. Nick's initial reaction was to reject him, but his perfect French, learned in an exclusive East Coast boarding school, and his photographic memory were too valuable to waste. Nick wasn't sure whether David's excitement would prove to be an asset—boosting morale after two years of covert missions and the loss of one of their own—or if his eagerness would ring hollow.

"Your landing point is five klicks south of the munitions dump," General Gibson said, pointing to the map. "Your contact will be waiting."

"Is it Jean?" Evelyn asked.

"It is," Gibson replied.

"Excellent! I haven't seen him in months."

Nick glanced at Evelyn. "Should I be jealous?"

"He is French," Carl said.

"And rakishly handsome," Evelyn added.

"And married," Nick said.

"Like I said," Carl replied. "French."

"Who's Jean?" David asked.

"The leader of the Resistance up north," Nick said.

David nodded as if filing that information away. His hands shook with nervousness. Evelyn remembered her first mission. No matter how many times she imagined what it would be like, nothing could compare to the reality of going behind enemy lines.

"You'll be fine," Evelyn said quietly to him. "You've done the jump before and it's a simple detonation."

"Nothing's simple," Nick snapped. He was thinking of Evelyn's fresh scar and what might have happened, had the bullet drifted a few inches to the right. This would be the third mission they had done since Theo's death, but his absence never got easier.

"After the explosion, you'll spend the night outside Rouen before rendezvousing with our boat at Le Havre," Gibson said. "Any questions?"

There weren't. Nick took Gibson's place.

"You know what I always say. 'Stay smart. Stay alert. Stay alive.'"

Carl quietly crossed himself in a silent prayer; then they made their way to the airfield. The plane shone bright in the moonlight. The crew waited at the bottom of the steps to greet them. While Nick joked with the pilot, Evelyn ran her hands along the silver steel of the plane's skin. As always, she walked carefully around it, checking its airworthiness.

"I know you'll keep us safe," she said to the machine. "I trust you to bring these men home."

The plane didn't respond, but she nodded in satisfaction as if they had an understanding. The crew watched her, standing respectfully aside. The first time she did this, the crew tried to hurry her along, but Evelyn never stepped onto a plane she hadn't checked herself. What began as an annoyance developed into a revered superstition. The average lifespan for a new soldier on a bomber crew was two weeks. Yet, after all their surveillance runs and parachute drops, the one constant was that Evelyn's planes always returned home. She climbed aboard and sat on the bench seat, her back resting against the cold wall. The interior was bare bones, loaded with only what was necessary to carry out the mission. Evelyn secured the belt across her lap and watched Nick talk to David.

"I need to know you're up for this," Nick said.

"Yes, sir," he responded immediately, a quaver in his voice.

"Now's the time to step off if you're uncertain. No one will think less of you."

"No, sir. I mean, yes, sir. I can do it, sir," he said, convincing himself.

"Good man," Nick said, clasping David on the shoulder. Then he took his seat beside Evelyn.

" 'Sir'?" she asked under her breath. "When was the last time someone called you 'sir'?"

"Maybe he'll be a good influence on you and Carl. Finally give me the respect I deserve as your commanding officer."

"Wanna bet how quickly we'll corrupt him?"

"No," Nick grumbled.

The pilot turned onto the runway and the plane picked

up speed, rumbling down the concrete until finally the wheels left the ground and they were weightless. Evelyn always loved the moment of freedom that came from breaking ties with the earth. It was an instant when anything seemed possible. As they climbed, it grew colder in the uninsulated cabin. She shivered slightly. Nick put his arm around her and she curled her body against his. The plane crossed high above the icy currents of the English Channel and they were soon in French airspace.

"Jump's in two minutes," the pilot called from the cockpit.

Everyone shrugged into their parachutes. Evelyn tucked her hair into her helmet and fastened goggles over her eyes. Carl hauled the door open and the bitter air swept over them in a wave. Evelyn looked at Nick and saw the slightest hesitation. She wasn't sure if he even noticed it. An antiaircraft gun sounded from the ground below.

"It's time," she said, pushing past Nick, into the night sky.

Nick followed her out, with David and Carl on their heels. Another round exploded as the plane turned back toward England. They free-fell silently to three thousand feet, where they pulled their chutes. Above them, the dark silk rippled in the wind. Drifting over to David, Nick shepherded him back into close formation. They landed just outside the tree line, gathered their chutes, and hurried under the cover of the forest.

"You know," Nick said, turning to Evelyn, "I'm leading this mission."

"If you wanted to be the first out of the plane, you should have moved faster," Evelyn replied.

"She's got you there, old man," Carl said as he unhooked his parachute.

"Whatever happened to military discipline?" Nick asked.

"I . . . I d-don't know, sir," David stammered.

"He's giving you shit," Carl said.

"No," Evelyn amended. "He's giving *us* shit. You're just along for the ride."

David glanced at Nick, Evelyn, and Carl uncertainly. Behind him, a twig snapped. Before David had time to react, the other three had their guns out.

"You're making enough noise for them to hear you in Berlin," a voice said.

"Jean!" Evelyn said as a man stepped out of the trees. She gave him a warm hug.

"You look marvelous, as always," Jean said to Evelyn. "Why you spend time among these ruffians is beyond me. Whenever you want to throw them over, let me know. I'll show you Paris as you've never seen it. The cafés. The boutiques. The hotels . . ."

"Nick won't mind," Evelyn said.

"Jean's wife might," Nick replied.

"Who can resist such beauty?" Jean asked.

"Flatterer," Nick said.

"I've been called worse."

"You could take lessons," Evelyn teased.

"After the war, we'll all go," Carl said. "Shouldn't be long now."

"What have you heard?" Jean asked.

"What everyone's heard," Nick said. "France will be yours soon."

"Not soon enough. It's been four very long years."

"Let's just worry about tonight," Evelyn said. "Gibson said the camp is five klicks north."

"*Oui,*" Jean said. "But there's a problem."

"Isn't there always?" Nick said.

"It's not just a munitions dump. It's a POW camp."

"Wow. Brilliant. Evil," Nick said. "But brilliant."

"Guess that's why we're here instead of bombing the shit out of it," Carl said.

"So, what's the new plan?" Evelyn asked.

"Same as the old," Nick replied. "Setting them free isn't in our mission parameters."

"You can take your mission parameters and shove them up your—" Evelyn started.

"Careful," Nick said. "You're a lady."

"Would it make you feel better if I said it in French?"

"It'd certainly sound nicer."

"Uh, guys," Carl started. "Nazis there. Us here."

"When we deviate from the mission, people get killed," Nick said.

"You know what happens in a POW camp," Evelyn replied.

It was hellish conditions: backbreaking work, little food, virtually no medical care. In the winter, the wind tore through the flimsy housing. In the summer, water was scarce, leaving more people to collapse from dehydration than from hunger. Whenever POWs escaped back to London, Evelyn sought them out, searching for news of Matthew, or at least a glimmer of hope he might still be alive. Inevitably, she left those meetings even more despondent. Afterward, Nick would find her in the back of a pub, bottle of scotch half-empty. This wasn't the happy buzz of having too many pints. This was the quiet drunk of a person who saw the morning's hangover as well-deserved flagellation.

"Every one of those POWs is someone's brother or son or husband," Evelyn pleaded to her team. "They all have families."

Nick looked to Jean. "It's your country. Your decision. We have no way of getting them back to England."

"The Allied forces will be here soon. They can aid from behind the lines," Evelyn said. "Please, Jean. We can't leave them in there."

"I do hate to disappoint a lady."

She threw her arms around his neck and kissed his cheek.

"Thank you!"

Nick understood Evelyn's reasoning, but he wasn't happy about it. Their mission just got a lot more complicated.

Chapter 8

Evelyn's darkroom was little more than a broom closet with a fan and running water. What was once a high school hobby had become a career necessity. The faint red light cast everything with an eerie glow. Around the room, wet photographs and long strips of negatives hung to dry. Evelyn centered an image on the enlarger. It showed the waitress sliding into the car with George Palmer. Carefully Evelyn expanded it to get a better view and adjusted the focus. Turning off the enlarger, Evelyn pulled a sheet of photo paper out of its black box and carefully slid it into the frame. As she was about to print the picture, the door opened, flooding the room with light.

"Damn it, Daddy!" Evelyn said to her father, Logan.

"Sorry, pumpkin," he said, closing the door behind him.

Logan Bishop was a solid man in his late fifties. His handsome face was tempered by the years he spent battling the sun and wind. He designed his own planes and insisted on testing each prototype that came off the line. It was a matter of principle to risk his own life before letting anyone else step into the cockpit. His dark hair faded to salt-and-pepper, giving him the distinguished look of a man who lived well. He possessed a warmth and kindness that made people instinctively trust him, and his mouth always seemed on the verge of a smile. Like all good businessmen, he took responsibility for failures and shared his success. The people he employed loved him with a fierce devotion and he returned their loyalty in kind.

Gently directing her father out of the way, Evelyn crumpled the ruined photo paper and tossed it into the bin. She set another sheet in the enlarger and exposed it before carrying it over to a wide, shallow developing tray. Logan watched her work. She had the same precision and attention to detail that made him so successful. It was just one of the many ways they were alike.

"You're up late," Logan said.

"Worried about me?" Evelyn asked, transferring the photo to the stop bath.

"Always," Logan said.

Evelyn looked up and smiled. Sometimes she wondered why he had not remarried after her mother died. There were plenty of options, but Evelyn suspected he could never quite give up the ghost of his late wife. The cancer was so fast, it took them by surprise, leaving a gaping hole in their family. Evelyn was only eight years old. Afterward, Logan had only two interests: ensuring his children grew up feeling loved and secure; and his business.

The day Evelyn left for England, they had the worst fight of their lives. With Matthew captured, Logan couldn't stand the idea of his daughter in harm's way. In turn, she argued that she was twenty-two years old and could do as she pleased. In retrospect, it wasn't true. Her death would have destroyed her father. Which was why she never told Logan about her work with the OSS. Instead, she let him believe she spent the war translating documents in London.

Logan looked at the pictures hanging from wires in Evelyn's darkroom.

"Why are you photographing George?" Logan asked, pointing to one from outside Ciro's. The two men had been friends for years.

"You know I can't tell you," Evelyn replied.

"I wish you'd give up all this investigator stuff. It's unseemly."

"Heaven forbid the Junior League gossips about me."

"They're a nice group of women. Your mother was in the Junior League."

"My mother hated the Junior League."

"Well, true, but she still did it."

"Is that supposed to be a recommendation?"

"Maybe?" Logan replied without any hope of persuading her.

Evelyn started to laugh.

"Yeah, that's about as well as I expected it to go over," Logan said with a sigh. "What about getting married? Starting a family."

"Are you that eager to be a grandfather?"

"Yes," Logan said. "But that's not what I mean. You love James, right?"

"Daddy, I don't want to discuss this with you."

"He's a good man, Evie."

"No one's arguing he isn't," she said. "I'm just not sure marriage is my cup of tea."

"I don't understand."

"Mom was so good at all of this. Keeping the house. Looking after Matthew and me. Being a wife. What if that's not who I am?"

"It could be."

"Despite what the world might think, not every woman is meant for that path."

"I just want to make sure you are taken care of."

"Daddy, I have money. I don't need a husband."

When her mother died, she left Evelyn a sizeable inheritance, believing that money could buy the freedom so lacking in most women's lives.

"It's not about need. James loves you," Logan said. "He's good for you."

"And the succession of Bishop Aeronautics would be secure," Evelyn replied.

"That's not—" Logan started.

"I'm sorry," Evelyn said. "I didn't mean that. It wasn't supposed to be James. Or me. It was supposed to be Matthew. He was the one to follow in your footsteps."

Logan closed his eyes, holding back the tears that still sprang forth every time he thought of his son.

"Sometimes I walk by his room and I think I can hear him grumbling about a math problem," Evelyn said. "I keep expecting to see him at breakfast in the morning. I even miss him teasing me about my inability to make eggs."

"You two are what I'm most proud of," Logan replied.

"I wish he'd never gone over there," Evelyn said. "I wish he had a bum leg or a bad eye or something to keep him out of that godforsaken war. Sometimes I hate him for being a hero."

"There is nothing anyone could have done to keep him from joining up," Logan said, gathering Evelyn in his arms. "Just like there was nothing I could do to stop you. You're both so goddamn stubborn."

"Like you," Evelyn replied.

"Like your mother," Logan corrected, ". . . and maybe a little bit like me."

"I'm not going anywhere."

"Not even to a house in Benedict Canyon?"

Evelyn looked up at her father, wondering exactly what James told Logan. Or more specifically, what he asked him.

"I'll support whatever you decide," Logan said. "All I want . . . all I've ever wanted . . . is your happiness."

"I know," Evelyn said. It was the one thing in life she never doubted.

Chapter 9

The perimeter of the German camp consisted of twelve-foot-high barbed-wire fences that were charged with enough electricity to stop a person's heart. Guard towers stood at the corners and midpoints of the fence, armed with machine guns. Their spotlights relentlessly prowled the grounds, searching for hints of insurrection. As Evelyn, Nick, and the others approached, Nazi soldiers shouted for them to halt. Dressed as a French farm girl, Evelyn called for help. Behind her, Carl and Nick, wearing American uniforms, had their hands loosely tied. David and Jean walked beside them, wearing large game bags packed with explosives.

"How do you always get your way?" Nick asked Evelyn as they drew near.

"You should be used to it by now," she whispered. Then, calling out in French, she announced, "We found American spies."

The gate swung open, admitting them to the compound. Nick and Carl were searched by the soldiers, while Jean and David were stripped of their rifles. Jean opened his bag and showed them the rabbit carcasses hiding the explosive charges at the bottom.

"I'd kill to have something other than rabbit stew," Evelyn said. "Perhaps there's a reward for finding these Americans."

"That's a question for the commandant," the soldier replied with a leer. "Drexler will definitely want to speak with you."

The soldier led Evelyn toward the command building in the middle of the camp. Nick hated letting her out of his sight. When she was gone, he was divided in two. One part was always with her, regardless of the mission. It was what he feared that first day she walked into his office. As she disappeared into the building, two other soldiers stepped up, grabbing Nick and Carl by the arms. Nick motioned to the cigarette one of them was smoking.

"Pity for a condemned man?" he asked in broken French. "The least you can do for someone about to enter Hell."

"You got that right," one of the soldiers laughed. Then he shook out a cigarette and handed it to Nick, lighting it for him.

Nick took a few puffs. It was disgusting. Inferior tobacco mixed with dried grass to make it stretch. This was reason enough not to let the Nazis win the war.

"Doesn't seem like there's many of you," Jean said. Then, motioning to Nick and Carl, he asked, "What's to stop these animals from breaking out and coming for revenge?"

"We have fifty men guarding the camps and another twenty in the woods patrolling the border," the soldier said.

"Good to know," Nick said. He grabbed the closest man, pulled the knife from his belt, and slit his throat. Jean withdrew his hidden silenced pistol and shot two more between the eyes. Carl dispatched the last one. They dragged the bodies into the guard shack. They stripped them of their uniforms and dressed as Germans.

"David, Carl. Head to the POW camp," Nick ordered. "Jean, you're with me at the munitions dump."

"What about Evelyn?" David asked.

Carl and Jean laughed quietly.

"She can handle herself," Nick said.

The command building had the industrial feel of a temporary shelter. Evelyn followed the soldier down a narrow hall. He knocked on a door and a loud voice barked for them to enter. A tall, fit man dressed in a crisp uniform sat behind a desk. He looked to be in his late thirties, with blond hair and cold gray eyes. In a different life, he might have been a matinee idol. His face was beyond handsome, and a person might look twice just to stare at its perfection. However, his expression forbore any sort of adoration. It was hard and unrelenting. He studied Evelyn for a moment, then nodded to the soldier.

"Leave us."

The commander stood up from behind his desk and approached Evelyn. Unlike most farm girls who found their way into this office, Evelyn did not shrink from his approach. Maybe, once upon a time, she was a woman who could be intimidated, but those days were in the far-distant past.

"Good evening, mademoiselle, I'm Commandant Drexler," he said in impeccable French. "What brings you to our camp this evening?"

"My brothers and I discovered American spies hiding in our barn."

"Brothers, not husband?"

"I'm unmarried," Evelyn replied.

Drexler smiled. It had an unnerving effect.

"Sit," he said, indicating a chair. He perched on the edge of the desk, his legs brushing against her skirt. "How did you come to find these men?"

"We secured the barn at night, as we always do. But the animals were restless. My brother went to check, fearing it might be foxes, only to discover these men. It was terrifying to find strangers—enemies—in our own home."

"You fought them?" Drexler asked.

"No. We offered them food. They set aside their weapons, thinking we were part of the Resistance."

"That's very smart," Drexler said. He put his hand on Evelyn's shoulder, his eyes dropping to where her blouse buttoned. "Perhaps we can help each other."

"How?"

"You're a beautiful woman," Drexler said. "Beautiful women should have nice things. Chocolate. Cigarettes. Silk stockings . . ."

Was that all it took for someone to betray their country? Evelyn wondered to herself. Aloud, she asked, "What would I have to do?"

Drexler studied Evelyn, his eyes running up the length of her leg as he smiled in anticipation.

"I can think of many things," he said. "But what I need first is information. There's a man called 'Le Reynard.' Perhaps you've heard of him."

Evelyn most certainly had. Jean was currently infiltrating Drexler's munitions dump.

"No," Evelyn lied. "Is he important?"

"We're offering a fifty-thousand-franc reward for information leading to his capture."

It was an impressive bounty.

"Do you know his real name? Or what he looks like? Where he's from?" Evelyn asked.

"He's a ghost. Works with the Resistance and seems to be everywhere at once. No one can tell us anything except that he's sly as a fox."

"I wish I could help," Evelyn said. "That money would mean the world to my family."

"Perhaps there's other ways to help your family," Drexler said, reaching toward her. She pulled away as if frightened.

"My hands. They're shaking," she said, lifting her palm to show him. It was an act she had performed dozens of times. Being a helpless woman made men lower their guard, and when they got too forward, she could plead her virtue to escape. If that didn't work, she also had a knife hidden in her boot.

"You've had a lot of excitement tonight. Can I get you something? Maybe coffee?" he asked.

"You have real coffee?" Evelyn asked with just the right amount of awe in her voice. Only part of it was forced. Even in London, coffee was a luxury.

"I'll go make a pot," Drexler said. He stood and his hand brushed her neck. "Then we can talk about some kind of arrangement."

Drexler stepped out into the hall, shutting the door behind him. As soon as she heard the lock click, she began rifling through his papers. The corners of several shipping manifests were marked with a white cross inside a blue circle. Evelyn pulled open the file drawers, her fingers skipping lightly over the labels. She glanced at a few, looking for secure communication and information about troop movement. It seemed the Germans had an idea about the Allied invasion. They just weren't sure when or where it would happen. Pulling a small camera from inside her blouse, Evelyn photographed everything. As she searched for anything else that might be of use, she discovered a prisoner manifest. Her eyes widened as she read and her heart stopped. The surprise was so great, she never heard the footsteps down the hall, or the creak of the door as it opened.

"I think we need to have a longer chat," Drexler said, setting aside the tray of coffee and pulling his gun from the holster.

Chapter 10

Evelyn's office sat above a small boutique on Rodeo Drive. The street was filled with tony stores selling dresses, shoes, and handbags that cost more than an average person's rent. The sidewalks were swept clean every morning and no one would dare consider something so gauche as spitting their gum on the pristine concrete. Even the palm trees seemed reluctant to shed their fronds.

Evelyn leased the space from Lily Shen, who owned the building and ran the downstairs boutique. Shortly after Evelyn arrived home from the war, she spotted Lily sobbing quietly in the corner of a coffee shop. Evelyn's nature warred between wanting to give this stranger space and the desire to make things better. Lily's grief wasn't something as simple as a husband lost at the front. He was an abusive son of a bitch, who had sent her to the hospital more than once.

When Lily received the telegram notifying her of his demise, she felt relief unlike any she had ever known. She took the money from her husband's life insurance and opened a small shop, importing the latest fashions. The store should have been a huge success, but she was on the brink of bankruptcy. Lily was Evelyn's first client and the thing that gave her a sense of purpose in those first few weeks back in Los Angeles. Evelyn discovered Lily's partner was embezzling, she convinced him to return the money in exchange for not going to prison. Lily's relief made Evelyn realize there might be something more for her than charity galas and tennis at the club.

Lily offered Evelyn space to start her own detective agency. She liked having Evelyn upstairs, calling her "the muscle," in case anything went wrong. Even more, she appreciated the nights, after the boutique closed, when she and Evelyn would put their feet up, drink whisky, and forget, just for a while, to be proper ladies.

The location was perfect for the kind of clients Evelyn attracted. The women—it was always women—who came to see her never needed to venture into a seedy part of town. Instead, they ducked up a private staircase, which was marked by a small brass plaque reading EVELYN BISHOP, INVESTIGATIONS. The walls were painted a soft, comforting blue. She had dove-gray couches on either side of an Art Deco coffee table. Tiffany lamps illuminated the space and a pale green Persian rug lay on the hardwood floor. Evelyn's mahogany desk stood discreetly by the window, as if the business side of her profession was an afterthought. When the women came to her office, she wanted them to think of her as an understanding friend, with whom they could share their secrets. Evelyn made hiring a private investigator feel almost respectable, as if it were just another errand to fit in between getting a haircut and buying new shoes.

Evelyn set a manila folder down on the coffee table. Inside were the photos she developed last night. Colette Palmer's manicured hand picked it up and laid the pictures across the table.

"She's pretty," Colette said, looking at the waitress.

"She's young," Evelyn replied. "Everyone's pretty when they're young."

"And when they're older?" Colette asked wryly.

"True beauty takes time to mature."

"I'm thirty-two," Colette said. "Shouldn't feel as old as it does."

"Neither should twenty-eight," Evelyn replied sympathetically.

Colette picked up the photo of George helping the waitress into the car. He had his hand on her lower back. It wasn't anything definite, but the familiarity was impossible to ignore.

"What do you suppose he's doing with her?" Colette asked.

Evelyn thought for a moment.

"I've known George since I was a child. Before you, there was rarely a woman in his life, at least not one he'd bring to dinner. He's never struck me as a man in search of conquests. You and I don't know each other well. I'd left Los Angeles by the time you arrived, and after the war . . ."

"I'm not much for socializing, either."

"I always imagined George with someone intelligent, sophisticated, and kind."

"And that girl?"

"I spoke with her briefly and found little to recommend her."

"Exactly how old is she?" Colette asked.

"Nineteen."

Colette just shook her head.

"Does it bother you, spying on George?"

"I suppose it should," Evelyn said. "But no. Not really. My father thinks what I do is unseemly, but it comes from a place of curiosity. I want to understand people. Uncovering their secrets is only the beginning. There's always a question of why they behave the way they do. It's rare that people are all good or all evil."

"I used to think that," Colette said.

"What does your gut tell you?"

"George's changed. We made plans to leave Los Angeles. Go somewhere no one could find us. Maybe even start a family. Then a few months ago, he put everything on hold. He began working late, coming home at all hours. He was angry a lot. For the first time in our marriage, he kept secrets. When I asked him about it, he lied to me. There was a tension I hadn't seen since the war. One day, he came home smelling of perfume. It was a cheap scent— vanilla. I thought maybe his secretary, but then I remembered she only wore lilac. I smelled it again a few nights later. That's when I came to you."

"You met George during the war, didn't you?" Evelyn asked.

"Just before. 1939. George came to France to sell weapons to the military, for all the good they did. Once the Nazis invaded, it was unspeakable. The fear, the violence, the uncertainty. You didn't know who to trust."

"I remember," Evelyn said. "I spent a lot of time in Northern France working with the Resistance."

"Le Reynard?" Colette asked.

Evelyn nodded. "Jean Mollet was a good friend. Did you know him?"

"Just by reputation," Colette said. "Maybe if I'd been braver, I wouldn't have so many regrets."

"When did you get out?"

"Not until '43," Colette said. "In the time it took to escape France, George's letters became the only bright spot in my life. I looked forward to them, and when mail became difficult, I re-read them until they were in tatters."

"You love him."

"With all my heart. I know how it looks—the difference in our ages and his money. But I'd be with George, were he penniless and we lived in a shack."

Evelyn looked at the pictures splayed across her coffee table.

"Are you sure you want me to keep going?" Evelyn asked. "This could be nothing more than an innocent flirtation."

"I have to know the truth," Colette said. "Find out everything about this girl. Who she is. Where she came from. Why she's here now. I need to understand what's happening."

Evelyn nodded. Having had her life fall apart, she could appreciate wanting to know why. Carefully Colette gathered the photos together. As always, her movements were graceful, betraying no emotion. She stacked them in a neat pile with the close-up shot of the waitress on top. Then she slid them back into the envelope.

"I'll call you when I have more information," Evelyn said, escorting Colette to the door. As her footsteps retreated down the stairs, Evelyn wished, more than anything, her suspicions were wrong. Unlike the war when uncovering secrets saved lives, now they often destroyed them.

Chapter 11

A thick hedge bordered the Palmers' extensive property in Hancock Park. The only clear view of the Colonial mansion was through the large metal gate securing the drive-way. Parked on the corner in her Alfa Romeo 6C 2500 convertible Evelyn watched as George Palmer opened the front door. He looked back at Colette with a smile and pulled her close for a kiss. It lingered several moments past a simple goodbye.

Nick approached and leaned against the side of Evelyn's car, eyeing her over the windshield.

"Didn't anyone tell you it's rude to spy on people?" Nick asked.

"No. In fact, I'm pretty sure you told me the exact opposite."

"Nice ride," Nick said. "Didn't Daddy have anything less conspicuous?"

"We Bishops have never been a subtle bunch."

Nick ran his hands over the smooth lines of the car. It seemed specially designed for driving along the coast on a summer day.

"California's the only place you can get away with this beauty."

"What do you want, Nick?"

"Could ask you the same thing."

"I'm just doing my job," Evelyn said.

"Who hired you?"

"The better question is why George Palmer needs security."

"You know I can't answer that," Nick replied.

Evelyn looked past Nick to see George step into his waiting Bentley.

"Your ride's about to leave you behind."

"Don't get caught up in this mess, Evie."

"You lost the right to tell me what to do a long time ago."

"I forgot how goddamned stubborn you are."

"No, you didn't," she replied.

"No," Nick said with a humorless laugh. "I didn't."

The car horn sounded from the driveway. Nick made his way back and slid behind the wheel. The Bentley pulled onto the street.

"Suppose there's no point in hiding," Evelyn said as she flipped a U-turn to follow George Palmer. Ahead of her, Nick cut over to Rossmore and followed into Vine. As the street widened, Nick sped up, weaving through traffic.

"Aw, Nick," Evelyn said to herself. "You should know better than to try to outrun me."

She steered around a slow-moving car, then into opposing traffic, to get around a bus. Ahead, Nick swerved between a fruit truck and a Packard. She had the feeling this was less about losing a tail and more about seeing if she still had her old skills. Nick pulled a sharp left at Franklin and cut over toward Cahuenga Pass.

"Where are you going?" she asked aloud as he turned up Mulholland Drive.

Nick roared around the sharp curves, disappearing over the hills. Within moments, Evelyn was on his bumper again. Near Laurel Canyon, he pulled onto a fire road. She followed him, realizing too late that he chose it because it was unpaved. The wheels of the Bentley kicked up dust and rocks, leaving a heavy cloud in its wake. In her open car, Evelyn choked on the dirt as it filled her lungs and stung her eyes.

"Well played," she said, accepting defeat.

Slowly she reversed up the hill onto Mulholland Drive, then drove down to Sunset.

Ciro's was just barely open when Evelyn pulled up outside. She parked her car at the curb and looked at her suit. The dark green was now a tawny brown from the dirt that coated every inch of her car. She brushed off her clothes, as best she could, then took the clean handkerchief from her purse and wiped her face. Flipping upside down, she shook out her hair, silently cursing Nick. She pulled her compact from her purse and checked her appearance. Not great, but it would do in a pinch. Glancing down, she spotted the diamond brooch she pinned to her lapel that morning. Slipping it off, she dropped it in her pocket before heading inside.

The main room was empty, aside from a couple sitting at a table drinking daiquiris. Nearby, waiters hovered at the edges, cracking jokes before the evening rush. A lone bartender, dressed in a short black jacket, vest, bow tie, and crisp white shirt, straightened the liquor bottles. He turned as Evelyn approached.

"What can I get you?"

"Not here for a drink," Evelyn said. "Though God knows I could use one. Actually, I'm looking for someone. There was a waitress here last night. Cute. Blond. Nineteen?"

"That describes most of them," the bartender said.

"She left around eleven, wearing a black dress with small white birds on it."

The bartender thought for a moment. "Sounds like Katie."

"She working tonight?"

"It's her day off. Was there a problem?"

"Not at all," Evelyn said. "Any chance you could give me her address?"

"Afraid I can't release that information," the bartender replied. "Get a lot of guys in here. Think the girls are flirting with them. Want to take it a step further . . . You understand."

"Gosh," Evelyn said. "How awful! Of course, you need to protect them. Thing is, I was in the ladies' room with her last night and I think she dropped this."

Evelyn pulled the diamond brooch out of her pocket and showed it to the bartender. His eyes widened.

"You can leave it with me," he offered.

"I would, but it seems like an heirloom. Pricey too. Unfortunately, I have to leave town tomorrow. I'll try again when I get back in a few weeks," Evelyn said. "What was your name? I just want to make sure I remember when I tell her how good you are at protecting her privacy."

"It's, uh, Arthur," he said.

"Thanks so much for your help, Arthur," Evelyn said, turning to leave. She was almost at the door when the bartender called out.

"Maybe I can make an exception."

Evelyn smiled to herself and turned back.

"I wouldn't want you to get in trouble," Evelyn said.

"Well, you don't seem like the type of lady to harass a person," Arthur said as he pulled an address book out from under the bar. He paged through it until he found what he was looking for.

"Katie lives at 631 South Cochran, apartment 8."

"You're a doll," Evelyn said, sliding a five-dollar bill across the bar.

Arthur smiled broadly and slipped the money into his pocket.

Chapter 12

Evelyn pulled up outside Katie's apartment. It was a two-story building covered in dirty white stucco, with an uneven Spanish tile roof. The lawn was mostly dead grass, with a few patches of weeds to liven things up. A cracked redbrick walkway led up to a glass door. Through a window on the second floor, Evelyn saw a woman with a slight figure, wearing a dress cinched tightly at the waist. Though the thin curtains blocked all but the shadow of bodies, Evelyn assumed this was Katie. She picked up her camera and shot a few frames. The figure disappeared, replaced by a large man—George. Evelyn rested her head against the back of the seat and wondered how long before they adjourned to the bedroom. A hot bath and a glass of scotch called to her.

Suddenly George began walking backward, his hands raised. Evelyn sat up and lifted her camera. Just as she snapped a picture, two gunshots rang out. George collapsed, the curtain behind him splattered red. Evelyn grabbed her handbag, pulled out her gun, and rushed toward the apartment. She yanked open the front door. There was a long hallway that led to a back door. Nick rounded the bottom of the back staircase.

"Nick?" she asked, surprised.

He met her eye, then ran out the back door.

Evelyn was tempted to follow, but George was the more pressing matter. She dashed upstairs. Using the muzzle of her gun, she nudged open the door to Katie's apartment. George lay with two holes in his chest. A thick lake of blood spread across the hardwood floor. Though it wouldn't tell her anything she didn't already know, she reached down and felt for a pulse. Nothing.

Quickly Evelyn searched the rest of the apartment. She was alone. Dropping her gun back into her handbag, she reached for the phone. Then she stopped, seeing a checkbook in the name of Katherine Pierce, showing regular deposits from George Palmer. The sums were significant and Evelyn wondered where the money went. She certainly didn't spend it on this place. The walls were bare and the furniture second- or thirdhand. Curiosity got the better of her. Evelyn opened up the desk drawer and rummaged through it. There were a few bills and a couple of matchbooks from clubs around the city. Nothing out of the ordinary. Scattered across the coffee table, there were glossy magazines with celebrity gossip. Seeing the photos made Evelyn realize no family pictures hung anywhere in the room. The kitchen itself was neat, with two sets of dishes, cups, and silverware. A small percolator sat on the stove, and the refrigerator was empty aside from a carton of milk and an apple.

Katie's bedroom was more of the same. Some dresses hung in the closet, with a few pairs of shoes lined up below them. The nightstand held another magazine and a bottle of lotion. Evelyn wondered about this girl who suddenly appeared in George Palmer's life. The apartment gave no indication of her personality. It struck Evelyn that this wasn't a home, it was a way station on the path to somewhere else. Was it stardom Katie sought, or something else?

Evelyn pulled the drawer from the nightstand and felt for a false bottom. She did the same for the dressers, searching for any clues as to the real Katie Pierce. She rummaged through the kitchen drawers and behind the refrigerator. She tested the closets for hidden walls and the floor for loose boards. It was a search she had performed countless times during the war and she executed it with quick, surgical precision. She found nothing other than a copy of *The Iliad*, translated by Samuel Butler, hidden in a small compartment under the desk. It was the original 1898 edition, published by Longmans, Green. Not only was it a relatively rare book, but it felt wildly out of place as the only work of literature in the entire apartment. Evelyn flipped open the front cover to see an inscription in German. It was a quote from *The Iliad*: "No man or woman born, coward or brave, can shun his destiny." Curious, Evelyn slipped it into her purse to investigate later.

Everything about this apartment nagged at her. Katie was too much of a blank slate for a woman her age.

"What did you get yourself into?" she asked George's body.

Evelyn picked up the phone and waited for the operator.

"I need the police at 631 South Cochran. Apartment 8," Evelyn said. "Tell them to bring the coroner."

Hanging up the phone, Evelyn sat on the desk chair to wait.

It only took ten minutes for the police to arrive. The patrol car carried a fresh-faced kid, barely out of high school. Though he strutted in with his gun on his hip, the bravado did nothing to hide the peach fuzz that grew instead of a proper five-o'clock shadow. His partner was older and filled out his uniform with a belly that strained the buttons of his shirt. He introduced himself as Officer Ryan and the kid as Officer Larson.

"Holy shit!" Larson said as his glance fell upon George's body. "Is he dead?"

"If not, he made an awful mess of the curtains," Evelyn replied.

Officer Larson looked to the blood-splattered walls and ruined carpet. There was a certain smell that a body gave off once it no longer served its purpose. It mingled with the lingering scent of cordite from the gunpowder. Larson stared for a long moment, his face turning green. Then he rushed out of the apartment and sounds of his retching came from the hall.

"I'll call in the cavalry," Officer Ryan said. "You all right?"

"Not the first body I've seen," Evelyn said as they listened to Larson lose his dinner.

Officer Ryan shrugged. "What can I say? The kid's new."

It was another twenty minutes before the coroner arrived with detectives and more police. Officer Larson, as if to make up for his previous conduct, took it upon himself to question Evelyn. He loomed over her, his back toward the forensic technicians near the body.

"How did you know the victim?" Officer Larson asked.

"He was friends with my father."

"And he invited you?" Larson asked.

"No," Evelyn said.

"Then why are you here?"

"As I told you before, I heard gunshots and came in."

"What were you doing outside?"

"It's a beautiful night. Why shouldn't I be outside?"

"But why here?"

"Why not here?"

"You're not being very helpful," Larson complained.

"You're not asking very good questions," Evelyn replied.

"I'll have you know I was at the top of my class at the academy."

"And it's been what? Three weeks on the job? Four?"

"Six months," Larson said.

"That's adorable. Can I talk to the grown-ups now?"

"I . . . I . . ." Larson stammered. "Let me see some ID."

Evelyn opened her handbag. As she reached for her wallet, Larson pulled his gun.

"Stop! Hold it right there! I found our killer."

Everyone turned to look at Larson.

"Excuse me?" Evelyn asked.

"Put your hands up. She's our killer."

Evelyn started to laugh.

"Hands up!" Larson said. His gun began to shake with nervousness.

"Get that thing out of my face," Evelyn said.

"No. You killed him. I saw your gun," Larson said. "Now put your hands up. I'm gonna cuff you."

With one hand still holding the gun, Larson reached out for his handcuffs, struggling to unsnap them from his belt.

"While I do appreciate a new set of bracelets," Evelyn said, "I prefer mine to come from Cartier."

"Be quiet!" Larson said, still struggling with the handcuffs.

"What the fuck is happening here?" a loud voice asked.

Larson turned abruptly, swinging his gun to point at Police Captain John Wharton. Wharton was a distinguished man, with dark hair and a booming voice. He was not a man to suffer fools lightly, and Evelyn imagined him being quite effective in interrogations. Standing beside him was Carl, his detective shield shining from the front pocket of his suit jacket.

"Son, put that thing down," Wharton said, swatting away Larson's firearm. "You're gonna hurt someone."

"But . . . but she has a gun!" Larson said.

"Ma'am, is that true?" Wharton asked.

"It is," Evelyn said. "I also have a permit."

"I'm gonna need to see 'em both."

Evelyn handed over her purse.

"It's a Beretta," Evelyn said. "From the size of the holes in that guy's chest, I'd say it was at least a .44."

"You know your guns," Wharton said.

"Girl's gotta have her hobbies," Evelyn replied.

"One of many," Carl said. "How are you, Evie?"

"Better than Mr. Palmer."

"You two know each other?" Wharton asked, looking between them.

"We jumped out of a few perfectly good airplanes together," Evelyn said.

"Shit," Wharton said. "OSS?"

"I can neither confirm nor deny."

Wharton was not amused. He reached into Evelyn's bag and fished out her gun.

"Hasn't been fired recently," he said.

"Not since I went to the range last week," Evelyn said.

Wharton pulled out Evelyn's ID.

"Evelyn Bishop," he read. "Don't see many socialites hanging around crime scenes."

"Maybe you need a higher-caliber crime scene," Evelyn replied.

"Why are you really here?"

"I'm a private investigator."

Wharton began to laugh. Sensing a joke, Officer Larson joined him.

"No, really," Wharton said.

"Really," Carl said.

Wharton flipped through Evelyn's wallet until he saw her detective license.

"I'll be damned. Guessing you're here on a job?"

Evelyn nodded.

"Care to tell me about it?"

"Nope," Evelyn said.

Wharton debated whether he wanted to push. Before he could decide, the door opened and Nick entered the apartment. His eyes caught Evelyn's and she thought she saw something akin to a plea.

"Nick Gallagher," Wharton said. "Why am I not surprised?"

"What the hell happened?" Nick asked.

"Could ask you the same thing," Carl said. "Thought you were working protection for Mr. Palmer."

Nick held up a bottle of whisky.

"He asked me to run down to Wilshire and pick up a fifth."

"While you were gone, Mr. Palmer got killed. Seems you're about as good in the PI racket as you were at being a cop," Wharton said.

Pain and embarrassment flashed across Nick's face. It was an expression only discernable to someone who knew him well. Evelyn wondered what Nick's life had been since the war.

"Where's the girl?" Nick asked.

"What girl?" Wharton asked.

"The one who lives here."

"She his dish on the side?" Wharton asked.

"Dunno," Nick said. "Palmer didn't offer up details about his private life."

Wharton turned to Evelyn.

"You see anyone when you came in?"

Evelyn glanced at Nick, then shook her head.

"Well," Wharton said, "this is a right fine mess if I ever saw one. Gallagher, you'll let us know if you hear from the girl?"

"Have I ever let you down?" Nick said.

"That's not a question you want to ask," Wharton said.

"So it's not just me," Evelyn said. "You have this effect on everyone."

"You know each other, too?" Wharton observed. "I must say, Miss Bishop, you do get around."

Wharton fished the car keys out of Evelyn's bag and tossed them to Nick.

"Gallagher, make yourself useful and drive the lady home."

"The lady can drive herself," Evelyn insisted.

"Ma'am, that's a dead body over there," Wharton said. "It's traumatic to someone with a delicate constitution."

"Carl, help me out," Evelyn said.

"I think Nick's the perfect person to drive Miss Bishop home," Carl replied. "Something tells me they have a lot to talk about."

"Miss Bishop," Nick said with mock chivalry.

"Judas," she whispered to Carl as she followed Nick outside.

Chapter 13

Nick drove Evelyn's Alfa Romeo almost as fast as she did. He appreciated its smooth acceleration and the way it handled as he rounded the corners. Money could buy nice toys. Beside him, Evelyn stared off into the distance as the Los Angeles streets passed in a blur. Nick offered her the bottle of whisky he had picked up on Wilshire. Evelyn took a look at the label and shuddered.

"Thanks, but I don't drink lighter fluid."

Nick tucked it in his pocket for later.

"Your car is filthy," he said.

"That was a nice trick," she replied.

"You didn't have to follow us."

"Maybe if you'd let me, Palmer would still be alive."

Nick was silent.

"Sorry," Evelyn said. "That was below the belt."

"Thanks for not ratting me out. Captain Wharton was never my biggest fan."

"You don't say."

"He's not a bad guy, it's just . . ."

"I know."

Keeping his mouth shut was not one of Nick's skills and radical honesty rarely made a person popular. In retrospect, it was amazing he lasted a whole year on the force. The one thing he regretted was that Carl stuck his neck out to get him the job. Though Carl rarely discussed it, the LAPD was filled with white men who had little tolerance for anyone different. There were insults, intended and not, that could be exhausting, cruel, and downright dangerous. The color of Carl's skin, combined with his last name, meant he had to work twice as hard to get half as far. Nick never meant to put Carl's position at risk.

"So you don't think I shot George Palmer?" Nick asked.

"Don't be stupid. I might hate you with every fiber of my being, but you're not a killer. At least not without a really good reason."

"Thanks?" Nick said.

"My guess? When I saw you, you were chasing after whoever did it," Evelyn said. "So, what really happened back there?"

Nick pulled up in front of a dive bar.

"What are you doing?" Evelyn asked.

"Maybe you're not into drugstore booze, but tell me you couldn't use a drink."

Nick got out of the car, still carrying her keys, and headed toward the door. Evelyn glanced at the low building in front of her. A neon sign reading HANK'S flickered precariously.

"To hell with it," Evelyn said, following him inside.

The interior of the bar matched the promise of the outside. The low ceiling and dim lights gave it a slightly claustrophobic feeling. The walls were covered in a dark paper whose pattern was indistinguishable from smoke stains. Sad tunes poured from tinny speakers of the jukebox, highlighting that this was not a place for celebrating. It was a place for forgetting. Nick grabbed a stool at the far end of the bar and Evelyn took the one next to him. He motioned to the bartender.

"I'll have a scotch and the lady will have . . . What was that thing? Mai tai? Daiquiri?"

"Macallan. Neat."

"We've got Johnnie Walker."

"Guess that'll do," Evelyn said.

"Maybe you haven't changed as much as I thought," Nick replied.

The bartender returned with two glasses and poured the scotch for them.

"You can leave the bottle," Nick said.

"Why did George Palmer hire you?" Evelyn asked.

"He was getting threats."

"What kind of threats?"

"Never said," Nick replied.

"Hard to protect a person who won't tell you what's after them."

Nick drank the rest of his scotch and topped up their glasses.

"This wasn't your fault," Evelyn said softly.

He looked into her eyes and saw something akin to sympathy. It wasn't as bad as pity, but it was close.

"Who hired you?" Nick asked.

"Give you three guesses."

"Ah, yes. The beautiful Mrs. Palmer. Suppose knocking him off's cheaper than a divorce."

"We don't know anything . . . yet."

Nick raised his eyebrows skeptically.

"Yeah, I get how it looks," Evelyn said. "But why kill him when she knew I'd be there?"

"Maybe she needed you to find Katie Pierce."

"Which leads me to my second question. You have a wife that looks like Colette, why the hell are you screwing around with a waitress from the middle of nowhere?"

"Thrill of the chase?" Nick offered.

"That the best you got?"

"Katie Pierce is cute enough, if you're into that type."

"Please," Evelyn scoffed.

"She's sweet, wide-eyed, innocent. Colette Palmer may be many things, but I highly doubt innocent is one of them. War breaks something in people."

"There's a missing piece you'll never get back," Evelyn said.

For a moment, the old familiarity returned. Nick wondered if he would ever stop aching for her. He wondered if she felt the same.

"You drove George to Katie Pierce's apartment," Evelyn said.

"The girl let him in. Palmer told me to wait outside."

"How chivalrous," Evelyn said.

"He was in there about an hour before I heard the gunshots. I felt for a pulse, but it was too late. There were footsteps by the back door and I chased them down the stairs."

"That's when I saw you."

Nick nodded.

"And Katie?" Evelyn asked. "Where was she?"

"Don't know. I was mostly focused on the fellow with a gun."

"You get a look at him?"

"He was a ghost. All I saw was a large man in a trench coat. I chased after him, but he disappeared on La Brea."

"You picked up the booze as an excuse."

"Seemed easier than trying to convince Wharton I wasn't involved."

"Did you know the apartment had a back door?"

"No. That's how the killer must have snuck in."

"Unless he was already there," Evelyn said.

"You think Katie Pierce was part of it?"

"You said he was getting threats. What better way to get him alone than in the apartment of a pretty girl?

"Please," Nick said.

"Come on, Nick. How many times did we run that exact same con?"

"You can't honestly think Katie Pierce killed a guy. She's . . ."

"Pretty. Sweet. Blond. Do I have to remind you that people aren't always what they seem?"

"Ev—" Nick said.

"If she's so innocent, then where the hell is she?"

Nick thought about that for a moment.

"She's the only one who knows what happened in there. Her boyfriend's shot, but she didn't call an ambulance or the cops. She just disappeared," Evelyn said. "Aren't you curious why?"

Nick nodded. "This whole thing doesn't sit right with me."

"Not sure I like my part in it, either," Evelyn replied.

"Our interests align on this one."

Evelyn looked down at her drink, studying it for a long moment.

"One case," she said.

Nick held his glass to hers and toasted her.

"You never know," he said. "You might have fun."

Evelyn tossed back the rest of her drink and poured herself another.

Chapter 14

Nick drove Evelyn's car through the empty streets of Los Angeles. She rested her head against the back of the passenger seat. Two drinks had turned into four. Four to six. Before she knew it, the bottle was empty. Nick had seen Evelyn drunk a few times. The alcohol cracked the cool reserve with which she faced life. Nick wondered if this relaxed openness was closer to her natural state—the one from before the war and Matthew's death. Hell, maybe even from before she lost her mother.

It still amazed Nick that he managed to break through Evelyn's guard. It happened slowly, chipping away a little bit at a time, until one night, it all crumbled. They had known each other six months. They were rescuing a scientist from Berlin, but their contact at the Swiss border never arrived. Instead, they had to sneak through France to get to Portugal. The weather was frigid and by the end of the third week, they were cold, hungry, and inching toward collapse. They found a twelfth-century cemetery outside Lyon that offered shelter.

The stone crypt was damp with the night air. The scientist fell asleep immediately, but Evelyn shivered relentlessly. Starting a fire was not an option. Instead, Nick put his arm around her, trying to impart warmth. For a moment, she sat rigid; then she curled into his chest, relaxing against his body. Despite the danger, he had the strangest feeling of coming home.

Nick had slept with his fair share of women. He lost his virginity at fifteen in the back of a truck parked down by the docks. The cackle of seagulls sounded like laughter at his hurried uncertainty. The intervening years offered plenty of opportunities. Some were sweet girls, looking at him as more than he was. Others were simply a night's company, their names forgotten by morning.

Evelyn was different. She was beautiful, but that wasn't why Nick fell for her. She was fearless and funny, stubborn and sarcastic. She was more alive than anyone he had ever met. For a man who existed in black and white, she was a sledgehammer over the head, telling him to wake up to all the colors in this world. As he held her close, they whispered softly, talking about nothing and everything at the same time. When the dawn broke and light spilled through the iron gate of the crypt, Nick knew something had changed. His life was irrevocably divided into before and after.

Sitting in the passenger seat as he drove her home, Evelyn sang "*La Marseillaise*," the national anthem of France. Last time he heard her sing was the Liberation of Paris. As they marched down the Champs-Élysées, there was a mass euphoria unlike anything Nick had felt before. Hearing their American accents, people handed them bottles of champagne and Evelyn drank until she was beyond giddy. That day made the end of the war seem inevitable and promised a future where anything was possible. The next morning, as Evelyn slept off the wine, Nick went to the only jewelry shop he could find and bought a ring. He carried it with him through the end of the war, promising himself he would give it to her the day Churchill declared victory. It still lived in his pocket, a constant reminder of what might have been.

"You don't know how much I wish things were different," Nick said, half to himself. His words were so quiet, he thought they were swept away by the wind. For a moment, Evelyn didn't respond. Then she turned to look at him and he felt the power of her gaze down in his bones.

"What am I supposed to do?" she asked.

"About what?"

"Life. Over there, we saved people. Now I'm chasing cheating husbands. One step up from useless."

"So find something else."

"Like what? You've had my cooking. I hate cleaning. Can barely sew on a button. Should I take up golf? Improve my tennis swing? Or should I get married and start popping out babies?"

Nick didn't have an answer.

"Don't you get it?" she said. "There's no place for me. Not here. Not there. Not anywhere."

"There aren't many opportunities for a street rat who never graduated high school," Nick replied.

"The war was supposed to change both our lives. It was supposed to change the world," Evelyn said. "Now look at us. Back where we started. I'm expected to return to my old life and pretend to be happy in a mold that never fit. Except now I know there's something more."

The scotch made her confess more than she intended. Nick couldn't tell if the streetlights reflected off her eyes, or if there was a sheen of tears clouding them. More than anything, he wanted to reach over and take her hand, but the distance between them felt much larger than the width of a car.

Nick turned down a broad, leafy street, then into a gated driveway. Evelyn gave him the code and they drove up the curving path to her front door. It was one of the largest houses Nick had ever seen. During the war, he thought he understood the extent of the Bishops' wealth. Now he realized exactly how modest Evelyn was in her description. Nick came around the car and helped her out.

"I'm fine," she said, but balance proved tricky. He picked her up and carried her to the front door. She dug in her bag for the key, but Nick simply rang the bell. It echoed through the house, and after a moment, Logan Bishop answered.

"Should I ask?" Logan said.

"Probably not," Nick replied. "Mind pointing me in the right direction?"

Logan led Nick up the curving staircase to Evelyn's bedroom. It was large, furnished with a canopy bed covered in crisp white sheets and a fluffy down comforter. A thick Persian rug muffled Nick's footsteps. Logan watched from the doorway as Nick set Evelyn down. He pulled off her shoes and tucked the covers around her.

"Do you remember those nights in France?" she asked.

"Of course."

"We were cold and hungry, but I never felt scared, because you were there," she said. "I loved you. So much."

Nick brushed the hair away from Evelyn's face.

"You broke my heart."

"Evie . . ."

She turned away and pulled the covers up to her chin. Lying here, in her childhood bedroom, she looked so fragile. Nick wanted to lie down beside her, as he had in the war, holding her until the morning light broke through the windows. But she was no longer his. He looked to Logan standing in the doorway, then stepped away from Evelyn's bed, into the hall.

"I always suspected Evie met someone during the war," Logan said.

"She didn't tell you about me?" Nick asked.

"She didn't tell me anything, apparently. What did she mean about France?"

"You should ask her."

"I have. She said she was a translator in London."

Nick couldn't hide his surprise.

"Why don't we have a drink?" Logan said. "Perhaps you can fill in the blanks."

Nick followed Logan down to his study. It was decorated with rich forest-green wallpaper, largely hidden behind shelves of books. Several lamps cast overlapping pools of light, giving the room a subtle warmth. Logan led Nick to two leather wingback chairs, sitting in front of a dying fire. He picked up a crystal decanter from the sideboard and poured them both scotch.

"This ain't bad," Nick said.

"It's from before the war," Logan said.

"Funny how war divides everything into before, during, and after."

"Before seems so long ago. I keep remembering Evelyn running around with pigtails."

"She never had pigtails," Nick said, laughing at the image.

"She did," Logan insisted. "And it's a father's prerogative to always see his daughter as his little girl."

"I often thought of her as Athena," Nick said. "Springing into the world fully formed and ready for battle."

"Well, she does have an opinion on things."

"That's putting it mildly."

"Before the war, we never kept secrets from each other," Logan said. "Now there's a space between us. I miss when Evelyn felt like she could tell me anything."

"It's really not my place," Nick said.

"I respect that," Logan replied. "I do. But, maybe it's a burden she shouldn't have to carry alone."

Nick sighed, debating with himself.

"When I met Evie, she couldn't type to save her life," Nick began. "Knowing her—she probably still can't. She wasn't cut out to be a nurse. Didn't mind the blood, but hated taking orders. Not one to stand on the sidelines, she joined the OSS. Best officer I've ever seen. She could get us into places no one else would attempt. When we found ourselves in trouble, she was scrappy and aggressive. Perfect shot from four hundred meters away. A platoon of men didn't stand a chance against her."

"You're saying she can take care of herself."

"She took care of everyone. There were all kinds of missions, but they usually started with parachuting behind enemy lines to aid the French Resistance."

"Where?" Logan asked, his voice suddenly alert.

"The mission you really want to ask about was in 1944. We liberated a POW camp outside Lille."

Logan's face went slack as he struggled to process the information.

"She was there?"

Nick nodded.

"I had no idea."

Logan turned to the fire, tears streaking down his face. Nick knew he should leave, but he had to ask.

"Why were crates from your factory in a Nazi munitions dump?"

The corners of Logan's mouth twitched in a bitterly ironic smile. He shook his head, as if having a conversation with himself. Then he looked to Nick.

"The past is in the past. Let it stay there."

Chapter 15

Dressed as German soldiers, the team split up. Carl and David headed toward the POW camp. Nick and Jean set off to the munitions dump. They entered a fenced-off area that was shrouded in camouflage netting. From their bags, they withdrew primer cord and explosives. They carefully set the charges among the boxes of artillery shells, guns, and bullets. Nick rounded a corner and stopped when he saw several wooden crates. He stared for a long moment in disbelief. Stenciled across the side were the words BISHOP AERONAUTICS. Seeing his expression, Jean approached.

"What's wrong?"

Nick nodded at the crates.

"Is that . . . ?" Jean started.

"Evelyn's father's company."

Jean let out a low whistle of surprise.

"How the hell did they get here?"

"That's a very good question," Nick replied.

"There could be a perfectly simple explanation," Jean said. "The black market, or traitors in the supply chain, or captured ships . . ."

"She doesn't need to know about this."

"I'll finish up here," Jean said. "Go find Evie."

Inside the commandant's office, Evelyn faced off against Drexler, his gun pointing at her.

"You're not a French farm girl, are you?"

Evelyn tried for her best innocent look. "Apologies. I thought you might have extra ration books in your desk."

"A nice lie," Drexler said. "But your accent is Parisian."

Evelyn could weave a story about fleeing Paris with her family four years ago, but based on the man's hard expression, it seemed a futile pursuit. Evelyn made her way from behind the desk until she was standing directly in front of Drexler's gun.

"Usually, Germans can't tell the difference," she replied.

"Unlucky for you," he said.

"You're not going to shoot me," Evelyn said.

"Why? Because you're so very beautiful?"

"Because you want information."

"And you're willing to offer that in exchange for your life?"

"No."

Lightning fast, Drexler grabbed Evelyn, wrapping his hand around her throat.

"Are you French Resistance?" Drexler asked. "MI6? OSS? What were you really looking for in my desk?"

"Chocolate. Cigarettes. Stockings," Evelyn taunted, mocking his earlier offer.

"I'm going to enjoy questioning you," Drexler said, tightening his grip. For a moment, she saw stars as he cut off her breath. She stepped hard on his instep, but he merely grunted in pain without slacking his hold.

"Tell me," Drexler said. "Who are you?"

"Le Reynard," Evelyn replied.

"No, you're not."

"No. I'm not."

"But I do think you know who he is," Drexler said, cocking the hammer of the gun.

Evelyn stopped struggling and went slack. The sudden shift in her body weight forced Drexler to loosen his grip. It was just enough for her to slide free. She grabbed the desk lamp and swung it hard. The heavy iron connected with Drexler's head. He fell to his knees, dazed. She swung the lamp again and he collapsed on the floor, unconscious. Quickly she tied him up, gagged him, and tucked his gun into the waistband of her skirt. She made sure his door was locked, then slipped out the window.

Nick approached from the munitions dump and saw the redness around her neck.

"What the hell happened?"

She waved off his concern.

"Matthew's here. I found his name on the prisoner manifest."

For a man who thought he knew all her expressions, there was a joy on her face Nick had never seen. After two years and an untold number of missions, they finally found her brother. They hurried toward the POW section of the camp where Carl and David were tying up a few Nazi soldiers.

"New guy's got a mean right hook," Carl said.

David beamed with pride. "What you get for having two older brothers."

"The guard tower near the gate is unmanned," Nick said. "The others need to be taken down before we liberate the camp."

Carl nodded and headed off.

"David, you're with us," Nick said as they approached the barracks. "We can manage what's inside the gates, but there's more Nazis patrolling the woods. Make sure the soldiers know that before we set them loose. We want them to have a fighting chance."

Evelyn slipped into the first barrack to find the POWs already on guard. The sound of the lock in the middle of the night was never welcome. The tense anger on their faces faded to confusion.

"Nap time's over boys. It's time to go," she said.

They glanced at one another, wondering if she was a delusion brought on by hunger and cold.

"Yes, I'm real. And we're breaking out of here. We can't get you home yet, though God knows you deserve it," Evelyn said. "For now, the French Resistance will hide you until the U.S. makes landfall. You'll get the chance to rejoin the fight."

"Hell yeah!" a few men shouted.

Their captain approached, holding his hand out to Evelyn.

"I don't know what angel sent you, but I think I speak for everyone. We'd rather take our chances with whatever lies beyond that fence than spend another day in here."

Evelyn smiled at their response, then she caught sight of the captain's last name as he threw on his jacket.

"Captain Dwyer? Of the 144th?" Evelyn asked.

"Yes . . ." he said uncertainly.

"You served with my brother, Matthew. Matthew Bishop."

"Wait, you're not Evelyn, are you?"

Evelyn nodded eagerly. Captain Dwyer let out a low whistle of surprise.

"He talks about you all the time."

"Do you know where he is? Is he still alive?"

"He's in the hospital wing," Captain Dwyer said. "I'll take you there."

They exited the barracks to find more Allied soldiers creeping out. A few broke down the doors of the other barracks as word spread about the escape. Nick and David handed out the extra guns they stole off the guards. The towers were silent with no lights tracking their movements. Evelyn and the captain hurried through the camp. The hospital was a wooden building, where rows of sick and injured men lay in the darkness. The smell of human waste and rotting flesh hung heavy in the air. Evelyn flipped on the light, though the weak bulbs barely illuminated the room.

"Matthew?" Evelyn called out as she made her way through the rows of beds. In the last one, a shadow of a man sat up. His chest had a wheezing rattle that sounded like pneumonia. What little flesh remained clung to his skeletal frame. His skin was pale from not having seen the sun in months and his eyes were hollow. Evelyn stared, trying to find the man she remembered.

"Matthew?"

"Evie?" he asked. "You're not real. You can't be."

"I'm as real as Mama's roses that still grow in the front yard."

She sat on the edge of the bed, taking his hand in hers. Matthew shook his head, unable to process her sudden appearance.

"I'm bringing you home."

"You shouldn't be here," Matthew replied. "Dad . . ."

"Will be so happy to see you. Now quit arguing. We have a boat to catch."

Evelyn helped Matthew into a jacket, then propped his arm over her shoulder. His tall frame was light as he leaned against her. He stumbled, dragging his feet as they walked. In front of them, Captain Dwyer had his arm around another man, and a few other soldiers streamed ahead of them. They had just stepped outside when they were confronted by several German soldiers pointing guns at them.

Captain Dwyer rocked back on his heels, preparing for a fight, but before he could move, a huge explosion sent flames into the night sky. Jean had blown the munitions dump. The guards turned in surprise and Nick used the distraction to sneak up from behind. In the blink of an eye, one guard was unconscious, with Nick in possession of his gun. He shot the other three.

A siren called the remaining guards to arms. They flooded into camp, firing indiscriminately at anything that moved. Yet, they underestimated the people they oppressed over the years. The POWs had little regard for their own safety and fought with a blinding rage. The Germans looked to the guard towers, only to find them empty. The sole occupied tower held Carl, who focused its machine gun on the approaching Nazis, mowing them down before they could reach the battle. Rivers of blood flowed across the hard-packed earth.

Evelyn looked to Matthew.

"We have to hurry."

Nick took Matthew's weight on the other side and they half-walked, half-dragged him toward the entrance.

"Leave me behind," Matthew said. "You'll be faster."

"You're the reason I'm here," Evelyn said. "I've come all this way to find you and I'd circle the world twice to do it again."

Beside the command building stood an open-top jeep.

"Nick," she said, nodding at the vehicle. They stumbled along, setting Matthew in the passenger seat. Nick crouched in the back, keeping watch on the chaos around them. Evelyn pried off the panel below the steering wheel. She pulled out the wires and began sparking them together.

"You know how to hot-wire a car? How do you know how to hot-wire a car?"

"Says the man who taught me how to dismantle an airplane engine when I was twelve."

Below her, the jeep roared to life. Carl, having used up all the ammunition in the guard tower, ran to them.

"Did you see David?" Nick asked.

"He escaped with Jean," Carl replied.

At first, Evelyn thought the sound was the muffler backfiring. Then she looked at Matthew and saw the blossom of red spreading across his chest. Commandant Drexler stood in the doorway of the command building, gun in hand. Carl shot back, driving Drexler inside. Evelyn moved over to cradle Matthew as Nick got behind the wheel. They roared out of the camp into the woods. Evelyn's hands covered the wound in Matthew's chest, but it wasn't enough. Blood oozed between her fingers as they raced over the bumpy road.

"Hold on," she said. "Just a little longer. We'll get you help."

"There's a safe house ten kilometers from here," Nick said.

Matthew looked up at Evelyn, his bloody fingers brushing her cheek.

"Thank you for coming for me," he said. "I didn't want to die in there."

"You're not dying," she said, but the blood staining her skirt told a different story.

"I thought about you when things got really bad. Remember all those days, with you, me, and James?"

"We were inseparable."

"You have to take care of each other," Matthew said, his breath coming out in short gasps. Bubbles of blood formed at the corner of his mouth.

"We will. All three of us," Evelyn said, trying to convince herself.

"Tell Dad I wasn't worth it," Matthew whispered.

"Worth what? What are you talking about?" Evelyn asked.

"I'm so glad I got to see you again. Love you, Evie."

"I love you, too."

Then he was silent.

"Matthew?"

It was not dramatic, but she felt the last breath leave his lungs. She knew the moment he let go. Though his eyes were open, they stared blankly at the trees blurring above them. His hand was still warm in hers, as it pressed over the wound in his chest. Tears streamed from her face, splashing onto his body and cutting inlets in the blood.

"No, no, NO! Please don't leave me. Matthew, please."

Evelyn was not ready. She had prayed to find her brother every day for the past two years. Never once did she lose faith he was alive. She knew she would feel it in her soul if he died. They were that closely linked. He was her best friend, closest confidant, and the one person who had always been there for her. When their mother had died and Logan fell apart, Matthew made her believe they would survive. He simply would not let her drown in her grief. Now what was she to do? How could she endure this? It was not fair for her to have gone through everything to find him, only to lose him forever in that same moment.

"Matthew!" she cried, as if her words could bring him back and hold him fast to his body. Yet, the essence that made him her beloved brother was gone.

Chapter 16

Los Angeles, 1948

Evelyn woke the next morning with a blinding hangover. Even the effort of cursing Nick and his scotch wasn't worth the pain of forming words. She stumbled into the shower and let the hot water run over her until she felt almost human again. Doing her hair was too much effort, so she pulled it back into a low bun and called it good enough. Exceptions had to be made for days when all the aspirin in the world could not make a dent in her headache.

In the kitchen, Evelyn found Logan reading the paper.

"You were in a fine state last night," Logan said.

Evelyn groaned in misery.

"I'll make you breakfast."

Logan handed her a cup of coffee, then cracked a few eggs into a pan. He put the bread in the toaster and fried some bacon. Evelyn sipped her coffee slowly. The caffeine began to loosen the knots behind her eyes. Logan set the plate in front of her and she picked up a slice of bacon.

"How come I never got your cooking gene?" she asked.

"Blame your mother. She couldn't boil water."

Evelyn took a few more bites, the food calming her stomach and soaking up the residual alcohol. When she finished all she could eat, she pushed the plate away and sat back in her chair. Logan studied her intently.

"This isn't going to be a lecture on the perils of whisky, is it?" Evelyn asked.

"Might be a bit late for that."

"Don't worry. I'm never drinking again."

"Famous last words," Logan laughed. "You must have had a few hangovers during the war."

"Nope. Never," Evelyn said. "I was always a proper lady."

"Back in London?"

"Yes."

"Where you worked as a translator."

Evelyn studied her father.

"You and Nick had a conversation."

"France?" Logan asked. "The OSS?"

"I didn't want you to worry. Sitting on the sidelines was making me crazy. I needed to feel like I was helping."

"I understand."

"You do?"

"Better than you know. But why didn't you tell me afterward?" Logan asked. "Was it because of Matthew? That POW camp?"

"Wow. You guys really bonded last night."

"He thinks you blame yourself."

"That's rich, coming from him," Evelyn said.

"Do you?"

"Yes. No. I don't know," Evelyn said. "I've replayed that night a thousand times in my mind. I keep wondering what I could have done differently. Maybe if I'd gotten there sooner? What if I'd killed the Nazi commander instead of just knocking him out? What if we'd just blown the munitions depot and left the POW camp alone? What if . . . ?"

"It wasn't your fault," Logan said.

"Matthew died in my arms," Evelyn said. "His blood ran through my fingers and I couldn't save him."

Telling her father everything felt like a confession. She described the mission. How it was her idea to liberate the camp. The way she found Matthew and the sound of the shot ringing out from behind.

"Do you hate me?" Evelyn asked. It was her darkest fear.

"No. God, no," Logan insisted. "I could never hate you. Nor do I blame you. Matthew died because a Nazi shot him. If it wasn't that, he would have died of pneumonia, sepsis, or a thousand other things. It was war. Terrible things happen in war."

"Yes, but . . ."

"No 'buts.' You found him and fought to bring him home. His last moments were with someone he loved."

"He was my brother," Evelyn replied. That simple explanation was more than enough to justify risking her life.

"You two make me so proud. Your bravery. Your loyalty to each other. You are the best things in my life," Logan said.

"I miss him so much," Evelyn said.

"I do, too," he replied.

They both started crying, mourning Matthew's death together in a way they never had before, with the weight of Evelyn's secrets between them.

An hour later, Evelyn stepped outside, cursing the beautiful California weather. Between the hangover and her tears for Matthew, her eyes were so red and puffy even her eyelashes hurt. It felt like her insides had been taken out and put back in the wrong place. Her skin ached at the gentle touch of her cashmere sweater and she considered going back to bed. James's car pulled into the driveway and he stepped out with the easy confidence he carried through the world.

"This is a nice surprise," Evelyn said, giving him a kiss hello.

"I read about George Palmer's death in the newspaper. You were working on his case, weren't you?"

Evelyn nodded, grimacing as the motion reignited her hangover. James raised his hand to shield her from the sunlight. It was just one of the many simple gestures he did without thinking. His unconscious concern made her feel so very loved.

"Are you okay?"

"Yes," Evelyn said. "It was awful seeing him like that."

"Wait, you were there?" James asked.

"Outside."

"You could have been killed!"

"Whoever did it was gone by the time I got to the apartment."

"But what if . . . ?" James broke off, upset. "I don't like you wrapped up in this mess."

"Didn't realize you had a say in the matter."

A flash of hurt crossed his face.

"Sorry," she said. "It was a rough night."

"I promised Matthew I'd look after you. Not that you need it, but I love you and concern comes with the territory."

Evelyn leaned up and kissed him.

"What's that for?"

"You're a good man," she said. "I don't tell you often enough."

James pulled her close, kissing her again. His arms were strong around her. His clean scent was familiar and reminded her of a time when life was more innocent. Behind her, the front door opened. Logan walked out and looked at the two of them. James blushed slightly.

"Morning, Logan."

Logan tipped his hat at James.

"James. See you at the office."

"Yes, sir."

Logan nodded at Evelyn, then got in his car and pulled out of the driveway. Evelyn giggled.

"I feel like a teenager again," James laughed.

"You never did that when you were a teenager," Evelyn said. "At least not with me."

"I wanted to."

"You did?" Evelyn asked.

"Of course. I had the worst crush on you," James said.

"Why didn't you say anything?"

"Matthew would've kicked my ass from here to Texas, and back, for looking at his baby sister."

"He was always a bit overprotective," Evelyn said. "I mean, sure, he taught me how to jump out of airplanes, but dating? Boys? No. None of them were good enough."

"Like poor Craig Wilson," James said.

"From freshman-year homecoming? I can't believe you remember his name."

"I was insanely jealous. You know, until Matthew pulled him aside and told him that you were a lady. He expected Craig to treat you like a lady. And if he didn't, Matthew would make sure he never walked straight again."

"No wonder he seemed so terrified," Evelyn said.

"Matthew did that to every guy who glanced in your direction."

"So that's why I couldn't get a date."

"If I remember correctly, you were beating them away with a stick."

"Okay, fine. I had dates, but they barely kissed me. All the other girls went parking and mine took me for ice cream, holding my hand like we were in church."

"Good," James teased.

"Would it matter if they'd done more?" Evelyn asked.

Whole books were written about proper decorum for women. Be delicate and sweet, a lady should never raise her voice. She should be demure and respectable, always crossing her ankles, never her knees. A lady shouldn't smoke or drink to excess and she should never, ever seem anything less than pure.

Nick was the first person Evelyn slept with, a fact that both surprised and terrified him. Taking her virginity felt like a huge responsibility, but she never bought into the idea that it was anything more than an experience. It was certainly not a reason to sort people into categories of good or evil. After the war, while Evelyn traveled Europe, she slept with a few different men. Sometimes the affairs were fevered and hungry. Others were gentle and tender. Those brief connections shot like flares into the darkness, reminding her she was still alive.

The first time she slept with James, there was an instant when he realized she was not a virgin. A fleeting look crossed his face and she wasn't sure if it was surprise, anger, disappointment, or a combination of all three. The moment passed and they never discussed it. Yet now, James sensed her uncertainty.

"Evie, I don't care about your yesterdays, so long as I get all your tomorrows."

Evelyn was startled at the relief she felt.

"Speaking of tomorrows," James said. "Come with me to see the house in Benedict Canyon."

"I'd love to," she said.

"And please think about what I said. Let this case go."

Evelyn made no promises.

Chapter 17

The frosted glass on the door of Nick's office was etched with his name and the words PRIVATE DETECTIVE. The chipped and peeling letters made the place feel decrepit long before a person crossed the threshold. As Nick entered, he kicked aside a few weeks' worth of mail that had fallen through the brass slot in the door. A cracked leather couch, rescued from a nearby curb, stood against one wall. Across from it was a wooden desk with drawers that swelled shut in the summer. A thick coat of dust covered almost every surface. Nick was tempted to blame his poor housekeeping on the time he spent at the Palmer mansion, but deep down, he knew it was a general apathy to this office, this job—hell, even this life—that made him too lazy to pick up a rag and wipe down the surfaces.

Gathering the mail, he sat down at his desk and began to sort through it. Magazines, newspapers, and weekly circulars went into the overflowing rubbish bin until only a few envelopes were left. All bills. He dropped the stack in his top drawer, promising to pay everything tomorrow. With what money, he wasn't certain.

There was a knock on the doorframe and Nick looked

up to see Katie Pierce. She still wore the same dress as the previous night and her unwashed hair was tucked behind her ears. Her makeup was smudged, making her look even younger than her years. The wide eyes, she had so often turned on George, now gazed at Nick, red-rimmed and pleading.

"Miss Pierce," Nick said. "Half the city's looking for you."

"I didn't kill George," she said. "I swear."

"Sweetheart, I've learned not to take the word of a pretty girl."

"Please, you have to believe me. I have nowhere else to turn."

It was a refrain Nick had heard a hundred times, yet it always touched a deep vein of sympathy. He understood the panic of feeling completely alone. He nodded toward his couch and Katie Pierce perched on the edge, tucking her skirt around her legs.

"What happened last night?" Nick asked.

"As you know, George stopped by to check on me. He's so kind and thoughtful. It's one of the things I love most about him."

Katie paused, as if realizing, for the first time, that those visits were a thing of the past. A few tears slid down her cheeks and Nick fished out a reasonably clean handkerchief and handed it to her. Grateful, she smiled at him and dabbed her eyes.

"Sorry, I just . . ."

"It's okay," Nick said. "Then what?"

"We were having drinks. I went into the kitchen to get us a refill and I noticed the back door was open. I always lock it. I don't know how that man got in, but when I glanced into the living room, he was standing there with a gun."

"What did he look like?"

"I only saw him from the back. He was big. Broad shoulders. Tall. Brown hair."

"Wearing a trench coat?" Nick asked. Katie nodded. "Same guy I chased out of there."

"He shot George, twice. I was terrified that he might turn around and see me, so I ran. I didn't know where to go and then I remembered you. I found your address in the phone book and hid across the street until I saw you come in this morning."

Her fear seemed genuine.

"Why not go to the police?"

"What if I go there and he finds me? What if they arrest me?"

"Here's what I know," Nick said. "You're a person of interest in a murder case. Maybe you can help the cops. Maybe they think you did it. Either way, the LAPD wants to talk to you. I'm inclined to pick up the phone and call them right now."

"Please, Mr. Gallagher. George trusted you."

"For all the good it did him."

"I trust you," Katie said.

She looked up at him with intense sincerity. He almost believed her.

"How do I know this wasn't a lovers' quarrel gone wrong?"

"Because George wasn't my lover. He was my father."

Nick let out a low whistle and leaned back in his chair.

"Why don't you start at the beginning?" he said.

Chapter 18

The butler opened the door and ushered Evelyn inside the Palmer mansion. He was an older man, with straight shoulders and a sense of stable dignity, as if he was the one immutable thing in a constantly changing world. Evelyn had known him since she was a little girl, visiting George with her father.

"Apologies, Miss Bishop, Mrs. Palmer is currently with another guest. There's been so much to do since . . ." the butler trailed off as if the words were too painful to say aloud.

"I'm so sorry for your loss, Peter. You've been with George a long time."

"Yes, ma'am. Started here before the Great War. Even went with Mr. Palmer to the front."

"I know how much he valued your friendship and guidance," Evelyn said.

"Thank you," Peter replied. "It means a lot to hear you say that."

There was a pause while Peter gathered himself and returned to his staid, professional persona.

"As I was saying, you're welcome to wait for Mrs. Palmer, if you like. I don't believe she will be long. Can I bring you anything?"

"No, thank you," Evelyn replied.

Peter nodded crisply and headed toward the back of the house.

Once she was alone, Evelyn took off her hat and gloves and set them on a table beside a man's fedora. The foyer was filled with bouquets of lilies, tulips, and roses all in funereal white. The cards attached to the vases were from a venerable Who's Who of Los Angeles society. Everyone from businessmen to socialites to politicians and movie stars sent their condolences. Telegrams from President Truman and General Eisenhower, commending Palmer's service to the war effort, were propped up against a vase of orchids. By all accounts, it looked to be a life well lived.

As Evelyn studied the display, she heard raised voices in the study. Quietly she crept down the hall to see Colette Palmer with Sam Wilder, the leading mayoral candidate and head of Wilder Artillery. He made his fortune during the war manufacturing the small arms and rifles that were provided to every soldier.

Wilder's height, build, and receding brown hair would have rendered him remarkably average, were it not for his flashy suit with wide lapels and a brightly colored shirt. His face bore a deep tan that spoke of a concerted effort to reach that particular hue. Evelyn had never been Wilder's biggest fan. His smile always felt a bit too bright and, like Logan, she felt a certain wariness toward politicians in general. At this moment, she thought her innate distrust was warranted. Gone was the ingratiating smile. Instead, his face burned with a rage Evelyn never suspected he possessed.

"It's your fault he's dead," Wilder spat at Colette.

"Get. Out," she replied with a quiet fury.

"Don't test me," Wilder said. "I can make your life unbearable."

"And I can burn the whole thing to the ground," she threatened. "I should have done it years ago."

Wilder grabbed Colette by the arm.

"Let go. You're hurting me," she said, struggling to break free.

"Good."

"George told me everything. There were no secrets between us."

"And look how well that worked out," Wilder replied. "This isn't over."

"For me, it is," she replied. "What more can they possibly take?"

Sam Wilder's face twisted into a sneer.

"You still have a sister, don't you?" he said.

His voice was cold and cruel as it dropped too low for Evelyn to hear. The color drained from Colette's face. She was more than afraid. It was pure terror. Sam saw her expression and nodded to himself, satisfied. Then he turned to exit. Evelyn slid away silently. In the foyer, she pretended to study a few more bouquets.

"Evelyn!" Wilder said, quickly composing himself. "What a surprise."

"I came to offer my condolences to Mrs. Palmer. Tragedy what happened to George."

"I swear," Wilder said, "world's getting more dangerous every day. How's your father handling the news?"

"We didn't discuss it."

"He and Palmer worked closely together during the war, didn't they?"

"If I'm not mistaken, so did you."

"This tragedy is hard on everyone," Wilder said. "I tried calling Logan at home and at the office. No answer."

"What did you want to talk about?" Evelyn asked.

"Nothing to concern yourself with. When you see him, tell him I need a word. Soon as possible."

Evelyn nodded. Wilder kissed her cheek goodbye, gathered up his fedora, and left. Evelyn waited until the door closed behind him, then made her way back to the study and peered through the open door. A large horse painting behind George's desk swung out to reveal a steel safe. Colette, armed with a screwdriver, was attacking the hinges.

"Mrs. Palmer?" Evelyn said.

Colette turned quickly.

"Miss Bishop. I didn't expect you," Colette said. Then following Evelyn's glance to the safe, she laughed humorlessly. "You must think me insane trying to get at George's papers."

"Not at all," Evelyn said. "Would you like some help? I've cracked more than a few in my time."

"Oh, no, thank you," Colette said quickly. "If I can't remember the combination, I'll get a locksmith out in a day or two."

After overhearing the conversation between Colette and Sam, Evelyn was desperately curious about what was hidden behind the steel door.

"Won't take more than a minute," Evelyn offered.

"That's quite all right," Colette replied. "What can I do for you?"

"I came by to check on you," Evelyn said. "George was a good man. Whatever he had going on with the waitress didn't change that."

"It doesn't seem real yet," Colette said. "I keep expecting him to walk through the door and ask me what madness I'm up to now. He was the best part of every day."

"You're lucky to have found that."

"More than you know," Colette replied. Then, hesitantly, "Were you there?"

"Outside. It was quick. He didn't suffer," Evelyn said, cutting to the heart of the matter.

Colette nodded, tears forming on her lower eyelids.

"What was he doing?"

"Nothing unfit for the newspapers," Evelyn replied delicately.

"And the girl?"

"She was gone."   .

"What did you find out about her?" Colette asked.

The fact of George giving Katie money did not seem like the thing to calm a grieving widow. The emptiness of her apartment, while noteworthy, was not exactly illuminating. Evelyn thought back to the copy of *The Iliad*. It wasn't anything definite.

"Her name's Katie Pierce. She's a waitress over at Ciro's. Seems she came to town fairly recently. Doesn't have much stuff and there was no sign of any family or friends," Evelyn said. "George hired Nick Gallagher to protect him. Do you know who was making threats? Why would someone want to hurt him?"

"I assume the girl killed him," Colette said.

"Too soon to say," Evelyn replied.

"George was beloved by everyone who met him. As for Mr. Gallagher, why George hired him was his own business. Clearly, it was not money well spent."

"I'd like to stay on," Evelyn said. "See if I can find out who killed your husband."

"I'm certain the police have it well in hand."

"There would be no charge. It's just, I've known George since I was a child. It feels personal that I was so close to his death and couldn't stop it. Please let me help you," Evelyn said.

"No. Thank you," Colette replied firmly.

Evelyn wanted to protest. There was nothing under the sun that would pull her off this case, but Colette's expression was resolute. For the first time, Evelyn wondered whether Katie Pierce was the real reason Colette showed up in her office. Colette reached into the desk and fished out a checkbook. Quickly she wrote out Evelyn's name and a large sum.

"That should cover your fee."

"And then some," Evelyn said. "This is too much."

"I appreciate everything you've done, and your discretion regarding this incident," Colette said. "Now, please, if you don't mind, I have funeral arrangements to make."

"Of course," Evelyn said as she left the office.

As she drove down Wilshire, Evelyn felt like she had been paid to walk away.

Chapter 19

Evelyn entered her office to find Katie Pierce sitting on the couch. Nick perched on the edge of the desk, poking around the miscellaneous supplies and photographs. Beside him was a large vase of newly delivered roses.

"I remember locking this door," Evelyn said.

Nick shrugged.

"Nice digs you got here," he said. Unlike at his office, everything here was chosen thoughtfully, was well cared for, and, most likely, didn't come from the curb. There was a sense of permanence and comfort.

"You know, normal people make appointments."

Nick plucked the card off the flowers and opened it.

" 'Evelyn, To all our tomorrows. Love, James,' " Nick read, wrinkling his nose. "Bit of sentimental overkill, don't you think?"

Evelyn snatched the card and read it with a smile. Then she turned back to Nick.

"It's nice being with a man who knows how to treat a lady."

" 'Lady'? You?" Nick said. "He obviously didn't see you last night."

"I have no idea what you're talking about."

"How much do you remember?" Nick asked.

"Everything," Evelyn said. "A lady doesn't get drunk."

"And she certainly doesn't sing '*La Marseillaise*' at the top of her lungs."

"She certainly does not."

"Well, I think the flowers are beautiful," Katie said, her broad Midwestern accent becoming more pronounced. "It's so romantic."

"Yeah, *romantic*," Nick said. "I could think of another word for it."

"Such as?"

"Desperate," Nick offered.

"Sweet," Evelyn corrected.

"Needy."

"Kind."

"Old-fashioned."

"Chivalrous."

"When did you become a woman who could be bought with a few stems?" Nick asked.

"When did you become a man who believes I could *ever* be bought?"

"Touché," he said softly.

"Plus, at your age, you must be so grateful that you're not alone," Katie interjected, breaking the tension.

"My age?" Evelyn asked.

"Oh, I'm sorry," Katie said in a tone Evelyn might have called simpering, were she more generous. Instead, she just found it bitchy. "I know in the big cities, women wait *forever* before settling down. I guess here it's okay to be old and not have a man. Back in my hometown, if you weren't married by twenty-two, well, folks began to wonder."

"Heaven forbid folks wonder," Evelyn said dryly.

Nick shot Evelyn a look of barely concealed amusement. He still knew her well enough to imagine her inner monologue.

"Now, then, with half of Los Angeles looking for Miss Pierce, how did you two end up in my office?" Evelyn asked.

Nick nodded to Katie. "Tell her what you told me."

"I moved to LA to find George Palmer. He met my mama when she was eighteen. It was just one night, but . . . here I am."

"So George was . . ."

"My father," Katie said.

Evelyn let out a low whistle of surprise, unconsciously mirroring Nick's reaction.

"George didn't even know I existed until a couple months ago."

"That's why he was at your apartment last night?" Evelyn asked.

"He was really good about checking on me and making sure I settled in okay. He gave me some of his old furniture. Got me the job at Ciro's."

"Mr. Palmer was a wealthy man," Evelyn said.

"What are you saying?"

"Do you have any proof you're his daughter?"

"Evelyn," Nick scolded.

"I spent my childhood wondering about my daddy," Katie said. "All the other kids had parents who came to school and were home for dinner. My mama did her best, but I always wanted something more than just us. After my mama died, I was all alone. I moved to Los Angeles because I wanted the chance to know him."

"Why didn't your mother reach out to George herself?"

"When it happened, she was engaged to someone else. They got married fast and everyone thought I was his daughter. He was a nasty son of a bitch. Took Mama years to work up the courage to leave. That's when she told me about George. I was ten and she didn't want my stepfather to be the only kind of man I knew."

"Makes sense," Nick said sympathetically.

"That was years ago," Evelyn said.

"Honestly, I think Mama was scared. What if George was married? Or didn't remember her? Woulda broken her heart. Instead, it was easier for her to imagine the perfect man who would have treated her kind and taken care of us. I had hopes, but no expectations, when I arrived in town. George was everything Mama promised he would be. Gentle, good, a person to admire. He is—was—the only family I have left. I didn't get nearly enough time with him."

"Come on, Evie, if anyone can understand, it's you," Nick said.

Evelyn understood, she just wasn't certain she believed it.

"Still doesn't answer why you're in my office."

"She needs a place to lay low until we can get this whole thing sorted," Nick said.

"Maybe I could stay with you, Mr. Gallagher," Katie asked.

"My place isn't exactly . . ."

"Clean?" Evelyn offered. "Fumigated? Livable?"

"Built for two," Nick said. "The Bishop mansion must have plenty of room. What do you say, Evie?"

They both looked at her with wide, expectant eyes. Every fiber of her being wanted to say no, but this woman was somehow tied to George Palmer's death. Keeping her close, as much as she loathed the idea, made sense.

"Fine," Evelyn said, already dreading her new houseguest.

It was a quick drive from Evelyn's office to her home in Bel-Air. Nick and Katie kept up a flirtatious banter that irritated Evelyn to no end. Instinct told her not to trust

Katie. She was the kind of woman who had no girlfriends and didn't understand why they were important. Evelyn wondered if it was a holdover from a rough patch in high school or whether she genuinely saw all women as threats. Katie's whole state of being revolved around men's approval and Nick was her current target. Not that he complained. He laughed a little too loudly at her jokes and was a bit too sympathetic to her plight. Evelyn hated that it still bothered her.

They pulled up in front of the house and Katie stepped out, looking around.

"You live here?" she asked in awe.

"It's my father's house," Evelyn replied.

"I don't think I've ever seen a place this fancy. And it's all just for you two? Goodness. That must be nice."

Katie's words were not a compliment.

"There used to be more of us," Evelyn said.

The pain in her voice momentarily silenced Katie. Evelyn led them inside and upstairs to a guest bedroom. Like most rooms in the house, it was filled with antiques and Persian rugs that were carefully collected through Logan's travels.

"Wow," Katie said, looking around. "I'm almost afraid to touch anything. It's like being in a museum."

"You should be comfortable here," Evelyn replied. "Bathroom's through that door. The kitchen will have all the food you need."

"Mr. Gallagher, you're my hero," Katie said, throwing her arms around Nick and smearing a thick lipstick kiss across his cheek. "I don't know what I'd do without you."

"Try to get some rest," Evelyn said, walking out to the hallway.

A moment later, Nick joined her, carefully shutting the bedroom door. She handed him a handkerchief.

"Bright pink was never your color."

"Are you sure?" Nick teased as he wiped away the lipstick. "I think I can pull it off."

"I can't believe you roped me into this," Evelyn said. "Remind me why we're not taking her to the LAPD?"

"Either they won't believe her story, and they'll toss her in a cell, or they do believe her story. She testifies and the killer comes back looking for her. Neither situation's exactly ideal."

"Even with those big, wide, innocent eyes?"

"Are you jealous?"

"Try nauseous," Evelyn said.

"I'm just being nice."

"Oh, so that's what they're calling it nowadays."

"If I didn't know better, I'd say she's getting under your skin."

"And if I didn't know better, I'd say you like her."

"Anything's possible."

"Maybe you two can ride off into the sunset."

"I could think of worse things."

"I'm imagining them happening to you right now."

Evelyn turned and walked down the stairs. She heard Nick laughing behind her. In the foyer, she opened the door and held it for him.

"You crack the case and you never have to see her again," Nick said.

"I let Carl arrest her and I never have to see her again, either," Evelyn said.

"Yeah, but where's the fun in that?"

"Fine," Evelyn said. "Meet me at the Palmer house tonight. Ten o'clock. Colette was desperate to get into the safe and I want to know why."

"Just like old times," Nick said.

Chapter 20

Evelyn and Nick snuck through the tall hedges surrounding the Palmer house. The lawn was lush and green, smelling of freshly shorn grass in the cool night air. Tiny blades stuck to their shoes as they crept across the wide expanse. A solitary light shone from a window in the back corner of the second story. Evelyn guessed it was Colette's bedroom. There was no way to be certain whether she was home, as the cars were tucked away in the vast garage. Evelyn made her way to a ground-floor window.

"I think this is the study."

Evelyn pushed hard against the lower edge of the window, but it wouldn't budge.

"It's stuck," Nick said, watching her struggle.

"Give me a boost. I can get some leverage."

Nick folded his hands together and she stepped into them.

"Almost there," she replied. "Just a little higher."

Nick boosted her a bit farther. Evelyn leaned forward and gave a hard push. The window slid up an inch, before it slammed back down. Evelyn lost her balance, toppling into the flower beds among the crushed peonies and mud.

"Well, shit," Evelyn said.

Nick held up the key George gave him when he was staying the night, working protection.

"Plan B?"

Evelyn gestured to her filthy clothes.

"Why wasn't that plan A?"

"Colette might be awake, or Peter straightening things up . . ."

Evelyn glared at him.

"It was fun watching you struggle," Nick admitted.

They opened the front door and slid off their shoes. More than the quiet, they did not want to leave tracks in the house. They tiptoed down the hall, alert for any sounds. They made their way to George's study and Evelyn pointed to the far wall.

"The safe is behind the ugly horse painting," Evelyn said.

"Reminds me of the one General Gibson kept at 70 Grosvenor."

"He was so proud of that thing."

"And his British roots from before the Revolutionary War," Nick said.

"Least it was better than when he tried to fit in with the locals," Evelyn said. "That accent!"

"It was a cross between Cockney and Oxbridge, without coming close to either."

Evelyn laughed at the memory as she went to the painting, and swung it away from the wall. She reached for the dial.

"You're kidding, right?" Nick said.

"Please, I was always better at cracking a safe."

"What about that time in Stuttgart?"

"I *knew* you were going to bring that up."

"You left me alone to guard the door in the Abwehr station."

"Because a woman would have been so much less conspicuous."

"It took you forever to crack that thing."

"It was a Hartmann Tresore. And it was four and a half minutes."

"Well, it felt forever. I was tap-dancing with that *Reichsmarschall* trying to explain my awful German."

"You couldn't speak German. Had terrible French. Abysmal Italian. How did you ever make it in the OSS?"

"My charming personality."

"Of course," Evelyn said. "How could I forget that?"

Outside the door, they heard the creak of a floorboard. They both ducked behind the desk. Evelyn looked to Nick.

"Your fault," he whispered.

She glared at him. After a minute, the footsteps retreated back down the hall. Nick went to the door and pressed his ear against it.

"I think they're gone."

Evelyn reached for the dial of the safe and twisted it slowly, waiting to feel the slight catch as the tumbler fell into place. She turned it the other way and back again. Cranking the handle, she swung the door open.

"So maybe you have a few skills," Nick said.

"But timing's not one of them," Evelyn replied as she looked inside. The safe was empty. "Colette must have figured out the combination."

Evelyn glanced over to the fireplace. Fresh ashes were in the grate. She got down on her hands and knees and began sorting through the charred remains.

"Aha!" Evelyn exclaimed as she pulled a singed fragment from the fireplace.

Just then, the footsteps returned. Nick swung the painting back into place and Evelyn ducked behind the sofa as Colette Palmer opened the door.

Chapter 21

Colette was shocked to find Nick standing behind George's desk. For the first time in their acquaintance, she wore no makeup. Her eyes were red from crying and her white-blond hair was pulled back into a chignon, carelessly run through with pins. None of that hid her ethereal beauty. Light seemed to gravitate toward her, and her perfection struck Nick, once again, with its coldness.

"What are you doing here?" Colette asked.

"I came for my things."

"And you thought they'd be in George's study?"

Nick looked trapped in his lie. Evelyn made a gesture he understood too well—she needed him to bluff their way out of this.

"Why are you really here?" Colette asked.

"Aw, hell," Nick said. "I came to see you."

He slid back into his shoes, stepped around the desk, and grabbed Colette in his arms. He kissed her hard. Pulling away in surprise, she slapped him.

"Tell me you never thought about it."

Her face softened slightly and he kissed her again. This time, she didn't pull away. Instead, she clung to him with a hungry, desperate need. Tears slid down her cheek, their warm saltiness flavoring his tongue. He felt a shiver run through her, but it wasn't passion. It was sorrow. Evelyn stood up from behind the sofa and stared at Nick. He motioned for her to exit. Shaking her head, she tiptoed through the open door of the study. When she was gone, Nick broke for air.

"I'm sorry," he said.

"I shouldn't have let you kiss me," Colette said, backing away.

"Grief makes people do strange things."

"With George dead, I feel so lost and alone. The fact that he was found in that girl's apartment . . ."

"He loved you," Nick said.

"Wouldn't that be nice to believe," Colette said.

"It was in the way he spoke of you. The way he looked at you when you didn't realize he was watching."

Nick took Colette by the shoulders and steered her in front of the window. The light of the room against the darkness outside turned it into an almost-perfect mirror.

"What do you see?" he asked.

Colette shook her head, not wanting to answer.

"I see a woman men write poetry about. You're Helen of Troy and Aphrodite all wrapped up into one," Nick said.

"Pretty words."

"Some women's beauty fades, but that's only because they never develop anything akin to a personality. Not you. There's something hidden there. A depth most people miss. You have secrets."

"Don't we all?"

Nick tilted his head in subtle acknowledgment of that fact.

"Care to share any of them?" he asked.

"They're mine to carry."

"You can trust me."

"That's what people always say before they screw you over," Colette replied.

Despite himself, Nick started to laugh.

"Tell me what you're really doing here," Colette said.

"I did. I came for you."

"I know the way a man kisses when he's in love," Colette said. "I know the way a man kisses when he's in lust. You kiss like you're thinking of someone else."

Nick couldn't deny the statement, so he went with the truth, instead.

"I failed George. He hired me to keep him safe. The only way I can make it up to him is if I solve his murder."

"You don't think it was the girl?" Colette asked.

"There's no motive. When George died, the checks stopped."

Colette stumbled back onto the edge of the desk, what little blood was left in her face drained completely.

"He was giving her money?"

Nick nodded.

"Ce putain."

"Is there anything you can tell me?" Nick asked. "Did George have any financial problems? Issues at work? I know he met with Norman Roth more than once. Does he have any dealings with the Mob?"

"No. God, no. He knew Mr. Roth from the war. That was all. George was kind and generous. He often helped his factory workers when they were having a rough time and made sure everyone could support their families. We have more money than a person could spend in a life-time."

"What about the threats?"

"George kept his worries to himself. The notes came to his office and he never told me what was in them."

Colette was a good actress, but Nick saw through the lie.

"Mrs. Palmer, I still feel responsible to George. Which means I feel responsible to you."

"I don't want you on this case. I don't want anyone on this case. George is gone. What good will it do?"

"Don't you want to know why?"

"Will it bring him back?"

Nick didn't answer.

"You're a nice man," Colette started.

"You only say that because you don't know me very well."

She laughed without humor, as if she understood that sentiment.

"Come to the reading of the will tomorrow. I could use the support."

"Anything to help," Nick said.

"Now go find whatever woman keeps you up at night and tell her how you feel."

"Trust me. She doesn't want to hear it."

"Trust me. She does."

Colette kissed him lightly on the cheek, and walked him to the door. On the threshold, she held out her hand.

"Key?"

Nick dug it out of his pocket and dropped it in her hand.

"Not that I don't trust you, I'm just not a fan of uninvited guests."

"I do, at some point, need my things."

"I'll have Peter put them together to take with you tomorrow."

Nick nodded then he walked out into the clear Los Angeles night.

Chapter 22

Nick found Evelyn leaning against her car, annoyed. Patience was never her strong suit.

"Twenty minutes?" she asked. "It took you twenty minutes to get out of there?"

"I didn't want to be rude," Nick replied. "Besides, it was time well spent."

"How well spent?"

Nick just smiled at her.

"You forget, I know what you can do in twenty minutes," Evelyn said.

"I remember what you can do in half that," Nick said.

A faint blush rose to Evelyn's cheek.

"What did you find out?" she asked.

"Not much, but I wrangled an invitation to the reading of the will."

"You used to be better at this," she said.

"Do you have anything to show for our little field trip?"

Evelyn held up the scrap of paper she found in the fireplace. It was a singed fragment of a letterhead and showed a white cross inside a blue circle. Nick frowned in confusion.

"That's it?"

"The same symbol was on a shipping manifest in the commandant's office at the POW camp outside Lille," she said.

"It could be anything."

"Same colors."

"Blue and white," Nick said dismissively.

"Same shape."

"You saw it, what? Four years ago?"

"Why are you fighting me on this?" Evelyn asked.

"I'm just saying it could be a coincidence."

"Coincidences don't get us anywhere. Conspiracy does."

"Conspiracy also gets people killed," Nick said pointedly.

"Yes, it does," Evelyn replied, looking toward the Palmer mansion. "Did you and Jean see anything when you wired the munitions dump? It was one of the few times we would have been close enough to see the shipping labels on the arms we destroyed."

"You think there was something from Palmer Munitions?" Nick asked.

"Both he and Sam Wilder made a fortune during the war."

"As did a lot of people," Nick said. "You'd better have rock-solid evidence if you're going to accuse those men of being traitors."

"I'm not accusing anyone of anything."

"Not yet," Nick said.

"I've known these people most of my life," Evelyn began. "George gave Matthew and me sweets when we were kids. He came over at least once a month for dinner and seemed genuinely happy to be around a family. When Colette came to me with her suspicion George was cheating on her, it didn't seem possible. He wasn't that kind of man. I was actually relieved to find out Katie was his daughter."

"Did you tell that to the grieving widow?"

"I've never found sharing information in the middle of an investigation to be advantageous," Evelyn replied. "Have you?"

"So, what are you thinking?"

"I don't know. I can't believe George would betray his country, but I also don't think this symbol is random," Evelyn said. "What do you think of Colette Palmer?"

"Why do I feel like I'm about to step into a trap?"

"Because you've gone a whole five minutes without saying something stupid."

"You know, I don't miss this side of you."

Evelyn cocked an eyebrow.

"She's clearly very beautiful," Nick began cautiously.

"And?"

"I don't know," Nick said. "French."

"Exactly," Evelyn said. "During the war, everyone in the occupied countries fit into one of three categories. Those just trying to survive. Those in the Resistance. And collaborators."

"You don't think . . ." Nick started.

"I always assumed she was the first, but when she was talking about the Resistance, she referred to Jean as Le Reynard."

"Only the Germans did that," Nick said.

Evelyn nodded.

"You think she was working to ship black-market weapons to the Nazis?"

"I don't know. I genuinely like her, but as you said, she's a beautiful woman. Beautiful women get men to do terrible things all the time."

Chapter 23

The next morning, Evelyn drove to City Hall. The building was a gleaming white testament to the city's recent infatuation with Art Deco. Designed in the 1920s, the architect received special dispensation to build the high tower, dwarfing its surroundings. The clean ivory lines stood in sharp relief against the cloudless blue sky. Along with the gilded pyramid atop the Central Library and the stately rectangles of the *Los Angeles Times* building, they formed a triumvirate guarding the city's values.

The clerk's office was at the end of a long hallway. The unassuming door announced its purpose with carefully stenciled letters on the frosted glass. Evelyn turned the brass knob and walked in to find a young man sitting at a long wooden counter. Behind him bookshelves containing carefully bound records stretched the length of the room. The clerk's eyes widened when he saw Evelyn and he sat up straighter. She smiled, turning up her innate charm.

"Good morning," she said warmly.

"Morning, ma'am," he said.

"'*Ma'am*'?" Evelyn said. "Goodness, how old do I look?"

"No," he quickly backtracked. "You don't look old at

all. You're young and pretty and . . . I was just trying to be polite."

"You seem very polite."

"Oh, well, th-thank you," he stammered.

Evelyn snapped open her pocketbook and withdrew the scrap of paper she discovered in George Palmer's office. She showed the clerk the white cross in the blue circle.

"I'm looking for a business that has this on their letterhead."

"Wow. Could be lots of companies," he said.

"That's what people keep telling me."

"Do you know who owns it? Or what it does?"

"This is all I have to go on," Evelyn said.

"That's not much," the clerk said doubtfully.

"True. But you seem so smart and capable. The kind of man who could help a girl like me," Evelyn said flirtatiously. "I'd be ever so grateful."

She took off her hat and shook out her curls. Slowly she pulled the fingers of her gloves off until her manicured hand lay unsheathed a few inches from his. Evelyn caught his eye and he swallowed hard.

"Sure, I, uh, could look into that," he said. "Might take a while."

"Perhaps I can help. We could start at the opposite end of the stacks and work toward each other?"

"I'm not supposed to let anyone back here."

"What's the harm?" Evelyn asked. "I mean, with you watching over me?"

"I, um, well . . . Some of that information is confidential."

"I promise to be good."

The clerk blushed and glanced over his shoulder. His eyes darted back and forth as he debated with himself. Finally he got off his stool and lifted the partition separating the reception area from the stacks.

"You can't tell anyone about this."

"It's our secret," Evelyn promised, slipping behind the desk.

"I'll start over here in the *A*'s," the clerk said.

Evelyn was less meticulous. She went to the *P* section and cross-referenced companies with Palmer on their board. Beyond his own and a few charities Colette patronized, there was nothing. Next Evelyn turned to international companies active during the war. There were few German organizations that still had contracts in the United States. Those not blacklisted in the early forties had yet to recover from the bombings that decimated many German cities. Evelyn looked through Russian, British, and French businesses, to no avail. She thought back to the German commandant's office. The paper on his desk was a shipping manifest. Turning into a different section, she began pulling records for shipping companies.

Nothing.

"What about this?" the clerk asked, startling her.

He held up a page for the American Red Cross.

"Well, it's a cross," Evelyn said. "Guess that's a start."

"But not the right one."

"No," Evelyn said.

"Everything has crosses," he sighed.

"Blame Jesus."

The clerk stared at her heresy.

"Good man," she amended quickly. "Big fan."

The clerk nodded, uncertain what to make of her. He refiled the heavy tome and plodded onto the next section. Evelyn returned to her search.

"Jesus," she said quietly.

Thinking of religion, she began pulling out more books. There were lots of crosses, mostly for hospitals or relief organizations. Evelyn began looking through charities, but there was nothing. By the end of five hours, she was exhausted and frustrated. Her feet hurt and her back ached. Between her and the clerk, they had searched most of the records.

"It's hopeless," Evelyn said.

"I can keep looking."

"I don't want to take up any more of your time."

"Maybe we could discuss it over dinner," the clerk offered.

"You've been too kind already," Evelyn replied. "Thanks again for all your help."

With that, she let herself out of the office, leaving the clerk forlorn, holding an open tome.

Chapter 24

Nick leaned against the wall as the guests milled about the Palmers' living room. The reading of the will was scheduled for two in the afternoon, but people arrived early to partake of Colette's impressive luncheon. Cold meats and salads lined the sideboard. People filled their plates high, then perched wherever they could find space. Silently Peter collected discarded utensils and refilled coffee.

Through it all, Colette Palmer sat on a couch in the center of the room. Her black dress was juxtaposed against her pale skin, red lips, and the silver blond of her hair, which was tucked into a sleek French twist. If sorrow were a fashion statement, she would be a trendsetter for the ages. Her makeup was perfect, as usual, but it did not hide the redness in her eyes that told of sleepless nights. She responded when spoken to, but did not seek comfort from those who orbited around her.

Across from Colette, on the other couch, sat George Palmer's sister, Meredith. She wore a Dior dress and a sour expression. Her rotund husband sat beside her, straining the seams on his bespoke suit. The two women were polar opposites and Nick wondered whether that alone accounted for the disdain in Meredith's gaze. If Colette noticed the hostility, she gave no sign.

The rest of the room was filled with George's business contacts. The manager at Palmer Munitions approached Nick and introduced himself as Sean Macintyre. He was a rough-hewn man in his fifties who served with George in the First World War. It was a bond they carried through their lives and into business. George had trusted Macintyre more than anyone else in the world, with the possible exception of his wife and Peter. Like many others, Macintyre was interested in the future of the company and, by extension, his job. George was the heart and soul of Palmer Munitions. Having proven itself through the war, the company stood poised for dominance in the second half of the century. So much hung upon the provisions of the will.

"George was a good man," Macintyre said.

"You knew him better than most," Nick replied. "Any chance his death was related to business?"

"How do you mean?"

"Have there been any changes at the company? Any strange people around?"

"Not that I noticed. And I woulda noticed. There was a little bit of a slowdown after V-J Day, but not like you'd think. Got a ton of new contracts for research and development. Suppose after last time, the government doesn't want to be caught with their pants down."

"Easy to read between the lines with Russia."

"Funny how quick allies become enemies," Macintyre said.

"Did you hear about George receiving any threats?"

"There's always the usual whack-a-doodles coming after rich men," Macintyre replied. "But nothing specific."

"In case you think of anything," Nick said, pulling a card out of his wallet.

Macintyre tucked it into his pocket and drifted across the room for another cup of coffee. It was approaching two o'clock and everyone gathered for the main event. Sam Wilder entered with his typical air of hurried importance. He shook a few people's hands and slapped a few backs before making his way to Colette.

"What are you doing here?" she asked, her voice iced over in anger.

"Just honoring an old friend," he replied, placing his hand on her shoulder. To a casual observer, it seemed a comforting gesture. However, the white tension in his fingers and the pained expression on her face belied any kindness.

"Let go of me," she said loud enough to turn heads.

Plastering a broad politician's smile across his face, he released her and went to sit beside Sean Macintyre. George's lawyer opened a briefcase and withdrew a large sealed envelope. The first order of business was to dispense with George's small gifts and benevolences. He gave paintings and collectibles to family members and friends. Meredith began to argue when it was clear she would not receive her mother's diamond brooch, which currently adorned the lapel of Colette's dress. Then the lawyer turned to larger issues.

" 'To my good friend and loyal companion, Peter, I bestow upon you five hundred thousand dollars. It should allow you to retire in comfort, buy that cottage in Santa Barbara, and spend the rest of your days fishing.' "

In shock, Peter looked to Colette for confirmation. The sum was more than a hundred times his already-generous salary and would make him a very rich man. For the first time all day, a genuine smile crossed Colette's face.

"It's well deserved," she said. "George loved you and valued your friendship. Of course, you'll always have a home here, should you want it."

"Thank you," he said, not quite believing his new reality.

The lawyer turned back to the will and continued reading.

" 'The house and all its contents not previously mentioned go to my beloved wife, Colette. As for Palmer Munitions, there are many good people I've had the honor to employ. To the best of my ability, I want to protect and safeguard those who have devoted their lives to this company. It should remain a beacon within the Los Angeles community. This is a complex business that needs to grow and change. To that end, I request Sean Macintyre continue on in his leadership position, taking over as president. In the hope he will enact the plans we discussed, I bestow upon him ten percent of Palmer Munitions.' "

Nick glanced at Macintyre, whose face showed stunned surprise at this generosity. Though a relatively small share, it was still worth at least 3 million dollars.

"Mr. Palmer adds a personal note to this bequest," the lawyer said. " 'Sean, I know the future will be difficult. I'm trusting you to protect my family and my life's work.' "

Macintyre glanced at Colette and she met his eyes. Her expression softened in a shared understanding. Nick wondered if there was more than just respect between them. As Nick's eyes traveled around the room, he noted Sam Wilder's reaction. His face flushed under his deep tan, his hands clenched at his sides. He tried to catch Colette's attention, but she steadfastly refused to look at him.

" 'The other ninety percent of the company will be divided equally,' " the lawyer continued.

Meredith sat straighter.

" 'Forty-five percent will go to my wife, Colette,' " the lawyer read. " 'The other forty-five percent will go to my daughter.' "

" '*Daughter*'!" Colette exclaimed.

"What is this?" Meredith insisted.

"It must be a mistake," Colette said.

"That's what it says here," the lawyer said. " 'Daughter.' "

Colette's cool reserve cracked, and for a moment, her absolute shock was visible.

"Don't you mean *sister*?" Meredith asked, ripping the will out of the lawyer's hands. She read down the page and stopped. "Who the hell is Katie Pierce?"

"How could he put a woman he barely knows into his will?" Colette asked.

"When George rewrote this a month ago, I was given to understand she was the product of a brief affair some years ago."

"He always was a useless bastard," Meredith said. "I begged him to marry a nice, respectable girl and settle down. But no, he always went after cheap whores."

"You will watch your tongue," Colette snapped, her anger temporarily redirected. "George was my husband and I loved him, which is more than I can say for you. If you can't speak of him with respect, the door is right there."

Meredith's dislike of Colette warred with her desire to see if the will held anything else. With an effort, she closed her mouth into a hard line.

"We have no proof she's actually his daughter," Colette said.

"He acknowledged her," the lawyer said. "According to the law, that's enough."

"I don't believe it," Meredith said. "My brother scratched an itch decades ago and now I'm left with nothing."

"It's not about the money," Colette snapped.

"Easy for you to say," Meredith retorted; then turning to the lawyer, she said, "There must be something more. I'll contest it."

"That wouldn't be wise," the lawyer said delicately.

"You must have his previous wills," she insisted.

"I do. The presence of Ms. Pierce does not affect your inheritance."

"That girl killed him," Colette said. "A woman comes into his life pretending to be his daughter. Of course, George acknowledged her. He was the best of men and could never see anyone's faults. All she wanted was the money. Once she convinced him to change his will, he was no longer of use to her."

"We shouldn't jump to conclusions," Wilder said.

"You're one to talk. If it wasn't for you, George would still be here," she said, standing to face Wilder. "You got him killed."

"This has been an emotional day for everyone," Sam Wilder said. "We should leave Colette to her grief."

"I don't want to be left alone. I want that girl to pay!" she said.

"It won't bring him back," Macintyre said softly.

She looked around the room, her eyes landing on Nick.

"You offered to help."

"I did," Nick said, stepping forward.

"Find her."

Chapter 25

Evelyn walked out of City Hall, onto Spring Street. She crossed First, plunging from the bright sunshine into the dark canyon of buildings. As she waited at the stoplight, a large man, wearing a brown wool suit, stepped up beside her. Evelyn initially noticed him waiting on the steps outside City Hall. He held a newspaper, its folds still crisp for having not been read. It would be easy enough to lose him by ducking into the nearby police station. However, that would not explain why he was following her and who sent him. Besides, she'd rather face him when she was prepared than have him catch her off guard at a later date. As long as his intention was to intimidate her, and not kill her, she felt confident in her ability to get through this with nothing more than a few scrapes.

The light changed and Evelyn hesitated a moment. He also waited. When she stepped into the street, he matched her pace. Halfway down the next block, they reached a gap between buildings. As expected, he grabbed her and dragged her into the shadows. Drawing his gun, he pressed it into her ribs.

"You shouldn't be sticking your nose where it don't belong."

"But it's such a pretty nose," she replied, turning so he could admire her profile. He wasn't amused, but his grip lessened and he stepped back, the gun still pointed at her chest.

"Listen, lady, I dunno what your deal is, but I'm telling you to leave this case alone."

"Or . . . ?"

"Or else."

"Can I get specifics?"

"I'll use this," the man said, nodding at his gun. "Give you a belly full of lead."

"Seriously? 'Belly full of lead'?" Evelyn said. "Who talks like that?"

"Well, I . . ." the man started. "Shut up."

"A poet, you are not."

"What's wrong with you?" the man said. "I got a gun."

"Yeah, about that," Evelyn said as she grabbed the muzzle of the gun and pulled it to the side, stepping out of its range. She drove the heel of her hand into his larynx. He gasped for breath as she kicked him hard between the legs. His eyes widened in pain as he doubled over. Using a quick jab, she broke his nose. He fell to the ground and she knelt on his chest, bending his wrist back to pry the gun from his hand. He struggled to get up, but Evelyn drove her knee harder into his sternum. Reaching into his jacket pocket, she withdrew his wallet.

"Daniel O'Brien, 2134 Colton Street, Los Angeles. Now, then, Mr. O'Brien, who do you work for?"

"Fuck you," he said.

"That's not a nice thing to say to a lady."

He struggled again and Evelyn grabbed his right hand, pulling his index finger back.

"Stay down or I'll break your finger and you won't be able to use this lovely piece of hardware," she said as she inspected his gun. "Colt .44. A little showy for my taste, but it gets the job done. Looks about the same caliber as the hole in George Palmer's chest."

Evelyn opened the chamber and emptied the bullets into her hand. Slowly she counted out all six, dropping the first five onto the ground.

"During the war, I learned a fun little game," Evelyn said. "Have you heard of Russian roulette?"

O'Brien shook his head. Evelyn showed him the last remaining bullet.

"It's pretty simple. Six chambers. One bullet."

"You're not going to shoot me," O'Brien said.

She inserted the bullet into the chamber, spun the wheel, and snapped it shut.

"Now, then, who do you work for?" Evelyn asked.

"Fuck you," he said.

Evelyn pulled the trigger. The click of the empty chamber resounded in the alley. O'Brien's eyes widened.

"Next is a one-in-five chance," Evelyn said, pointing the gun. "Who do you work for?"

"You can't just—"

Evelyn pulled the trigger again. Beneath her, O'Brien struggled, but Evelyn just drove her knee down harder.

"One in four."

"You're insane," O'Brien said.

Evelyn pulled the trigger again.

"Stop!" O'Brien said. "Stop."

"You know what I want," Evelyn said. "There's a thirty-three percent chance you're not getting through the next round. How do you like your odds?"

"Please," O'Brien said. "Please don't do this. If I talk I'm dead!"

Evelyn pulled the trigger again. It clicked.

"One out of two chances," Evelyn said of his new odds. "Fifty percent. Not something I'd bet on, but to each his own."

"I got a brother. His daughter, my niece, is my whole world. I'd do anything for that little girl," O'Brien said. "Now, you can pull that trigger, but if I talk, I'm dead. Before it happens, that little girl'll be tortured in front of me."

There was only one person in the city Evelyn thought capable of that kind of retribution. She looked into this man's eyes and knew his fear was real.

"Tell me about George Palmer."

O'Brien shrugged. "Whaddya wanna know?"

"Why did you kill him?"

O'Brien seemed at war with himself, debating whether to answer. Evelyn shifted just a fraction. It was what he was waiting for. He twisted and threw her off him. Her head slammed into the concrete and he was on his feet in a second. For a man of his size, he moved quickly, racing out of the alley. No way she was catching him in heels. At least she still had the gun and his ID. Opening her hand, she let the sixth bullet drop to the ground. Russian roulette was a messy game and she had already ruined two outfits that week.

Chapter 26

Nick walked into his office to find a burly man sitting on the couch. Nick didn't recognize him, but his bruised fedora and size told Nick this probably wasn't a new client. The fact that the office was completely ransacked was his other clue. Overturned drawers sat next to empty filing cabinets. The contents of the desk were scattered across the floor, with papers covering every surface. The man raised his gun. Nick reached for his own, but the door slammed shut behind him. He turned to see a small, wiry man with quick, shifty eyes. He stepped up to Nick and pulled his weapon from its holster.

"Careful," the large man said. "Vito's got an itchy trigger finger."

"Has he tried calamine lotion?" Nick asked.

"You're a funny, funny man."

"I try. Haven't quite perfected the comedy routine, but come back in a few weeks."

Vito drove the barrel of his gun into Nick's ribs.

"Sit," said the burly man.

"Where? You made a god-awful mess of this place and the maid isn't coming for another week."

" 'Maid'?" the man said. "This place hasn't seen the business end of the broom in months."

"I never said she was good at her job."

Vito righted an overturned chair and set it in front of Nick.

"We haven't been properly introduced," Nick said to the man on the couch.

"You can call me Francis."

"I had an Aunt Frances once. You and she would look about the same in a dress."

"Vito," Francis said.

Vito tucked his gun into the holster behind his right hip. His hand shot out and caught Nick's jaw. For a small man, he packed a powerful punch. Nick's head snapped back and pain radiated throughout his skull. It took him a minute to stop seeing stars. Slowly his eyes returned to focus and he rubbed the side of his face.

"That was more a criticism of her than you, but I see now that you're feeling a bit touchy," Nick said. "So tell me, what can I do for you gentlemen?"

"Word is, you've been poking around where you're not welcome," Vito said.

"Don't be silly. I'm welcome everywhere."

The man snorted a humorless laugh. The phone on the desk began to ring.

"Who's that?" Francis asked.

"How the hell do I know?" Nick said.

The phone rang six times before it finally stopped.

"Where were we?" Nick asked.

"We were talking about that big nose of yours and how you keep sticking it where it don't belong. Keep it up and Vito breaking it will be the least of your problems."

"I believe you guys, I really do. The last thing I need is

blood on this shirt. It's my only one that's anything close to presentable."

Francis looked toward Vito, but before he could hit Nick, the phone rang again.

"Fuckin' hell," Francis said. "Answer it. Vito, listen in."

Pushing aside a sheaf of papers, Nick unburied the phone and picked up the receiver.

"Gallagher here."

"Hey, Nick," Evelyn said.

"Your timing's impeccable," Nick replied.

"I ran into a spot of trouble."

"Funny that. Remember our weekend trip to Rouen a few years ago?"

The "trip" was an assignment working with the French Resistance. They came back to their safe house to find the Gestapo surrounding the building.

"What would you do without me?" Evelyn asked.

"Let's not find out."

There was a soft click. The phone went dead in Nick's hand as Vito pressed the switch hook, disconnecting the call.

"Who was that?" Francis asked.

"Ex-girlfriend."

"Why's she calling?"

"She missed me. You guys might not know it, but I can be a charmer."

"Ha!" Francis responded.

"Probably wants money," Vito said.

"Good luck. Look around this dump," Francis said. "What I want is information."

"Can you be more specific?" Nick asked.

"Don't play fucking games," Francis said.

"Seriously. This is my specialty," Nick said. "Finding things, people, whatever you need. Somewhere there's a retainer agreement. I get twenty-five dollars a day plus expenses. Let me just look in here."

Nick reached around the desk to find an empty hole where his drawer usually sat. Francis held up a gun.

"Looking for this?"

"Honestly, yes."

Vito hit him again. As he doubled over, the thought crossed his mind that maybe a steady diet of whisky and sleepless nights wasn't quite the healthy lifestyle his doctor prescribed.

"Jesus Christ!" Nick said. "There's no winning with you guys."

"Tell us about the girl," Francis said.

"I know lots of girls," Nick said.

"Katie Pierce," Francis said.

"Oh . . ." Nick replied. "That's a pretty common name. But again, fill out the retainer. Then I'm off to the races. Metaphorically speaking, of course. I'm not actually going to the track. Not that I have a problem with gambling, it's just—"

Vito hit Nick again. Evelyn warned him about opening his mouth too often. He had a sneaking suspicion that she found it rakishly charming. Then again, maybe it only worked on her.

"You know, fellas," Nick gasped, "I was really hoping we might be friends."

This time, he saw the punch coming. He just didn't see anything after.

Nick came around to find himself lying on the floor. Vito and Francis were arguing.

"Told you not to hit him so hard. You always do this. Knock 'em out before we get what we need."

"How's I supposed to know he'd wuss out?"

For a moment, Nick debated defending his honor versus simply waiting to see if they would leave. He never counted gallantness among his attributes, firmly believing discretion was the better part of valor.

"I'll shock him awake," Vito said. "A little prod never hurt anyone."

From the corner of his eye, Nick saw Vito rip the wire from the back of a lamp and spark the two sides together. He sat up so quickly, he cracked his head on the corner of the desk.

"Goddamn it," he said, bringing his hand up to the wound. He felt the sticky warmth of his own blood.

Vito picked Nick up and propped him back in his chair.

"So . . . Katie Pierce," Francis said. "What do you know about her?"

"Pretty, blond."

Francis sighed as if the whole thing exhausted him. He nodded toward Vito, but the door flew open and four policemen entered with Carl. Francis pointed his gun at them.

"Don't be stupid," Carl said.

Realizing they were badly outnumbered, Francis relented. A policeman pulled his wrists firmly behind his back and slapped handcuffs on him. Captain Wharton and Evelyn entered, looking at Nick.

"Christ, Gallagher," Wharton said, looking at the bloody, bruised state of him.

"I had it under control."

"Tell that to your black eye," Evelyn said.

Carl turned to Vito and Francis.

"Who are you working for?" he asked.

"Fuck you," Francis said.

"They're always so creative," Evelyn said. "Just once, I'd like them to say something different."

"Maybe the St. Crispin's Day Speech," Nick offered.

"Or Hamlet's Act Three soliloquy," Carl suggested.

"What does that have to do with the price of beans?" Wharton asked.

"Almost anything by Churchill is a barn burner," Evelyn added.

Wharton rolled his eyes and turned back to Vito and Francis.

"You're either going to give us answers now. Or down at the station. The only question is what condition you'll arrive in."

"Nothing you can do will be worse than what we've got coming if we talk . . ." Francis said.

Carl nodded to the policemen holding Vito and Francis. "Take 'em away."

"What do you got for me?" Wharton asked Evelyn.

She reached into her purse and pulled out Dan O'Brien's wallet and gun.

"Took these off an unpleasant gentleman today. Dollars to doughnuts this is the gun that killed George Palmer. O'Brien wasn't exactly a font of information, but he's genuinely afraid of someone. Not sure if it's Mickey Cohen or a new outfit. Whoever it is, they seem to have no problem going after family."

"Let me get this straight," Wharton said. "Miss Bishop managed to disarm what I'm assuming was a large thug. And Gallagher, you . . . what? Spent a few rounds as a human punching bag?"

"I was subtly interrogating them," Nick said.

"Right. And what, exactly, did you discover?"

"Guys seemed awfully curious about Katie Pierce. She got a sizeable chunk of George's estate."

"Wouldn't be the first time a person was shot over a fortune," Carl said.

"Maybe Miss Pierce got in with the wrong people," Wharton said. "Threatened the whole racket. Maybe she could ID the shooter. Maybe Mickey just wanted the girl for himself. Doesn't take much to piss him off."

"You gonna talk to Cohen?" Nick asked.

"Yep. And before you say anything, no, you can't come."

Wharton left with Carl, slamming the door behind him.

"So this is your office," Evelyn said, looking at the destruction.

"It's usually neater."

Evelyn raised her eyes questioningly.

"Sometimes," Nick admitted. "You think Cohen's behind it?"

"I wouldn't put anything past that man, but I don't know. Something doesn't add up."

"We don't need Wharton's permission to talk to him."

"True, but he's not going to tell the truth, so why bother?" Evelyn said. "I think I might know another way."

"What?"

Evelyn didn't reply. Instead, she reached for her car keys.

"Come on. I'm taking you home."

"That sounds promising," Nick said.

"Don't get your hopes up."

Without another word, she headed out the door. Nick stumbled through the files scattered across the floor. At the threshold, he turned and surveyed the wreckage. No point locking the door now.

Chapter 27

Evelyn pulled up outside Nick's apartment. The building was five stories, with a tattered awning marking the entrance. The front door hung crooked on its hinges and the windows hadn't been cleaned since the day they were installed.

Nick rested his head against the back of the seat as blood trickled from his nose. Evelyn snapped open her purse and fished out a handkerchief.

"Here."

"Thanks."

Nick took it and dabbed at the blood.

"You just couldn't keep your mouth shut," Evelyn said.

"It's a highly overrated virtue."

"Says the man with a broken nose."

"It's not broken," Nick said. "I know broken."

"Not something to brag about," Evelyn replied. "How many times has it been?"

Nick thought for a moment.

"Five, counting the time in Paris."

"That's right. The bar fight."

"I was protecting your honor."

"My honor needs no protection."

"Those French soldiers would say otherwise."

"The day I can't handle a few drunks is the day I hang up my hat and retire," Evelyn said. "God, that was a lot of blood."

"My point exactly."

She looked at the flat center of his nose, already swelling. "You should put some ice on it," she said. "Does it hurt?"

"I've had worse."

"I know, but worrying about you is a surprisingly hard habit to break."

He caught her eye and for a moment felt the flicker of possibility. Then she turned away and looked through the windshield again.

"I'm guessing this place is even worse than your office."

"It's temporary," Nick replied.

"How long you been here?"

"Three years."

Evelyn resisted the urge to point out that was longer than he had lived almost anywhere. The hopelessness of the place felt at odds with the man she knew during the war. Back then, Nick was always fighting for something better. He was always in motion. This building and the surrounding neighborhood felt resigned to its own bleakness.

"You need help getting up the stairs?" she asked.

"Only if you're planning to stay, once we get to the top."

"I'll call when everything's set for tomorrow," Evelyn said.

Nick got out and walked to the front door, his shoulders hunched, each step exposing his pain. When he disappeared inside, she put the car into gear and drove across town to see James. He lived in a small bungalow in Culver City, not far from the MGM lot. It amused Evelyn that they often shared the local diner with movie stars, whom neither of them recognized. Though they both enjoyed a good film, they were largely indifferent to the entertainment industry that defined the city.

Evelyn parked her car on the quiet street and walked up the narrow path. Before she could reach the door, James opened it and stood waiting for her on the threshold. Just the sight of him brought a sense of calm. Until this moment, she had not realized the toll of the past few days. Though James was dressed to go out, he took one look at Evelyn's face and gathered her in his arms.

"I'll make us drinks and you'll tell me what's going on."

"The house you wanted to show me . . ." Evelyn began.

"It'll wait," James replied.

She leaned up and kissed him.

"Have I ever told you how much I love you?"

"I never get sick of hearing it."

James led her inside and Evelyn kicked off her shoes, curling her feet under her on the couch. His home was the epitome of a bachelor pad, but Evelyn found it cozy. A single story, it contained a living room, bedroom, and small kitchenette. James rented it shortly after returning from the war, when Logan offered him a job at the company. It was close enough to Bishop Aeronautics to be convenient, while also being near the rest of the city. The furniture was simple, but comfortable. Posters and prints James had gathered on his travels hung on the wall. None were expensive, but they gave the room a certain harmony. A tartan throw, undoubtedly picked up in London to fight the foggy chill, lay over the back of the couch, and a variety of lamps banished the shadows. On the end table were photographs of his parents, a snapshot of Evelyn taken on the beach, and a picture of her, Matthew, and James, from when they were children.

James went to the kitchen and mixed martinis. He brought one to Evelyn and sat beside her. Gently they clinked glasses and she sipped the icy cold liquor. He took her hand and held it lightly in his as she told him about her day. He reacted sharply to the fight with Dan O'Brien, but knew enough not to interrupt.

"Sounds like a lot," James said when she finished.

"I expected you to tell me to stop this investigation."

"That's worked so well in the past," he replied. "So, what's next?"

"Actually, I was hoping you could help me," Evelyn said.

"I don't know how, but . . . sure. Anything."

"The other night you mentioned you knew Norman Roth in the war," Evelyn said. "Can you get me a meeting?"

"You're not getting wrapped up with Mickey Cohen, are you?"

"That's what I'm hoping to avoid."

"Fine," James said. "But I'm going with you."

Evelyn nodded and he picked up his address book. Flipping through it, he found the number and dialed. The conversation was short, and when he hung up, they had a breakfast meeting at Canter's on Fairfax. Evelyn called Nick to relay the information. There was something in her voice. It was light, teasing, and a bit too familiar.

"Nick?" James asked after she hung up. "Don't think you've mentioned him before."

"We knew each other during the war. He was guarding George Palmer when all of this went down."

"Now you're working on this, together. Was he . . ."

James could not quite put his question into words. He thought Evelyn was with someone during the war, but the details never seemed to matter. As far as he knew, everything that happened across the Atlantic was left there when she returned home.

"One case," Evelyn said. "Then the past goes back where it belongs."

James nodded, uncertainty still etched on his face. Evelyn kissed him and slowly felt his tension unwind. They finished their drinks; then she took his hand and led him into the bedroom. She kissed him again as he slowly slid down the zipper at the back of her dress. As she shrugged out of it, the soft wool pooled on the floor around her feet. She kicked off her shoes and he knelt down, unrolling her silk stockings. Her fingers found the buttons of his shirt and she traced his broad shoulders as the fabric fell back. Like the rest of his body, his chest was well defined, the muscles carving lines under his skin. Their caresses built, until her skin quivered at nothing more than his breath. He laid her down on the bed and she gasped softly. Meeting his eyes, she shared a smile with him. In this instant, they were the only two people in the world.

When they finished, lying spent beside each other, Evelyn luxuriated in the liquid feeling of her body. He pulled the pins from her hair and ran his fingers through it, letting it trail down her back. He traced the knife scar along her ribs and the shredded skin of her shoulder, from when she got caught crawling under barbed wire. Just above her hip was the pucker of a bullet wound. Gently James kissed each patch of healed skin, and she knew he was thinking about the times he might have lost her.

"What was the worst part of the war for you?" Evelyn asked, rolling onto her side to face him.

James's fingers fluttered along her skin as he thought.

"The loneliness. Every day I went to work, processing numbers and organizing papers. Sometimes I went out for drinks afterward, but then I came home to my empty room."

"I'm sure there were more than a few nurses who volunteered to keep you company," Evelyn teased.

"They weren't who I wanted," he replied. "You were in London, but not really. I almost never saw you."

"Everything was classified," Evelyn said. "And I didn't want to lie to you."

"I missed you."

She knew he wanted her to say that she had missed him, too. The truth was that during that time, there was no room in her life for anything other than her team and their missions.

"I wasn't in London very often," she said. "The people I fought with were like family. We did everything together and they were the only ones I didn't have to keep my guard up around."

"What was the worst part for you?" James asked.

"The fear," Evelyn replied. "It wasn't so much that I was afraid of dying. It was a fear of failing Matthew. Then a fear of what might happen if I didn't return home. My father wouldn't have been able to handle it if . . . I should have come back to Los Angeles after I lost my brother, but at that point, I hated myself. I hated everyone else. I was so goddamned angry I couldn't see straight. I didn't know what to do with all that rage."

Just thinking of that time brought a flush to her cheeks. Inadvertently, her fingers curled into fists and her muscles tightened. No one knew that sometimes, even now, she saw Matthew's blood seeping through her fingers. Underneath everything else, the rage still thrummed in her chest.

"But it wasn't all bad," Evelyn said.

"I guess not," James replied.

"What was the best part?"

"London. Paris. I got to see the world. Granted, it wasn't like before the war, but it was a chance I wouldn't have had, otherwise. Rarely do gardeners' sons grow up to travel Europe."

"You were never just a gardener's son."

"Because your father paid for my education."

"Because *your* father is a good man, who taught you to be kind and instilled a drive for something more. You were always going to make something of yourself, no matter what."

James reached for Evelyn's hand and brought it to his lips. It felt like chivalry, but the look in his eyes was pride.

"What was the best part for you?"

"Strangely, the fear."

"How so?"

"Growing up, I always felt like I was trying to find myself. I'd read books about grand adventures or heroic knights and wondered what I would do in that situation. Of course, it never felt real, because I was a girl and therefore I'd never get to do any of that. I was supposed to become an adult and host tea parties and play tennis, slowly dying of boredom. Then, one day, I found myself curled up against a mudbank, German bullets pinging the dirt around me. I was terrified, but not immobile. My hands shook, but I could still reload my gun. I could still take aim. When it was over, I knew I'd go back again. I knew I could face the fear. For the first time in my life, I felt like I knew who I was."

"Did you ever kill anyone?" James asked.

Evelyn nodded.

"I hated it. When I could, I avoided it, but there were times when that wasn't an option. If it came down to Nick, Carl, Theo, or David, I didn't hesitate. I regretted the need for us to be there, and I regretted the lives taken, but I never regretted my actions."

"You were lucky, then."

"I don't know that I'd describe it as 'lucky.' "

"War can be a time of compromises. Things you never thought you'd do, for reasons you never thought you'd see."

"Like what?" Evelyn asked.

James waved his hand as if to banish the memory.

"I wish . . ." he started, then broke off. A look of sadness crossed his face, before he looked up and met her eyes. "I wish we hadn't been in such a rush to join the fight. If Matthew had stayed home, I would have, too. Sure, we would have been drafted, but we would've had more time. Maybe everything would be different."

"There's no point in wondering what might have been. We're here now," she said, kissing him to drive away his demons. He pulled her into his arms and tried to drown the past in the present.

Chapter 28

Canter's was the kind of Jewish deli most often found on the Lower East Side of Manhattan. Its name was scrawled boldly across the front of the restaurant. A Star of David, showing pride in the deli's heritage, was located on each edge of the sign. James parked in front and turned off the engine.

"Thanks for doing this," Evelyn said.

"It's not often you ask for my help," he replied. "Who knows? Maybe I'm secretly cut out for a life as a private eye."

"My father would never forgive me for taking you away," Evelyn teased.

They opened the doors of the car and stepped onto the sidewalk. From a distance, Evelyn saw Nick shamble down the street. Though he had changed his suit, his clothes still looked slept in. She wondered if he even owned an iron. His fedora was pulled low, and it was only when he reached them that she could decipher the purple bloom of his black eye.

"You look like shit," she said by way of greeting.

James raised an eyebrow. He almost never heard Evelyn swear. In fact, he had almost never heard her speak to anyone with such irreverance. The implied intimacy pained him in a way he did not want to admit.

"Head's ringing like a gong," Nick replied.

"Hangover or concussion?"

"Yes."

Evelyn laughed. Then she turned to James.

"Nick Gallagher, James Hughes."

James stuck out his hand.

"Pleased to meet you," he said.

Nick shook James's hand, grasping it a moment longer than necessary. He didn't try to hide his assessment of James, nor the fact that he found him wanting.

"So you and Evie are going steady."

"Nick . . ." Evelyn warned. He just fired a shot across the bow, but James was not one to back down. He slid his arm around Evelyn's waist, pulling her closer.

"Sure. You could call it that," James replied. "After all, we did go to high school together. In fact, we've known each other our entire lives. That kind of history is nice, don't you think?"

"You can spend a lifetime barely touching the surface of a person. Or you can understand them intimately after less than a day."

"Enough," Evelyn said.

"What?" Nick asked with false innocence.

"I hear you two served together in the war," James said. "What exactly did you do? Evie doesn't like to talk about it."

"You know what it was like on the front lines, don't you?" Nick said. Then, noting James's tight expression: "Or were you comfortable behind a desk while the rest of us risked our lives?"

"I did my part."

"Ever fire a gun? Hand-to-hand combat? Anything more than a paper cut?"

"The skills I learned during those years served me well

when I got home," James replied. "How about you? Was it an easy transition to civilian life?"

Nick looked murderously at James.

"Stop it. Both of you," Evelyn said. "A man died and we are trying to figure out why. If you can't focus on that, then leave."

They both looked chastened. Leading the way, Evelyn threw open the door to the deli. She was greeted by a long counter of smoked meats, platters of fish, and trays of kugel. There were fresh bagels and hanging rows of thick kosher salami. Norman Roth sat in the booth farthest from the door, with his back against the wall. He was dressed in khaki pants and a brown plaid shirt. Showing nothing of his deadly associations, he looked like an off-duty banker enjoying his morning coffee and the cross-word. He glanced up at their approach, not bothering to stand.

"Thanks for meeting us," James said, ushering Evelyn into the seat across from Norman. "This is Evelyn."

"I've heard a great deal about you," Norman said.

Evelyn glanced at James, who slid into the booth beside her.

"Not just from James. Mickey Cohen is impressed with your moxie."

"That's quite the compliment," Evelyn replied.

"Indeed."

The year before, she worked a particularly ugly divorce case. Rather than hide in the shadows, she went to see Cohen herself. He was tickled by the idea of a lady detective. She convinced him that a domestic violence charge for one of his employees would bring unwanted attention. Evelyn's client was granted a quick divorce with a generous settlement. Ever since, Evelyn and the Mafia held a grudging respect for each other, realizing their paths might cross more often than either would like.

Norman looked up to Nick, who was standing awkwardly beside the table. With no chairs nearby, he was faced with the option of sitting in an adjoining booth or pushing in next to a stranger. Norman seemed amused at Nick's predicament; then he picked up his newspaper and pencil and slid over to make room.

"Please sit, Mr. Gallagher," Norman said.

Nick did as he was told.

"Apologies," Nick said. "I didn't know we had met before."

"We haven't," Norman said. "But your business has, tangentially, approached ours, which made you a person worth knowing."

The waitress arrived with a pot of coffee. Norman nodded to his cup. Evelyn and Nick turned theirs over to be filled.

"Whatcha havin'?" she drawled with a thick Brooklyn accent.

"I'm good with coffee, thanks," Evelyn replied. James and Nick nodded their agreement and she drifted away to another table.

"So, what brings you to see me, instead of visiting Mickey with the police?" Norman asked.

"How'd you know they were going there this morning?" James asked.

Norman smiled at his naïveté. It was common knowledge that Mickey Cohen had informants at every level of the LAPD. Similarly, Evelyn also knew he had signed off on this meeting, otherwise it would not have happened. Gently she laid her hand over James's and he took the cue to let her handle things.

"Mr. Cohen and I have a fine working relationship," Evelyn said. "Besides, he's not going to tell them anything worth knowing. And why would he? I'm not convinced he's involved."

"He'll be glad to hear that."

"Couple of guys came to see us yesterday," Nick said. "Kind of heavy hitters."

"Your face shows the evidence," Norman replied.

Nick shrugged.

"We were wondering if there's a new outfit in town," Evelyn said.

"There's always some upstart looking to take on Mickey," Norman replied. "They learn quickly enough. Far as we know, there's nothing significant, or at least nothing coming at us head-on."

"The name Dan O'Brien mean anything to you?" Evelyn asked.

Norman shook his head. The waitress reappeared with a toasted onion bagel, a heap of cream cheese, and smoked whitefish piled onto a plate. She set it in front of Norman, then disappeared back to the kitchen. He picked up his fork, skewering a sliver of fish to taste. Approvingly he began assembling his bagel.

"Sounds Irish," Norman said.

"Name is. He didn't have an accent, though," Evelyn replied.

"The other guys were Vito and Francis," Nick added. "Guessing Italian origin."

"These things are rarely agnostic," Norman said before taking a small bite of his bagel.

"It's more than that," Evelyn continued. "I can't say for the others, but O'Brien seemed genuinely frightened. Not just for himself, but he mentioned having a niece. Seemed she was fair game."

"It isn't wise to underestimate Mickey, but I've never known him to go after kids," Norman said carefully. He wiped the corners of his mouth, then folded the napkin beside his plate. "I've been authorized to tell you certain things. The first is that we had nothing to do with George

Palmer's death. I wasn't aware you both had run-ins yesterday. To the best of my knowledge, they were not our people. The second thing I am to tell you is that we don't know anything about George Palmer's death. Usually, with something this high profile, there's some buzz. This is exceptionally quiet. The third thing is that I wish to help you as much as I can. As James told you, I knew George during the war. He was a good man. I enjoyed his company and he was kind. After we returned home, not everyone acknowledged our former friendships. George did."

Evelyn reached into her pocketbook and pulled out the charred slip of paper with the white cross on a blue background.

"Do you know anything about this?"

"I've seen it," Norman said after a moment. Then he looked to James. Evelyn followed his gaze.

"It showed up during the war," James said reluctantly. "On some of the manifests."

"What kind of manifests?" Evelyn asked, feeling like she was pulling teeth to extract information.

"The kind where items went missing," Norman said.

Nick sat up straighter. "You mean the black market?"

"Black market was silk stockings, chocolate, and coffee," Evelyn said. "George produced weapons."

"I originally noticed the stamp after America joined up," James began. "Before then, I was working for the British Army. As you know, I hoped to go into the field, but it turned out I'd made an impression. My superiors deemed me too valuable to let go. So I spent the war behind a desk. Initially, I didn't really think anything of the symbol. Some of the manifests came in with dozens of different stamps. Some from customs. Some from receiving. Some from God only knows where. Eventually I started getting calls. I wasn't the first person they called. Nor the second. There was a whole chain of command, and by the time it reached me, the red tape was so thick it was near impossible to get through."

"What kind of calls?" Evelyn asked quietly.

"Things were missing. Supplies never arrived."

"James came to me," Norman said. "Admittedly, I'd been known to make a fair bit of cash off luxury items. Whisky, satin negligees, French perfume . . . pretty much anything you wanted. But this was guns, ammo. Items our soldiers needed to fight. I'd never risk their lives. I did what I could to help unravel the mystery, but there was something larger at work."

"Most of the missing crates had that stamp on their invoice," James continued. "I tried to trace their origins and shipping routes, but I kept running into roadblocks. Then the war ended and it didn't seem quite so important. I wrote reports, passed it up the food chain, and came home. Maybe I should have pressed harder, but honestly, I just wanted to put it all behind me."

James looked to Evelyn, as if seeking absolution. She took his hand in hers.

"How do you think the crates got diverted?" Nick asked.

"I don't know," James replied.

"Where do you think they ended up?"

"I don't know," James repeated.

"Was it just ammunition?" Nick asked carefully. "Or other things?"

James's eyes narrowed as he looked at Nick. The two men studied each other across the table. Evelyn glanced to Norman to see if he understood what was between them, but he shook his head.

"What else do you think went missing?" Evelyn asked.

Nick waited for James to answer, and when it was clear that he wouldn't, Nick shrugged, as if to play off his question.

"Who knows?" he asked. "I can imagine a lot of things that might be of interest during the war."

Evelyn knew she wouldn't get more information while these two were together. Turning to Norman, she asked, "Is there anything else you can think of that might be helpful?"

"All I have are rumors and conjecture," he said.

"Then you're a step ahead of me," she replied.

Norman took another small bite of his bagel, chewed it, then swallowed some coffee. Again he dabbed his mouth with the paper napkin, before folding it and setting it beside his plate. All his moves were studied and precise. It had the effect of making him seem like a cautious man, when it actually gave him the time to study others.

"It was always curious to me that George Palmer's ammunition was the type that went missing. We had dozens of suppliers, but his invoices were the only ones with the stamp," Norman said. "You know his wife is French. He managed to get her out of the country in 1943. No easy feat. I know nothing definite, but her means of escape might be worth looking into."

Norman took another sip of his coffee, then picked up his pencil and turned back to the crossword. The meeting was over. Evelyn thanked him for his time and asked him to send her regards to Mickey Cohen. He nodded without looking up. She, James, and Nick slid out of the booth and headed back into the bright sunlight.

Chapter 29

Nick, Evelyn, and James stood outside Canter's, watching the early-morning traffic amble by on Fairfax.

"So, what's the next step?" James asked.

"The next step is for you to head into the office," Evelyn said.

"But . . ."

"I can't tell you how much I appreciate your help," she continued with finality.

Gently James pulled her away, dropping his voice low.

"I know you're the best at this," James began. "I trust you, I love you, and I would never tell you what to do. But there's something about this that doesn't feel right. Maybe that it's so close to home, with George Palmer being a friend. Maybe it's that you could have been killed yesterday. Maybe it's that I don't know what I'd do if I lost you."

"You're not going to lose me."

"Please," James said, "consider walking away."

Gently she cupped his face in her hands and they both knew her answer. He gathered her into a hug and she felt the strength of his arms around her. When James finally released her, she smiled up at him.

"I'll see you tonight," Evelyn said. "You can finally show me the house."

James kissed her, then got into her car. Putting it into gear, he pulled out of the parking space and headed south. Evelyn stood on the curb, watching until he turned the corner onto Beverly.

"What the hell was that?" Evelyn asked, turning to Nick.

'What?" Nick said with a forced innocence.

"You and James were going at it like a couple of kids on the schoolyard."

"He—"

"Is who I'm with and has every right to be protective," Evelyn snapped. "You're just behaving like an ass."

For a moment, Nick looked like he wanted to argue; then he pulled his car keys out of his pocket.

"What do you say we have a chat with Palmer's foreman. I met him at the funeral and got the sense he knew more than he was letting on."

Evelyn was surprised by Nick's capitulation, but didn't want to push her luck. They got into his car and drove through Hollywood, which always looked somewhat diminished during the day. Tourists gathered to fit their hands into the molds of Clark Gable's and Joan Crawford's, as if the concrete still held a hint of their magic. Grauman's Chinese Theatre seemed gaudy and small without the klieg lights announcing a new premiere. The whole area gave the impression of a flat, pasteboard film set rather than a Technicolor movie.

Evelyn and Nick headed over Cahuenga Pass, north toward Burbank. Large manufacturing plants, such as Moreland Trucking Company and Lockheed Martin, one of Bishop Aeronautics' major competitors, were nestled among the orange groves at the foot of the Verdugo Mountains. George Palmer's factory was a three-story redbrick building, with smokestacks rising to the sky in regular intervals along an angled roof. In front, the asphalt parking lot held cars of every variety.

Nick and Evelyn walked to the front door, where a young man sat at a desk. He looked up at them with a polite smile.

"Morning. What can I do for you?"

"We'd like to see Sean Macintyre."

"Is he expecting you?"

"No," Nick said, handing over his business card. "But we met at Mr. Palmer's home."

The man nodded and picked up the phone. He spoke into it, giving all the relevant details in a crisp, precise fashion. A moment later, he hung up.

"If you'd like to take a seat, Mr. Macintyre will be with you shortly."

"Thanks," Nick replied, moving to an olive-green vinyl chair.

Evelyn drifted around the room looking at the framed newspaper clippings that adorned the wall. The largest was from December 8, 1941. The headline of the Los Angeles Times read: JAPS OPEN WAR ON U.S. WITH BOMBING OF HAWAII. It was the moment that took George Palmer from a successful businessman to an essential part of American history. Other clippings mentioned Palmer Munitions by name or had photos of their bombs strapped into the belly of a plane making its way over the English Channel. Somehow none of the pictures showed the end results of the factory's creations.

After a few minutes, Sean Macintyre entered with a slightly harried look. He shook Nick's hand and winced at the sight of the black eye, but was too polite to ask for details.

"Sorry to keep you waiting; it's a struggle around here without George."

"Not a problem," Nick replied. Then, gesturing to Evelyn, he said, "May I introduce Evelyn Bishop?"

"A pleasure, Miss Bishop," he said. "I know your father by reputation, of course."

"You had a common cause," she replied, gesturing to the walls.

"Thank God those days are behind us," he said. "Come on back."

They walked onto the main floor. Large machines ferried munitions from one station to the next. At each, workers in coveralls carefully added new elements all leading up to a deadly cylinder that would, hopefully, never be needed again. Macintyre led them through the factory to an office overlooking the assembly lines. He closed the door behind them, reducing the noise to a muted thrum that faded into the background. All around were stacks of papers, invoices, and accounting books.

"Sorry for the mess," Macintyre apologized as he cleared off two chairs for Evelyn and Nick.

"I've seen worse," she replied. Then, gesturing to Nick, "Specifically, his office last night."

"That wasn't my fault," Nick protested half-heartedly.

"Now, then," Macintyre said, taking a seat behind his desk. "How can I help?"

"Evelyn and I are trying to figure out exactly what happened to George," Nick began. "Got a couple of questions you might be able to answer."

"Anything," Macintyre replied.

"A lot of Palmer Munitions were used during the war," Evelyn began. "How did you get them where they needed to go?"

"I'm sure much the same as your father. Packaged them up, then a truck from the U.S. Army arrived. They were out of our hands after that."

"Did you ever hear of any going missing?" Evelyn asked.

Macintyre's face tightened.

"What are you accusing me of?"

"Nothing," Nick said quickly. "We just spoke with someone who served at HQ in London. He mentioned that sometimes shipments didn't make it where they were supposed to go."

"Like I said, once the army got hold of them, they were out of our hands."

"Did George seem like he'd changed at all recently?" Evelyn asked.

"How do you mean?"

"He say anything about life at home? Was he different at work?"

Macintyre thought about that for a long moment.

"When I started working for George, back in the 1920s, he loved this business. I know that's strange to say, considering what we do, but George was always first into the office, last to leave. He constantly tried new ways to streamline the process and make it safer for our workers. He wanted to make bombs more precise, to help reduce civilian casualties.

"Sometime during the war, that energy faded. I chalked it up to the fact that it became impossible to separate the pure creation of a thing from its ultimate purpose. After the war, it took a few months for him to come back to himself. He started taking meetings again and talked about shifting the plant to manufacture consumer goods instead. He'd go down to the floor just to chat with the lines men. Even Mrs. Palmer came with him sometimes. Then, I don't know, about six months ago all that faded."

"You know why?"

Macintyre shook his head no.

"He just stopped talking about new innovations. It was almost . . . This is going to sound crazy. It was almost like he had given up."

"On the business?" Nick asked.

"On life," Macintyre replied. "I was worried about him."

"How was his relationship with his wife?" Evelyn asked.

"Good, so far as I could tell," Macintyre replied. "George was smitten from the start, but between the age gap and the fact that she was so very attractive, he never thought he had a chance. Even so, he figured what the hell? No harm in writing her a few letters. When he got a response? Man, his face was like sunshine."

"From what I saw, it was mutual," Nick said.

"Most people would have appreciated her looks. They're almost impossible to ignore, but George was never that kind of guy," Macintyre continued. "Instead, he talked about how smart she was and her kindness. You'd never know it, but she's got a dry sense of humor that'll catch up with you a day later. George would've moved Heaven and Earth just to see her smile."

"Do you know anything about how George got Mrs. Palmer out of France during the war?" Nick asked.

"George was a well-connected man," Macintyre said.

"Which would explain a visa into this country," Evelyn replied. "But it was a struggle to leave occupied territory. Nazis weren't exactly known for being generous in that department."

"What are you implying?" he asked sharply.

"Did you know that my brother got captured early in the war? 1941," Evelyn said. "It was awful. Having him in a POW camp, unable to get him out . . . I would have done almost anything to save him. When it comes to the people we love, sometimes we're willing to do things we never imagined just to keep them safe."

"Don't know what to tell you," Macintyre said, standing up to end the meeting.

Evelyn gambled on the fact that he was too much of a

gentleman to actually throw them out of his office. She pulled the slip of paper from her handbag.

"Have you seen this symbol before?" she asked, showing him the white cross on the blue background.

"I want you to leave."

"Apparently, it was stamped on some of Palmer Munitions' manifests," Evelyn persisted.

"Get out," Macintyre growled. There was a low rumble of something more than impatience.

"If you know anything about George's death," Nick began, "don't you owe it to him to help find who killed him?"

For a long moment, Macintyre didn't say anything. Evelyn realized the look in his eyes was not anger. It was fear.

"I have a family," Macintyre finally said. "I loved George, but I have to protect them. Now please go, and don't come back. I can't help you."

Evelyn wanted to promise they could keep them safe, but she had no idea what they were up against. She and Nick left Macintyre's office and headed out through the rumbling beast of a factory that felt more dangerous than ever.

Chapter 30

Nick and Evelyn agreed that talking to Colette Palmer was the logical next step. As they drove to her house, a question kept nagging at Evelyn. Finally she turned to Nick.

"At breakfast, you asked about other things going missing during the war. It seemed like you were thinking of something specific. What was it?"

She could not be certain, but it looked as though Nick tensed just a fraction.

"Anything," he replied. "Guns, medicine, who knows?"

"We made a few runs to blow ammo dumps during the war," Evelyn began. "Did you ever see anything from Palmer?"

"No, but we blew most of them up from outside."

"Except for one," Evelyn said.

"Except for one," Nick agreed.

The night Matthew died.

"Did you mean what you said to Macintyre?" Nick asked. "About understanding how someone might do anything to keep those they love safe?"

"You should know the answer to that question," Evelyn replied.

"Yes, but you fought the bastards. What if someone was blackmailed or paying ransom for a hostage?"

Evelyn thought for a long moment.

"Part of me wants to say it's selfish to give supplies to the enemy in order to save someone you love. Each person killed by those weapons, or fighting without the supplies they need, has loved ones back home. Another part of me realizes that not everyone could pick up and join the OSS. If you told me the only way I could help Matthew was to plant a Victory garden, I would have gone insane."

They drove on in silence for a few miles. Nick thought over their history and all he knew about her. Finally he said, "I need to tell you something . . ."

Evelyn turned to face him. He slowed the car as they rounded the corner onto Colette Palmer's street. Several police cars were in front of the house.

"I . . .um."

Nick wanted to continue, but their attention was caught up in the chaos. They got out of their car and found Carl and Captain Wharton.

"Jesus, you're everywhere, Gallagher," Wharton said with exasperation.

"What's going on?" Evelyn asked.

"We're arresting Colette Palmer for arranging a hit on her husband," Carl said.

"You got that from Mickey Cohen?" Nick asked.

"Bastard's a brick wall. Not that I expected anything different," Wharton grunted. "Nah, while we were there, a lawyer came in to see those two goons. After that, they couldn't shut up. Said Mrs. Palmer hired them to get rid of her husband and frame the girl. When Katie Pierce disappeared, they went looking for her at your wreck of an office."

"Was it Sam Rummel?" Evelyn asked, naming Cohen's lawyer.

Carl shook his head.

"No one we recognized."

"What are you two doing here?" Wharton asked. Nick opened his mouth to answer, but Wharton held up his hand. "You know what? Never mind. Just stay out of our way."

Wharton motioned to the other police officers to fan out around the house, while he marched up to the front door.

"Wait in the car. I'll see if I can get you in for a chat before we take Mrs. Palmer downtown," Carl offered.

"Thanks," Evelyn said.

She and Nick watched Carl and Captain Wharton knock on the front door. Colette's car was parked in the circular driveway. The lights in an upstairs bedroom were on and the breeze fluttered the curtains from an open window. Still, no one answered Wharton's insistent pounding.

"She's gone," Evelyn said. "She must have seen the police arrive or was tipped off by someone at the station."

"You don't know that," Nick said.

"You don't *always* have to disagree with me."

"You're not always right."

Evelyn cocked an eyebrow at Nick.

"Just most of the time," he conceded. "Where do you think she went?"

In the distance, a streetcar rumbled past.

"Not where. How," Evelyn said. "That line goes straight to Union Station."

"From there, she could catch a train to Mexico."

Nick drove to the end of the street and turned to follow the tracks. As they passed the first streetcar, Evelyn looked in the windows.

"You see her?"

"No," she said. "Had she caught this one, we would've seen her leave the house."

In the distance, they could just make out another streetcar. Nick pushed the pedal down as far as it would go. He swerved around a slow-moving Packard and then into the other lane of traffic to get around a fruit truck.

"Are you trying to get us killed?" Evelyn asked.

"I'm trying to catch the streetcar."

Nick shifted into the next gear just as the stoplight turned red. He sped through the intersection, with Evelyn clinging desperately to the dashboard.

"If I didn't know better, I'd say you were trying to make up for Hamburg," Evelyn said.

"Oh, you just had to bring that up."

"I got there a full hour before you. Even my grand-mother didn't drive as slow."

"There was snow!"

"You steer into a skid. Everyone knows that," Evelyn said as Nick swerved around another car. The distance be-tween them and the streetcar was narrowing.

"Some of us didn't vacation in the Alps."

"And some of us have a working knowledge of physics."

In response, Nick shifted up another gear.

"Nick, *slow down*," Evelyn insisted.

"We're almost there."

Ahead, the streetcar pulled away from its stop and moved into traffic. Nick drove up next to it.

"There!" Evelyn said.

Nick glanced where she pointed, only to see the back of a woman's head. Her burgundy hat was pulled low, hiding any trace of her hair.

"It could be anyone."

"That's a Reboux."

"Of course . . . ?"

"The woman who can afford that hat does not ride the streetcar," Evelyn said. "Get ahead of it."

"Sure, *now* you want me to speed."

Evelyn glared at him and he gave her a cocky smile.

"Eyes on the road," she growled, hating how his lips curled up.

Nick wove through traffic until he was ahead of the streetcar. Then he yanked the wheel sideways and pulled his car across the tracks. With a screech of brakes, the streetcar ground to a halt.

The conductor was already yelling by the time Evelyn got to the door.

"What the hell, lady! Move your car!"

"Sorry," Evelyn said, trying to open the door.

The conductor kept it firmly shut.

"Promise, I'm not crazy. I just need to get on board," Evelyn said.

"That's what the stops are for," the conductor replied.

"It couldn't wait."

"The stop's in two blocks," the conductor replied.

"Do I look like a person who regularly takes the streetcar?" Evelyn asked.

"You're not helping your case," Nick yelled.

"It could be my job," the conductor argued.

"I won't tell if you won't," Evelyn replied.

Irritated, the conductor motioned to all the witnesses in the back of the streetcar.

"Oh, right."

From inside the streetcar, people craned their necks, trying to get a look at the commotion. Evelyn banged on the door again. From the corner of her eye, she saw two traffic cops approaching Nick's car.

"That guy won't move his car until you open the door. He's even more stubborn than I am," Evelyn said. "What's worse? Letting one little person on your streetcar or keeping all these people waiting?"

"Christ on a cross," the conductor swore under his breath. "What did I do to deserve this?"

Evelyn smiled as the conductor opened the door. She stepped on board as the traffic cops reached Nick's car.

"What do you think you're doing?" the first cop asked Nick.

"Not now," he said, waving them away. The conductor leaned on his horn again, his side of the bargain complete.

"You can't be here," the traffic cop insisted.

"Yep. Absolutely. You're completely right," Nick agreed, shutting off the engine.

"Move the car or we're taking you in," the second cop said, reaching for his handcuffs.

"That doesn't work for me. Kinda in the middle of something," Nick replied as he got out and walked to the streetcar. The conductor sounded the horn again, motioning to the traffic cops in exasperation. Nick's sole focus was Evelyn as she approached Colette. Silently he willed her to be careful.

Evelyn was only four rows away from the Reboux. Now three. Two. Colette's face was hidden, but the massive rock of her Cartier engagement ring was unmistakable. She finally looked up, meeting Evelyn's eyes. In them, Evelyn saw the panic of a trapped, terrified animal.

"I just want to talk," Evelyn said.

With strength that surprised both Evelyn and Colette's seatmate, she shoved him into the aisle and ran toward the back entrance. Evelyn stepped over the man, struggling to get up.

"Sorry," she apologized as her heel accidentally crushed his hand.

Nick moved to intercept Colette, but the traffic cop grabbed his arm.

"You have to stop her!" Nick said.

"Your car," the traffic cop growled, holding tight to Nick. Ahead of him, Colette ran down the street, with

Evelyn close behind her. Nick tossed his keys to the second traffic cop as he broke free of the first.

"Make yourself useful."

Evelyn ran after Colette, their heels pounding down the pavement. Evelyn was fast, but Colette had a head start and was making the most of it. Nick chased after them. Colette hazarded a glance over her shoulder to see them both following. She hiked up her skirt and threw her leg over the railing to the steep embankment of Echo Park. Evelyn followed, skidding down the hill, her heels digging up gravel, the tiny rocks irrevocably scuffing the leather. Silently she cursed Colette Palmer. These were her favorite shoes. Ahead, Colette reached the flat path and began running again. Nick overshot the angle of the hill and tumbled ass over teakettle downward. Evelyn didn't have a moment to spare for him. He'd always had a thick skull and she was certain it wouldn't fail him now.

Running after Colette, they cut through the tree-lined path. Lovers sneaking late-afternoon picnics gaped at the strange sight of the two women sprinting across the park. Behind them, slightly worse for wear, sleeves torn and gravel dusted, Nick hurried to catch up. The tumble twisted his ankle and he limped slightly as he ran. Colette ducked toward the *Nuestra Reina de Los Angeles* statue, with Evelyn close behind. Nick dashed through the trees attempting to cut her off. Colette turned left, only to find Captain Wharton, Carl, and two other police officers. The lake was at her back. To her right was Nick, and in front of her stood Evelyn. The Reboux was long lost and her hair framed her face in wild disarray.

Evelyn approached Colette slowly, like tending to a wounded deer.

"I didn't kill George," Colette said. "I loved him."

"No one knows what happens in a relationship, besides the two people in it," Evelyn said, glancing in Nick's direction. "It doesn't have to make sense to those on the outside. Hell, sometimes it doesn't make sense when you're on the inside. You know your heart and you don't care what anyone thinks. Because to you, this love is real and precious. It's the only thing in the world that really matters."

Colette nodded.

"Why did you run?" Evelyn asked.

"I had to."

"Why?"

Colette shook her head, sealing her lips.

"Please, Colette, let me help you."

"George rescued me. And now . . . it's all my fault."

"What is?" Evelyn asked. "His death?"

Colette nodded. Her eyes still carried a raw panic, but Evelyn began to suspect it wasn't just fear of being trapped. There was something more. Evelyn took another small step toward Colette. Behind Nick, the two traffic cops from the street approached. Wharton turned at the noise, waving them away. The sudden movement made Colette realize exactly how close Evelyn stood. Reaching into her bag, she pulled out a gun. The police pulled theirs.

"Everyone relax," Evelyn said. "You don't want to hurt me, do you, Colette?"

"Stay back!" she said, swinging her gun so it pointed at Evelyn. Then to Wharton. Then over to Nick. "Everyone just stay back."

Obliging, Evelyn took a step back, raising her hands. Nick moved so he was standing beside her.

"Colette," Evelyn began. "The police have to bring you in for questioning. You say you loved George, and I believe you. But right now, your actions aren't that of an innocent person. They say you hired a man to kill George."

"I'd never!" she insisted.

"They say you hired people to come after Nick and me . . ."

"What people?" Colette asked with a confused frown.

"Dan O'Brien," Evelyn said.

Colette's eyes widened.

"Colette, please. Let me help you. Tell me what's going on."

She looked at the assembled police and glanced at the lake behind her. For a moment, she turned her face up toward the brilliant blue sky, watching the clouds drift lazily across it. Then she looked back at Evelyn. A sad smile played across her lips.

"Wahlstatt," she said.

With that, she raised the gun to her temple.

"No!" Evelyn yelled.

Nick moved instinctively, diving for Colette. They fell back into the shallow lake, struggling for a moment before the gun went off with a resounding bang. Blood stained the water red, trickling out in gossamer threads. Nick lay limp, face down in the water. Evelyn stared, shock and fear rendering her immobile. During the war, death was always a possibility. But this was Los Angeles. They were supposed to be safe.

The police secured Colette.

"What have I done?" she asked, horrified, staring at Nick.

Carl rushed to Nick, hauling him onto the bank. Blood gushed down his face. The sight jolted Evelyn into action. She knelt down beside Nick and pushed back his hair, looking for the wound, but all she found was the deep gash on his forehead from the previous day that had reopened in the chaos. Carl put his ear to Nick's chest, hearing the faint breath stir in his lungs.

"Where was he shot?" Evelyn asked, panicked.

Her hands moved over Nick's body surveying the damage. She tore open his shirt, looking for the bullet's entry, but she couldn't find it. Even worse, she didn't see the exit.

Her worst fear was it rattling around inside him, tearing up his vital organs. Some of the deadliest wounds did not bleed.

"Nick, wake up!"

He didn't move.

"Carl?" Evelyn asked. "I don't see anything."

Carl looked over Nick's body.

"I don't, either."

"Then why won't he wake up?"

Carl didn't know, but he began chest compressions. Evelyn lay down next to Nick, her mouth close to his ear.

"Please come back to me," she whispered, tears springing to her eyes. "I can't lose you. Not like this. Nick, please."

She took his hand and prayed to all the gods she didn't believe in to make him wake up. The only response was the sound of Carl trying to coerce Nick's heart to beat and his lungs to breathe. After an interminable wait, Nick began to cough. Water rushed from his throat and he sat up. It took a moment for Nick's eyes to focus, and when they did, he looked between Evelyn and Carl.

"Christ, I could use a drink."

Evelyn kissed him long and hard. Her need driven by fear.

"That'll do, too," Nick said when she finally broke off.

Then she slapped him. The red handprint just another in a long string of wounds he racked up that week.

"Definitely woulda preferred the drink," Nick said.

"Don't you scare me like that."

"I thought you didn't care."

"I don't," Evelyn replied, but the tremor in her voice betrayed her.

Gently Nick reached out and brushed away Evelyn's tears.

"I'm all right."

Their eyes met and it felt like it was during the war.

They were perfectly in tune, understanding one another without effort. Then Evelyn shook her head and stood up.

"You'd better be."

Nick smiled briefly, but did not stand. He needed another minute to come back to himself. In the distance, the cops led Colette to the waiting police car. The fight had drained out of her. She looked broken, her elegant head slumped forward. The thick blond hair shielded her face.

"That was some stunt you pulled," Captain Wharton said to Nick and Evelyn.

"Car's in the middle of the intersection," the traffic cop grumbled.

"You're still whining about that?" Evelyn asked. "I would've had the damn thing towed by now."

Nick glared at her, and for a moment, the cop looked chagrinned at not thinking of that option himself.

"Can I take 'em in?" the traffic cop asked.

"Technically, that wouldn't solve your problem of my car in the middle of the intersection," Nick said.

"And technically, I wasn't driving," Evelyn added.

Wharton looked sorely tempted to let the cop slap handcuffs on both of them.

"With these two aiding in the capture of Colette Palmer," Carl began, "perhaps you could overlook this one incident. After all, if it wasn't for them, Mrs. Palmer might be on a train to Mexico right now."

"It's a good thing I like you," Wharton said to Evelyn. Then, to Nick, "Get your goddamned car out of the middle of my street."

"Yes, sir," Nick said.

He stood up, only to realize his legs didn't function quite as well as they should. Evelyn threw one of his arms over her shoulder. Carl took the other and they slowly maneuvered Rick back up the road.

Chapter 31

Evelyn pulled into her driveway and turned off the car. She looked to Nick, who was slumped in the passenger seat. His face was a mosaic of purple and yellow bruises. The bleeding had stopped, but the cut across his forehead was ragged and deep.

"Might leave a scar," Evelyn said as she brushed her fingers lightly over the wound.

"Just another reason not to lose my hair," Nick said. He reached for her hand, but she pulled away.

"Evie . . ." he started.

"What do you think Colette meant by 'Wahlstatt'?" Evelyn asked.

"You're changing the topic."

"You'd prefer we discuss your bruises?"

"You know what I mean."

Evelyn did.

"I'll head to the library tomorrow," Evelyn said. "See if I can find anything new."

"I was planning on being drunk tomorrow. Maybe the next day, too."

She looked at him, the way only she could. It was a

glance that was at once affectionate, but also spoke of the idiocy of his statement.

"Let Carl do his thing," Nick said. "Colette is with the police. They'll figure it out."

"No, they won't," Evelyn said. "She's terrified."

"She's going to jail."

"It's more than that, and you know it."

"Think about it," Nick began. "You're a grieving widow, what are you going to think when the cops show up at your doorstep?"

"That they have a lead in the case."

"Exactly! Only a guilty conscience would assume the worst."

"But that's if one car shows up. If it's a whole squad . . ."

"I'd still want to know what they had to say," Nick insisted.

"You really think she did it?" Evelyn asked.

"Hell, I don't know. Maybe theirs wasn't a fairy-tale marriage. A young woman grows tired of an older man. She leaves, she gets nothing. If he leaves her for another woman, she gets nothing. But if he dies . . ."

"So, why hire me?"

"To find Katie," Nick replied. "Figure out exactly what her husband was doing with this girl. Maybe give her some cover with the cops? Another person to pin it on? Maybe you were meant to be there that night, so it looked like a lovers' quarrel gone wrong. Or maybe . . ."

"Or maybe she genuinely didn't do it," Evelyn said as she got out of the car.

Nick followed her up to the doorstep. He grabbed her arm and spun her around to face him. Her breath caught in her chest as she looked up into his eyes.

"Do you think that maybe you can't let this go because it reminds you of the war?" he asked. "Of how good we are together?"

"Nick, don't."

"Working together again, being this close . . . I thought I'd made peace with everything," Nick said. "But I still miss you like a drowning man misses air. That pain is the only thing that feels real."

Evelyn tried to pull away, but he held her close.

"Admit it. You still miss me, too."

He leaned down and kissed her. In that kiss was everything they once had and lost. The love, the future, and the emptiness that replaced it. He tasted the salt of her tears and felt the confusion in her heart as she pulled away.

"How can I trust you?" she asked. "After everything that happened."

"Take a leap of faith," he said.

Nick looked down and saw her face soften. There was a quiet sadness in it, but also a desire to believe. He leaned down to kiss her again, but the front door opened, revealing James, who was waiting for her so they could go see the house in Benedict Canyon. Evelyn pulled away quickly.

"My God! Are you all right?" James asked, stepping in front of Nick to gather Evelyn in his arms. "You're covered in blood!"

"It's not mine," Evelyn said, nodding to Nick.

James checked her over, once more, to reassure himself, then gently kissed her forehead.

"Come inside," James said.

He led them into the foyer, where Katie Pierce was waiting. At the sight of Nick, she launched herself into his arms. He stumbled back—partially from the surprise of her onslaught, partially from the pain in his bruised ribs.

"You poor thing!" she exclaimed, looking at his face.

He stepped away from her prying fingers, attempting to minister to his wounds.

"I'm fine," he said.

"Oh, Nick! I was so worried," she said, crushing him in a hug.

"What happened?" James asked.

"We caught Colette Palmer," Nick said.

"Colette?" James asked with a frown.

"The guys from yesterday said she hired them," Evelyn explained. Then, turning to Katie, "It's safe for you to go home."

"But . . . so soon?" Katie asked. "Who knows what might be waiting for me?"

"Worst thing you'll find are the cops with a few questions, but that's inevitable," Evelyn responded.

"Are you sure I shouldn't stay for another night or two?"

"You're in no danger," Nick assured her.

"If you're certain," Katie replied, turning toward him. "I knew you'd take care of me!"

"Evelyn deserves the lion's share of the credit," he said.

"You're too modest," Katie said.

"That's not something anyone's ever accused me of before."

"Nick," James said, "why don't you take Katie back to her apartment?"

"I can call her a taxi," Evelyn said.

"Oh, no. Nick, please," Katie begged. "It won't take me a minute to gather my things."

"Sure, I guess," Nick said, and she ran upstairs.

"She seems fond of you," James said.

"I've always had a way with women," Nick replied.

"Too bad they don't stick around."

"Sometimes they come back."

"For what, exactly?" James asked. "You don't seem the type to offer any sort of stability. House? Family? Future?"

"James, stop," Evelyn warned quietly. Though Nick rarely mentioned it, those were exactly the things he most wanted. The story of his life had come out in small bits and pieces throughout the war and she wasn't certain if Nick realized how much he revealed. After a childhood of loneliness, he was desperate for someone to love. Someone who would love him in return. More than anything, he wanted a family that would not leave. His greatest fear was that he did not deserve it.

"Does anyone want a drink?" Evelyn asked. "I could use a drink."

She headed into the living room, picked up a decanter of scotch, and poured some into a crystal glass. In the foyer, no one spoke, but Evelyn still felt the tension. James was smart enough not to continue baiting Nick, but he also wasn't willing to surrender the field. The silence was oppressive, with only the sound of the grandfather clock, marking each moment. Evelyn heard Katie return, her perky voice sending waves of irritation through Evelyn. Katie's goodbye to James was a bit too familiar. The front door closed and James came to Evelyn.

"I really hate that guy," James said.

"Nick has that effect on people."

"You must be exhausted," he said.

"I'm all right," she replied.

"In that case, let's go see the house. The agent wants me to put in an offer."

The only thing Evelyn really wanted was a long, hot bath and another glass of scotch, but she had put him off long enough.

"Give me a minute to freshen up," she said.

She turned to leave, but James pulled her close and kissed her. It was long and deep, reasserting his claim over her heart. When they finally broke apart, Evelyn lingered in his arms. A slow smile eased across her face and she breathed in the warm scent of James's cologne.

"Go change," he said. "I'll wait."

Upstairs she washed the grime from her face and stripped

off her filthy clothes. When she looked in the mirror, all she saw was exhaustion. She brushed her hair and tied it back in a low ponytail. She pulled out slacks and a warm sweater from her dresser. A photograph floated out from between the woolen folds. It was her, Nick, and Carl, standing in front of a pub in London. They had their arms around each other, laughing with the easy joy of being young and alive. Back then, death stalked them on every mission, so each minute felt precious. It was terrible to admit, but she missed the rush of war. Peace carried too many questions, and the future stretched out toward infinity. She glanced down at the picture again. Damn Nick for getting into her head. She shoved the photo far back into her drawer, then went downstairs to James.

Chapter 32

It was unseasonably warm and James put the top down on his car. As they wound through the canyon roads, the stars shone brightly through the overhanging trees. Evelyn relaxed back into her seat and looked over at James. He took her hand and gave it a soft kiss.

"Penny for your thoughts," he said.

"I was thinking about you," she replied.

"Then it was definitely a penny well spent."

"Do you think love is a leap of faith?" Evelyn asked.

James thought about it for a moment. She appreciated how he always gave her questions serious consideration before answering.

"No," James said eventually. "I think love is built on strong foundations. It's trust and kindness. Compatibility and reliability. I know that doesn't sound sexy."

"Certainly not what comes across in the movies."

"Movies never go past the wedding night," James replied. "Love shouldn't hurt. It should be the thing that takes away the pain. It's the person who holds you close at night and makes you believe everything will work out for the best. And if it doesn't, love makes it so you'll never have to face those challenges alone."

"You're such a good man," Evelyn said.

"Sometimes when you say that, it doesn't sound like a compliment."

"It is. You make me feel like I have solid ground under my feet," Evelyn said. "You make me feel safe."

"It's what you deserve," James said.

"Why do you love me?" Evelyn asked.

James glanced over at her, concern written across his face.

"That's a question you should never have to ask."

"Humor me . . ."

"I love you because you're smart and independent. You're funny and you know who you are. Doesn't hurt that you're the most beautiful woman I've ever met," James said. "But mostly, I love you because I can't remember a time when I didn't."

Evelyn could not have come up with a better answer, had she tried. James pulled up to a darkened gate.

"Is this it?" Evelyn asked.

James nodded, then came around to hold Evelyn's car door. Opening the gate, he revealed a beautiful two-story mission house topped by red Spanish tile. The wide green lawn was enclosed by white stucco walls. At their base, wild rosebushes and jasmine perfumed the night air. To the side stood a three-car garage, with a fountain set into the driveway. A terra cotta walkway led up to the heavy wooden door.

"It's beautiful," Evelyn said.

"I know it's not as grand as your house . . ."

"That doesn't matter."

"I want you to like it," James said as he reached under a flower pot and fished out a key. Opening the front door, he ushered Evelyn into the shadowed living room. The dark cherry floors had a soft luster. The walls were the same whitewash as the exterior and one featured a fire-place, surrounded by colorful tile.

James moved toward one corner and traced the outline of a nonexistent bar.

"This is where I'd mix us martinis after work."

With an imaginary shaker, he rattled the vodka and spilled it into an invisible glass. Carefully he handed the stem to Evelyn and she laughed, holding it between her fingers. She tasted it.

"Mmmm. Very good. Not too much vermouth."

"I do my best."

Still carrying their imaginary drinks, James led Evelyn into the dining room.

"Here's where your mother's table would stand. Room for eight, should we decide to have that many people over. Otherwise, it's perfect for weekly dinners with Logan."

Evelyn was touched that he carved a place for her father in the life they would share. James brought her into the kitchen and Evelyn couldn't help but raise her eyebrows. This was definitely not a room in which she was comfortable.

"What exactly do you have planned for here?" Evelyn asked.

"This is where we unpack takeout every night," James replied.

"How well you know me."

James threw open the back door, leading to a wide backyard. A long pool rippled blue and green.

"We can spend our weekends relaxing with a swim," James said.

"And do all the things we never dared when we were teenagers," Evelyn suggested.

"I love the way you think."

He took her hand to continue the tour, leading her upstairs. Just off the landing were two bedrooms connected by a bathroom. James traced the outline of a small bed.

"If we decide to have children, this is where we'll tuck them in at night. I'll read them stories and you'll banish their nightmares."

Evelyn smiled at the image. In his description, she could almost see a little girl with his eyes and her nose, hugging a tiny stuffed bear. It was something she never really considered until this exact moment. Growing up, Evelyn preferred toy planes to dolls. Plus, her mother died before Evelyn realized she had not been perfect. It was a high standard and Evelyn felt certain of falling short. Mostly, though, the war had shown her exactly how vulnerable people became once they had children. Their hearts resided outside their bodies and she did not know how to choose that feeling. Yet, standing here with James, it all seemed possible. Going into parenthood, she would have a partner to share the work and the worry. They could choose to make raising a child an equal endeavor. James looked into her eyes and saw the effect his words had upon her.

"You'd make an amazing mother," he said.

"You don't know that," she said.

"Even if you don't trust yourself," he said, "trust me. I've given it a lot of thought."

"What if I don't want kids? Or I couldn't have them?"

"We'll figure out what's right for both of us. Whatever we decide, our life will be filled with love."

James guided her down the hall to their bedroom. He threw open the drapes, revealing French doors that led out to a balcony. In the distance, the lights of Los Angeles glittered in the darkness. This house promised peace and refuge from the constant drive of the city.

James slipped his arms around her waist and pulled her close.

"This is where I'd hold you as we fall asleep at night."

This vision of their life was so beautiful. So perfect. So surprising to Evelyn that it might make her genuinely happy. James sank to one knee and pulled out a diamond ring.

"Evelyn Bishop," he began. "I love you. I've loved you all my life and I will keep loving you until the end of my days. I know who you are and I don't ever want to change you. I just want us to build a life together because I think it can be a very, very good one. So, what do you say, will you marry me?"

Evelyn stared down at James and the ring in his hand. This proposal had been coming for the past year. Yet, her lips couldn't quite form the word "yes." James's face fell slightly at her hesitation. He slid the ring onto her hand.

"You don't have to answer right now," he said. "Just think about it."

"I love you," she said.

It was the truth. What other man would give her the time and the space she needed? Who else would understand her fear of losing herself in the title of "wife"? She glanced down at the diamond on her hand. The ring felt heavy, but not as much as she once expected.

Chapter 33

As James drove, Evelyn looked down at the glittering diamond on her finger. It drew light from the darkness and refracted it outward. He chose well. Its beauty came from the craftsmanship and the detailing of the platinum, rather than the size of the stone. James pulled up in front of his house, where her car was still parked from the night before.

"Can I come in?" she asked, pulling him close.

"You have some thinking to do and I don't want to distract you."

"What if I want to be distracted?" she asked.

He groaned slightly, his desire palpable.

"When you say yes, we'll never have to sleep apart again," he replied. "Until then, I want you clearheaded. I know this is the right decision, but I want you to know it, too. My whole life I've been waiting for you. I can wait a few more days."

"Fine," she said. "If you want to be all mature and grown-up."

"Just this once," he said, releasing her.

With a kiss, Evelyn got into her car and headed to Bishop Aeronautics, where she knew her father would be working late. The main building was six stories high, with walls of corrugated steel. The factory covered several acres with a variety of structures. It sat on the shore of the ocean, with a deep-water dock extending into the Pacific. During the war, it was used to facilitate the shipment of airplane parts to both Europe and the Pacific. It also allowed for the import of raw material. Sometimes Evelyn was awed by the sheer tonnage of steel that Bishop Aeronautics managed to turn into something beautiful.

Evelyn loved airplanes. They were in her soul, instilled there by her father's passion. When she was a child, Logan often allowed her to sit on his lap while he piloted a plane. Later on, Logan let her take the controls and feel the rush of air beneath her. With privilege came responsibility. By the time she had her license, she could take an engine apart and put it back together. She understood the physics behind flying and could perform most repairs. Even at her debutante ball, there were grease stains on her knuckles. Logan only had himself to blame for why Evelyn did not fit into the typical mold of a proper young lady.

Evelyn walked through a door on the side of the main building and climbed the stairs to her father's office. From his vantage point, he could see the entirety of the production line. There were at least six planes in various stages of construction. Though it was dark and shuttered for the night, the light from her father's office poured across the silent floor.

"Daddy?" Evelyn said, knocking on the open doorway.

Logan was hunched over his desk. It took him a moment to focus, but when he did, he greeted her with a warm, tired smile.

"You look exhausted," she said.

He was not one for complaining, but he could not help rubbing his eyes. Then he noticed the ring on Evelyn's finger.

"It looks good," he said.

Evelyn held it up, turning her hand this way and that, so the diamond caught the light.

"Did you know he was going to ask?"

"Everyone knew he was going to ask," Logan said. "The only question was when. I'm so happy for you, honey. James is a good man."

"He is," Evelyn said. "But I didn't say yes . . ."

"What?"

"I didn't say no, either," she said. "I didn't know what to say."

"Why not?" Logan asked.

Evelyn shrugged. She didn't know how to put her hesitation into words.

"What was it like for you and Mom?"

Logan smiled, his eyes wistful as he thought back thirty-five years.

"When I was with her, time stopped. She was my favorite person and the one who saw parts of me I didn't realize existed. Somehow I managed to make her laugh and she made me feel like I could take on the world. The best part of my day was coming home to her."

"See? That's the problem," Evelyn said. "You spoiled me with your fairy tale."

"It wasn't magic. Nor was it perfect," Logan said. "We respected each other and did our best to be kind, even when we were tired and angry. Evie, you're one of the most amazing people I've ever known. You're smart, talented, and you chart your own course. How many men would understand that? Most would take you for granted or try to fit you in a box. James sees exactly who you are and loves you because of it."

"I know," Evelyn said.

"So, what is it?" Logan asked.

Evelyn didn't answer. Logan studied her for a long moment, then asked the question that was hovering near the edge of her brain. The question she couldn't acknowledge.

"Is it Nick?"

When they fell in love, it was all-consuming. Every moment they were apart, he was on her mind. Their fights were legendary, but making up afterward was worth it. With him, Evelyn felt more alive than she ever had before. Maybe it was the war. Or maybe it was just the fact that she felt like the person she was always meant to be.

With James, love was a slow burn—the familiarity and comfort that came from knowing a person forever. She rarely admitted it to herself, but after the war, she was in mourning. Not only for Matthew, or even for Nick, but for a different version of herself. When she came home, James was there, never asking more than she could give. In time, her childhood crush grew into something much deeper. She just wondered if it would be enough to carry her through the long years of her life.

"I don't know," Evelyn finally said to Logan.

"James deserves an answer," Logan said.

Though Logan was right, she would not let herself be pressured into marriage. She glanced down at Logan's desk and something caught her attention. Pushing aside a few papers, she found one with a white cross inside a blue circle. She pulled it up to find a shipping invoice.

"What's this?" she asked.

"Nothing," he said, taking it from her and shuffling it into a stack.

"Doesn't seem like nothing," she said.

"Just work. New orders for old customers."

"How old?"

Logan didn't answer.

"What is Wahlstatt?"

"Where did you hear that name?" Logan asked, an edge in his voice.

"They had something to do with the war, didn't they?"

"Why all the questions?"

"Why aren't you answering them?" Evelyn asked.

"What did Nick tell you?"

"Nick?" she said. "What does he have to do with this?"

"Nothing. It's nothing."

"Daddy, what are you involved with?"

"I'm trying to protect you," he said. "Please just let it go."

"No."

"Evelyn, I'm your father. I'm telling you to stop this nonsense."

It was a tone he rarely used with her—for good reason. All it did was make her angry.

"Fine. If you won't tell me, I'll find out somewhere else."

With that, she walked out of the office, quietly furious, but also more concerned for her father than she had ever been before.

Chapter 34

Nick's attempt to drive Katie home didn't go as planned. When he pulled up outside her apartment, she refused to get out of the car. Her gaze was fixed upon the window, where the spray of George's blood had stained the curtain.

"Have you been back since that night?" Nick asked.

She shook her head.

"After everything, I came straight to your office. I couldn't . . ." she broke off, her voice strained. "It's all still up there, isn't it?"

Nick thought of the door, the cheap lock broken and the frame splintered from where Nick had kicked it in at the sound of gunshots. Mud from the policemen's shoes was tracked all over the hardwood, and fingerprint powder coated every surface. The broken flashbulbs of the crime scene photographer's camera created a minefield of crushed glass.

"The body's gone," Nick offered.

"But not the rest?" Katie said.

"No. Probably not. Cops aren't known for cleaning up after themselves."

"I can't go in there."

"You'll have to face it sometime," Nick said gently.

"Then let it be in the morning. Everything's easier to face in the daylight."

"All right," Nick said. "We'll find you a hotel."

"Can I stay with you?" she said. "I don't want to be alone."

"My apartment's small and, honestly, a disaster. I wasn't expecting company."

"I don't care," she said. "Please, Nick."

He knew this was a bad idea, and yet . . .

They drove to his building. Nick opened the door to a foyer lit by a weak bulb. While the floor tiles might once have been white, they were faded to an irregular gray, marred by cigarette burns and decades of shoes dragging in the outside world. The narrow stairs had a creaky wooden banister that looked ready to splinter at the slightest touch.

Nick led Katie up four flights to a claustrophobic hallway. The green carpet was faded and the bowls of the sconces were dotted black with dead flies. Nick unlocked the door and ushered Katie inside. It was a small room, with a bed in one corner and a kitchenette in the other. In the center stood a table piled high with unpaid bills, an empty cereal bowl, and a mug of cold, stale coffee.

"Told you it was a mess," he said by way of apology.

Nick pulled the bedcovers over the worn sheets. Then he took a pile of clothes off the room's only chair and shoved them into a closet. Dumping the dishes into the sink, he pronounced it good enough.

"I can't thank you enough for doing this," Katie said, sliding up to him.

"You take the bed and I'll sleep . . . somewhere," Nick said.

He looked around his apartment. It wasn't built for two. The few times he brought a woman back to his place, it was always so late at night, it verged on morning. They were both raging drunk and the shabbiness didn't seem to matter. This was a place to sleep, not a place to live. Katie crawled onto the bed and looked up at Nick. Seeing her here made the place seem worse by comparison.

"Aren't you going to offer a girl a drink?" she asked.

"God, yes," he said. "A drink sounds good."

He went to the cupboard and pulled out a bottle of whisky. It was cheap stuff he picked up at the corner store, chosen for its price, rather than its label. Grabbing his only glass and rinsing out the coffee mug, he poured. Handing the booze to Katie, he watched as she downed it in a single swallow and held her glass out for more.

"Might want to slow down, there," Nick said, pouring another round. She tossed it back and held out her glass again. When he hesitated, her eyes filled with tears.

"I've lost the only father I've ever known. I'm all alone in this world," she said. "What better excuse is there to get drunk?"

"Hate to break it to you, kid, but we're all alone."

"Don't you ever feel lonely?" she asked.

"Something tells me you'll do just fine."

Katie stood up, walked to Nick, and pressed herself into him. Though his mind resisted, the pull he felt was instinctual.

"I could use someone like you to take care of me," she said.

"Sweetheart, I can barely take care of myself."

She leaned up and kissed him. It took an impressive amount of self-control to break away.

"I don't want to take advantage of a situation," Nick said.

"I'm no virgin in need of your chivalry," Katie said as she began undoing the buttons of her dress.

Nick stepped back so there was a table between them.

"That much is clear," he said. "I'm flattered, really, but I can't."

"Why not?" she asked.

"Because I can't," he said with a circular logic that barely made sense to him as she slid her dress to the floor. Even the pain of his recent beating was momentarily forgotten.

Katie teased the strap of her slip off her shoulder. Nick could not remember how long it had been since he was last with a woman. It took all his willpower to grab a blanket from the back of a chair and throw it over her shoulders.

"You should get some sleep," Nick said.

Before she could argue, there was a knock at the door.

"Who's that?" she asked.

"Hide in the bathroom."

"Is it another woman?" Katie asked.

"It's late and I'm not expecting anyone. With the way my luck's been going, you really wanna chance it?"

Frowning, she slunk out of sight. Nick picked up his gun, checked the chamber, and released the safety. He opened the door to find Evelyn. The air left his lungs in a soft whoosh.

"What are you doing here?" he asked, then immediately amended his question. "That came out wrong. I'm glad to see you, but it's late and—"

"What are you hiding from me?"

Inadvertently, Nick glanced over his shoulder.

"Wahlstatt?" she asked.

"Today was the first I've heard about it."

"What does it have to do with my father?"

"I don't know."

"But you do know something about him."

Nick hesitated.

"You ask me to trust you," she said. "But you're keeping secrets."

Behind Nick, Katie stepped out.

"Nick, who's there?"

Evelyn pushed open the door to see Katie standing in her slip. Though Evelyn had no right to criticize, it hurt more than she wanted to admit.

"You have company," Evelyn said.

"Evie, wait," he said.

She turned and fled down the hallway. Ignoring Katie's calls, Nick ran after Evelyn, rushing down the dark stairway and out onto the street. Nick reached her just as she opened her car door.

"That wasn't what it looked like."

"I should have known better," she said.

"You do know better. Nothing happened with that girl."

"What about everything else?" she asked. "What are you hiding?"

"I'm trying to protect you."

"You say that. My father says that. All I'm left with is secrets. You say you love me. Then tell me the truth."

He didn't answer.

"Right," she said, stepping into her car.

"Evie, please."

His eyes held a sorrowful gaze that had not been there since their early days in London. Where she once felt the need to comfort him, now all she felt was the sharp stab of regret for allowing herself to believe again.

"James asked me to marry him," she said.

For the first time, Nick noticed the ring on her finger

and it felt like a gut punch worse than any he had ever taken.

"You said yes . . . ?"

"I have to go," she said. She closed the car door and turned the key in the ignition.

All Nick could do was step aside as she drove off into the night.

Chapter 35

The exterior of the Bradbury Building was not impressive. The brown brick facade blended perfectly with its neighbors in downtown Los Angeles. Evelyn pushed open the nondescript door to discover unexpected beauty. The central atrium rose to a vaulted glass ceiling, giving it the feeling of a cathedral. The muted red walls served as the perfect backdrop to the intricate wrought iron that wove through the atrium. The building was a jewel hidden inside a plain velvet box.

Evelyn had swung by the library that morning. Turns out Wahlstatt was a Prussian general who helped rebuild the German Army and defeat Napoleon. He was among the first to be awarded the Iron Cross. She also returned to the clerk's office and, armed with an actual name, was able to discover the company's address. It was listed as a charity with the stated mission of aiding refugees during World War II.

Evelyn headed to the third floor, where an office held a small sign, WAHLSTATT. She rapped smartly on the door, but heard no movement inside. After a moment, she did it again, to make sure it was empty. Then, glancing over her shoulder, she pulled a small lockpick kit from her purse.

Sliding a shim into the frame, she wedged the tongue down and turned the handle. Sitting behind the desk was a man who could drive a nun to blasphemy.

"What the hell are you doing here?" she asked.

"You invited me," Nick said.

"When?" Evelyn demanded.

"It was implied."

"Then it's also implied that your invitation was re-scinded."

"You always use big words when you're mad."

"Rescinded is only a big word for a troglodyte like you," Evelyn said. "And I'm not mad."

Nick smiled his infuriating grin and Evelyn turned to look around the small office. It was utilitarian at best. Just the one room with a map of Europe tacked to the wall. There were four filing cabinets. Evelyn pulled on the clos-est one, but it was locked.

"Nothing happened last night," Nick said. "With Katie. She didn't want to face the crime scene at her apartment, so I let her stay with me."

"It's none of my business."

Nick went to Evelyn and turned her so she was fac-ing him.

"Nothing happened."

Evelyn searched his eyes. Despite him being a skilled liar, she could always see through his bullshit. He was telling the truth.

"I don't care," Evelyn said.

"Awful lot of angry for not caring," Nick said.

Evelyn turned her attention back to the locked filing cabinets.

"Evie, please," Nick pleaded. "Trust me."

"That's the thing," she said. "I don't."

Evelyn picked the lock, pulled out a file, and began flip-ping through the pages. She took out another and another.

"Anything interesting?" Nick asked.

Evelyn handed them to Nick.

"Shipping manifests from before the war to 1945," Evelyn said.

"Tinned beef. Wool. Coal. Consumer goods. Nothing out of the ordinary."

"Also, nothing George Palmer produced."

"Who are these people?" Nick asked.

Evelyn went to the desk and opened all the drawers. There were the usual office supplies: scissors, staplers, paper clips. She checked for false bottoms, but found nothing out of the ordinary.

"I don't know," Evelyn said with frustration. "I found documents from Wahlstatt on my father's desk. He's covering something up and let it slip that you know more than you're telling me."

Nick struggled with how to respond. Evelyn took his silence as confirmation of his secrets.

"And we're back to square one."

Evelyn turned to leave, but as she did, she felt the slight shift of the floorboard under her shoe. The squeak was almost imperceptible.

"Evelyn—" Nick began.

"Shhh."

She stepped on the floorboard again. Again it moved slightly. She knelt down and jimmied up the wood. There, hidden among the dust and cobwebs, was a black ledger. Setting it on the desk, she began to flip through. It was all in code.

"More complicated than a substitution cypher," Nick said. "Maybe a transposition cypher?"

Evelyn pulled out the copy of Samuel Butler's *The Iliad* from her purse.

"Where did you get that?"

"I borrowed it from Katie Pierce's apartment."

"Borrowed?" Nick asked.

"It's possible I forgot to return it."

Evelyn opened the book and began matching up numbers on the sheets with the pages. At first, she thought they were looking for words, but she quickly realized it was just single letters.

"The book could have been left there by George, or something random she picked up at a flea market," Nick said. "It might not even be the right book. You can't actually think she's wrapped up in this."

When Evelyn finished translating, she stared down at the paper for a long moment, then looked to Nick.

"You still think I'm crazy?" she asked.

"I think you have a fine knack for getting us into trouble," he replied.

Chapter 36

Los Angeles spread out far below Griffith Observatory. The seediness of Hollywood appeared as an array of neon beckoning the hopeful to its church of possibility. The distinctions between up-and-coming, already-there, and never-would-be were muted by distance until it all seemed beautiful. The crisp white exterior of the Art Deco building stood bright against the dark night. The two wings were each domed with telescopes pointed at the cosmos. The thing Evelyn most loved about the observatory was its silence. The wind whistled through the trees and it felt removed from space and time.

Tonight, however, that quiet was nowhere to be found. Draped over the central door was a large banner reading: SAM WILDER FOR MAYOR. This was yet another fundraiser in his quest for public office. Everyone who mattered in Los Angeles Society was here, along with photographers to capture the moment. The valet opened Evelyn's car door as James handed over his keys. Her dress, a deep crimson silk, stood out in a sea of pastel and crinoline. She bought it in Paris before returning home from the war.

After armistice, Evelyn felt like a nomad wandering the earth with no star pointing north. Drawn by the familiar, she spent a few weeks with Jean and his family. He organized a reunion of Resistance fighters, who were finally able to identify themselves. Nick was not there, a fact for which Evelyn was both grateful and sad. She missed him with a hollow ache. Not even her memories were safe, having been tainted by the way things ended. Restless, unable to remain in any one place, she began traveling.

Evelyn steered clear of the major cities, not yet ready to plunge into old memories of innocent childhood vacations. Instead, she found herself welcomed in small towns, where strangers opened their homes to her. She felt a freedom that came from anonymity. There were no expectations, no history, and no future. Evelyn basked in their kindness and the comforting routine of the day. She traveled to Italy, and from there, she took a fishing boat from Naples to Greece. Then she turned north toward Vienna, where the first hint of spring appeared like a breath of fresh air across the continent. That feeling of hope drew Evelyn westward, with the initial stirrings of homesickness. She stopped in Paris before heading back to Los Angeles. On her last day, Evelyn discovered this dress in the back of a small shop. She was captivated by its brilliant color. The silk flowed over her body, with an open back and a neckline just short of scandalous. It was something she never would have bought before the war, but now it fit like a second skin.

Beside her, dressed impeccably in a tuxedo, James took her hand in his.

"You look beautiful. Distant, but beautiful," he said, proving once again he was perfectly attuned to her moods.

"Sorry," she said. "A lot on my mind."

"I should hope so," he said, lightly fingering the ring he gave her last night. She wore it on her right hand, a declaration of her indecision.

"Do you remember when we used to come up here before the war?" Evelyn asked. "You, me, and Matthew. We waited in line for hours just to look through the telescope. Matthew said the heavens were so close he could almost touch them."

James dabbed away a tear threatening to streak Evelyn's perfect makeup.

"He wanted to build rockets to space, so he could look down from above and show how fragile and precious we are," she said.

"We don't have to do this," James said, nodding toward the people streaming toward the music.

"Yes, we do," Evelyn said.

"Your father would understand."

Evelyn gave him a look. They both knew better. The next mayor of Los Angeles held the keys to Bishop Aeronautics' future. The factory needed to expand and that would be impossible without the necessary permits.

"Okay, maybe he wouldn't, but he'd forgive us. We can go somewhere else. Or just get in the car and keep driving."

"Doesn't that sound nice."

Evelyn took James's arm and they joined the procession of well-heeled guests. The side patio of the observatory was decked out in colorful paper lanterns, burning a rainbow across the sky. The twelve-piece band stood tall in their white dinner jackets, while waiters circulated through the crowd with trays of crab puffs and champagne. The party felt less like a fundraiser and more like the celebration of a foregone conclusion. Evelyn almost envied Sam's confidence.

"Los Angeles is one of the world's greatest cities," he crowed. "For too long, it's been overshadowed by New York, Boston, and Chicago. Mark my words, the second half of the century will see us propelled to our rightful place. Not only do we have the glamour and excitement of

Hollywood, but we have deep-water ports few can match. I promise to revitalize the South Bay, improving roads and clearing the shipping lanes."

"And approve the expansion of Bishop Aeronautics?" Evelyn asked.

Sam turned to her with a smile.

"Especially that. Bishop Aeronautics is among this city's most important industries," Sam intoned. Then turning to the assembled audience, "Did you know Logan Bishop is one of the largest employers of returning veterans?"

"After my brother died, my father thought it was only right to find jobs for those who fought beside him," Evelyn said.

"Your father, along with your brother and this handsome gentleman at your side, are patriots!" Sam said. "We all did our part during the war, but it's a true hero who continues to support our servicemen after the conflict has ended and our attention turns back to the routine of daily life. It's our job, as politicians and good citizens, to never, ever forget the sacrifice of those who fought for our freedoms!"

The supporters applauded loudly. Evelyn was impressed by Sam's masterful appropriation of soldiers' heroics.

"Smooth son of a bitch, isn't he?" James asked under his breath, mirroring Evelyn's thoughts.

"The kind of people who should be running the country are the ones who would never want the job," Evelyn said.

"The problem of politics since the days of Aristotle."

Evelyn supposed she should not be too critical, seeing her father's company hoped to be a direct recipient of this particular quid pro quo. By the time Sam got back to her and James, she wore an appropriate smile.

"Good to see you," Sam said, kissing her gently on the cheek. "Planning on contributing to the campaign?"

"My father would never forgive me if I said no," Evelyn replied.

Sam laughed, appreciating her honesty.

"I truly believe we're heading into a great age of air travel. This world is growing ever smaller and Bishop Aeronautics is directly responsible."

"Logan will be thrilled to hear you say that," James replied.

"He's lucky to have you," Sam said to James as he turned toward another couple.

"Sam," Evelyn said, drawing him back. "One more thing."

"Of course."

Evelyn reached into her purse and withdrew the torn paper bearing the cross she discovered in George Palmer's study.

"Have you seen this before?"

Sam's smile flickered slightly. Had Evelyn blinked, she would have missed it.

"No. Sorry. No idea what that is."

"We should let Mr. Wilder attend to his guests," James said.

"It's from a company called Wahlstatt. I found it in George Palmer's study after he died. Made me curious. Especially after I discovered you're listed as one of their suppliers."

"My company works with so many different institutions. Can't expect me to remember them all."

"This one would stand out," Evelyn said. "They shipped black-market arms during the war."

"Evelyn," James hissed. "Enough!"

A panicked look flashed from Sam's eyes before his cool politician's demeanor returned. He dropped his voice to little more than a hiss as he leaned in toward Evelyn.

"Now is neither the time nor the place."

"Tomorrow. Ten a.m. Your office."

Seeing no other way to end the conversation, Sam nodded curtly and moved on to other guests.

"What the hell are you doing?" James asked. "That man is going to be Los Angeles's next mayor and your father needs his approval to expand."

"He'll get it. The city council is on his side."

"For the vote, sure," James said. "But the mayor can slow permits to a halt. He can impose water studies and land studies that bog down construction from now until the end of time. Were you even thinking about that when you chose here and now to dive into God only knows what?"

"Something's not right. This case—"

"Is supposed to be over."

"Not everything gets wrapped up in a tidy little bow," Evelyn said. "Dad had this same symbol in his office. Did you know that?"

"Logan doesn't share all his business with me," James said.

"You said that during the war . . ."

"The war's over, Evie," James said, touching the ring he hoped would mean more than the sum of its parts. "I wish you could realize that. Not just for you, but for us."

Chapter 37

Evelyn stood at the railing of the upper deck, watching the party revolve below her. James's words so perfectly mirrored Nick's. The war was over. During it, she wanted nothing more than peace, but now it felt like a part of her still remained in Northern France. Sometimes she wondered how life would be different if Matthew had never been captured. She would have stayed in Los Angeles, organizing food drives and attempting to grow a Victory garden. Maybe she still would be contemplating James's proposal, the diamond ring resting on the correct hand. Maybe they would be long married, with her pregnant and content. As she looked over that alternate future, it wasn't the details Evelyn envied. It was the certainty that came from never knowing a different life.

Lost in her thoughts, she didn't notice Nick's approach until he was standing beside her.

"How did you get in?" she asked.

"Friend of yours," Nick said. "Sally Whitehall."

He nodded down at a blond woman in the crowd.

"Good God," Evelyn said. "That woman hates me enough for two lifetimes."

"She said she knew you through debutante class," Nick said.

"It's called finishing school. Though the thought that anyone could be *finished* at eighteen is horrifying."

"The thought anyone could be finished at thirty-two seems unlikely as well."

"You'll never be finished," Evelyn said.

"Isn't that a better way to live?"

"Probably," she admitted.

Sally Whitehall circled the party, looking for Nick. Then she glanced up and saw him beside Evelyn. A dark scowl crossed her face.

"What exactly did you do to her?" Nick asked.

"I *may* have stolen her boyfriend in high school."

"You little minx. Was he that irresistible?"

"Oh, God, no. He was a complete idiot."

"The thrill of the chase?"

"You know me better than that," Evelyn said. "She promised to go to prom with Matthew. Two weeks before the dance, she threw him over for that lug."

"So you took him away."

Evelyn shrugged.

"You Bishops certainly are a loyal bunch."

Evelyn was about to retort that loyalty was a thing Nick knew nothing about, but after all this time, what was the point?

"You get a little crease between your eyes when you're overthinking something," Nick said. "Personally, I find it adorable, but I also know it's exhausting."

"Maybe you're right," she said. "Maybe I am holding on to this case because I can't let go of the war. I can't let go of Matthew. I can't let go of . . . anything."

"In my experience, the things we hold on to are the most important ones."

"Why Colette and Wahlstatt?"

"I don't know," he said. "But I've never known your instincts to be wrong."

"Except once," she said.

Behind Nick's eyes, she saw his guard come up, already protecting himself against a battle lost long ago.

"Dance with me," she said, surprising them both.

"All right."

Nick led her down to the floor and held her close as they swayed to the music. She felt the weight of his body against hers. His arms encircled her back, comforting and familiar. The tart bite of his aftershave, mingled with the unique smell of his skin. It was a scent she would know anywhere. It told her not to worry when she heard footsteps behind her. It lulled her to sleep on cold winter nights and silenced the fear in her mind. She inhaled it deeply and felt a profound sadness for what might have been. It was amazing, even after all these years, that the pain was still so fresh. Once, she thought time had healed it, or at least stitched over it. But having him so close was a physical ache that brought tears to her eyes.

The music switched over to "It's Only a Paper Moon" and Evelyn looked up at Nick as he began to sing softly. The lyrics told how paper moons and cardboard seas, canvas skies and muslin trees, could all become real, if only two people believed in each other. It had once come so easily, but now . . .

"Everything with you is make-believe," Evelyn said. The tears slipped down her cheeks and Nick gently wiped them away.

"Not this. Not us," Nick said. "I love you. Of everything else that's screwed up in this world, of all the mistakes we've made, of all the things we've lost—it's the one thing that's true. That, and the fact that you still love me."

"I do," Evelyn replied.

Nick's face lit up, but Evelyn shook her head.

"I'll probably always love you. I keep thinking about everything that might have been, and everything our future could hold. Then I remember how much you hurt me. I don't know how to trust you because I can't go through that pain again. I don't think I'd survive."

Evelyn looked into Nick's eyes and they mirrored her own startled realization of finality.

"Please," she said. "Because you love me, let me go."

She kissed him gently on the cheek, then stepped out of his arms. He stood on the dance floor, alone among the bright, swirling couples. She could not look back because she did not trust herself to walk away. Crossing to James, she interrupted his conversation with a businessman in a well-tailored tuxedo.

"Will you take me home?" she asked.

"Of course."

He put his arm around her and led her away from the party.

Chapter 38

London, May 8, 1945

Peace was declared in Europe. In the streets of London, the word "celebration" barely began to describe the euphoria. It seemed as though not one person stayed home. Dressed to the nines, people waved British and American flags. They sang and cheered, their voices radiating through the alleys and sidewalks, amplifying into a single cry of joy. On this day, anything seemed possible.

Nick stood in Trafalgar Square with thousands of others, listening to speeches. Churchill told the story of how British strength endured through the long months of the Blitz, to stand strong as the defender of freedom. King George praised the great sacrifices of the brave men and women who fought and died to end the long darkness of war. When it was over, Nick pushed through the crowds toward the OSS and up to General Gibson's office. He had served four and a half very long years. The caution ingrained in him by the experience would be his constant companion. However, he had to admit, the war changed him for the better. Fundamentally a selfish man when he signed up, he found a purpose beyond his own needs and desires. It was more than a devotion to God and country. It was an abiding loyalty and love for those with whom he fought. Carl allowed him to trust people. More than just having Nick's back, he kept his promises, both small and large. It was a novel experience and Carl became the first person Nick truly considered a friend.

Evelyn brought him hope and happiness in measures he dared not dream of in the dark days of his youth. She gave him a reason to live beyond the simple reflex of taking his next breath. Now that peace was finally here, their life together could become official. Tucked into the pocket of his jacket was the gold ring he bought in Paris. It wasn't much—his OSS salary being paltry at best—but he didn't think she'd mind. Had Evelyn been the type of person who needed baubles for happiness, she never would have spent three years behind enemy lines. He had booked them a table at the Savoy and there was a bottle of champagne chilling in a room above. As soon as they finished their final debrief, they were free.

In the quiet of General Gibson's office, Nick heard the soft clink of a bottle meeting the rim of a glass. He turned as Gibson handed him a scotch.

"To fallen brothers," Gibson said.

Nick toasted Gibson and downed his drink.

"This is the best scotch I've tasted . . . maybe ever," Nick said as Gibson refilled his glass.

"Been saving it for a special occasion," Gibson said.

"They don't get much better than this," Nick said.

"There were times I wasn't sure this day would ever come."

"After everything, maybe we'll finally figure out how to get along."

"It'd be nice, wouldn't it?" Gibson said.

"You don't sound convinced."

"The Russians are already carving up Germany, and

we're in a race to claim what we can. They were allies of convenience, nothing more."

"Who knows? There could be a few good years ahead of us," Nick said.

"When did you become such an optimist?" Gibson asked.

"Blame Evelyn."

"I knew she'd be good for you," Gibson laughed. "I'm hoping you'll continue on with us."

"War's over. I enlisted because . . . well, because it was better than the hellhole I'd been living in. And I joined the OSS because . . ."

"You're an ornery son of a bitch."

"True," Nick admitted. "Back in Los Angeles, it's sunny and seventy-five. There are palm trees and wide, open streets untouched by bombs. The ocean stretches all the way to the horizon and the sunset is the most beautiful thing you've ever seen. I want to retire to a nice cabin on the beach somewhere. Spend a few years reading books. Maybe plant a garden. Just put all of this behind us."

"But . . . ?" Gibson asked.

"Evelyn loves being a spy."

"So, OSS it is."

"I keep trying to change her mind, but she's not ready to give it up."

"Glad to hear it," Gibson replied. "You two were among our best assets in the field. Though how you managed with your French . . . ?"

"I think Evelyn liked it. It was the only time she could get me to shut up."

"Smart woman."

"What's the new mission?" Nick asked. "Are we headed to Berlin?"

"Eventually," Gibson said. "But we have to clean house first. During the war, a few people made a lot of money. As you know, the American government doesn't pay that well."

"The black market was mostly harmless. Silk stockings. Cigarettes. Coffee."

"Where do you think this scotch came from?" Gibson asked. "That's not our concern. We don't want it to get out, but when we marched through France and Germany, we found huge caches of American weapons and machinery."

Nick thought back to the munitions depot and the crates labeled Bishop Aeronautics. It was the one secret he kept from Evelyn.

"There could be any number of ways those ended up there. The war's over. Let it be over. Send us to Berlin to find Nazis who are still in hiding. Hell, send us to Russia to make new friends. Evelyn knows the language and I look great in a fur hat."

"Investigating traitors not exciting enough for you? Think you're going to miss parachuting behind enemy lines?"

"Yes," Nick deadpanned. "I'm going to miss jumping out of a perfectly good airplane, having no idea what we'll find on the ground."

"Then what is it? What aren't you telling me?"

Nick hesitated.

"I just don't think it's right for us," he said eventually.

"I know we're a little bit more lax when it comes to discipline, but there's still a chain of command. A reckoning is coming for all those who aided the enemy. Because of them, good men died. We'll hunt down those traitors and punish each and every one of them."

With crates from Bishop Aeronautics turning up in German munitions dumps, Evelyn's missions might be seen in a dangerous light. Her work gave her unprecedented access to classified information that would be invaluable in the wrong hands. She was one of the few people who could get into and out of occupied territories on a regular basis and whose job had little oversight. All of that would add up to a damning picture of a woman who may have colluded with the enemy. Nick knew this wasn't the case. He could probably convince Gibson of her innocence, but what about those who didn't know her? Those who didn't see her strength and understand the depths of her loyalty? The army wasn't famous for appreciating the fine nuances of a situation. Unlike the rest of the country, it usually treated people as guilty until proven otherwise—an impossible task in the fog of war. Outside the OSS, Evelyn might be beyond their reach. If they stayed, she could be subject to a court-martial and a firing squad.

Slowly Nick set his glass down.

"I have to tell you something," he said to Gibson.

As Evelyn approached 70 Grosvenor, she saw Nick waiting for her. A broad smile lit her face. He returned it, but it didn't quite meet his eyes.

"Your mood certainly doesn't match the day," she said lightly.

He gathered her in his arms and kissed her. It was long and deep, the kind usually reserved for behind closed doors. When he finally let her go, she looked at him with confusion.

"Let's leave," he said.

"We have the debrief."

"Screw it. Let's get on a train or plane or anywhere that isn't here."

Evelyn thought about it for a moment.

"A few days in Scotland would be nice. I've always wanted to see the Orkneys."

"No. Not a few days. Permanently. The war's over. Let's put it behind us. Start fresh. Just the two of us."

"We talked about this."

"You did absolutely everything you could to save Matthew, but it's over now. Let's move on. We could travel the world or go back to Los Angeles. It wouldn't matter, so long as you're with me."

"What would we do?" she asked.

"Get married. Start a family."

Nick pulled out the ring from his pocket and grabbed her hand. He knelt down on the sidewalk. There was a sort of desperation in his eyes.

"You're proposing to me on the steps of the OSS?" Evelyn asked.

Nick nodded.

"Did you hit your head?"

"Please just say yes. We'll walk away and never look back. But we have to go now."

Evelyn pulled her hand out of Nick's and stared down at him.

"What's going on?" she asked. "You're scaring me."

"Haven't you had enough of this? The war. The fighting."

"I love this. I'm *good* at it. And so are you."

"The only thing I've ever been good at is loving you," Nick said sadly as he got to his feet and slipped the ring into his pocket.

"You do have skills in that area," she replied. "Don't worry. Wherever they send us, General Gibson will make sure we're together."

She kissed him, then took his hand to lead him inside. He hesitated and she looked back, searching his face for answers.

"I love you, Evie. Don't ever forget that."

"Nick . . . ?"

"Everything I've done is to protect you."

General Gibson led them to a small conference room. Director Benjamin Reynolds and Major Lindsey Harris sat on one side of the table. The director was a politician, straight down to his Savile Row suit and his polished oxfords. Major Harris worked in personnel and had a perpetually angry expression. Evelyn took a seat across from them with a bright smile. Nick hesitated in the doorway.

"So, boys, where you sending us next?"

"DC," General Gibson said.

"*Washington, DC?*" Evelyn asked, stunned.

"We have a translator position open," Director Reynolds said.

"Are you fucking kidding me?" Evelyn asked. "That's a glorified secretary."

"I'd like to remind you that you're a lady," Major Harris admonished.

"And I'd like to remind you that we went on over forty missions since the beginning of the war."

"You have a proven inability to follow orders," Director Reynolds said.

"Only when they're wrong," Evelyn said.

"And an apparent attitude problem," Major Harris added.

"Where's this coming from?" Evelyn asked Gibson.

Director Reynolds flipped open the file in front of him.

"March 1944. Your mission was to blow up a munitions dump. You defied your superior officer and freed the POW camp."

Evelyn shot a glance at Nick, but he wouldn't meet her eyes.

"You know as well as I do that those men were invaluable behind the lines during D-Day. They aided the Resistance and helped cut a path straight to Germany."

"It wasn't the mission," Major Harris said.

"Have you been in the field? Even once?" Evelyn asked them. "Of course not. You're bureaucrats sitting behind desks, playing chess with other people's lives. Out there, you have to trust your gut. You make hard decisions."

"Unfortunately," Director Reynolds said, "one of those decisions resulted in the death of Matthew Bishop."

Evelyn sat back in her chair, stunned. The idea that she was careless with her brother's life cut straight to the heart of her guilt.

"How dare you?" she whispered.

For a moment, the room was silent. General Gibson had the decency to look away, while Major Harris and Director Reynolds watched her carefully as if fearing feminine tears. Evelyn was far too angry to cry. She reached across the table and took the file, wanting to know who sat in judgment of the worst night of her life. NOT RECOMMENDED FOR FIELD WORK was stamped across it in red letters. Underneath was Nick's signature.

For a moment, Evelyn forgot to breathe. Then she pushed back her chair and stood up.

"We're not done here," Director Reynolds said.

"Yes. We are."

"Please, Evie," General Gibson said. "Think about DC."

"Maybe when Hell freezes over."

She threw open the door and walked out.

Nick caught up with her at the corner of Grosvenor Street.

"Evie, wait!" he said. "Let me explain."

She turned to face him.

"I can't tell you why I—"

"Betrayed me?" she interrupted.

"Please, you have to understand . . ."

"I do. I understand perfectly. You were done with this life. You wanted the house, the kids, the white picket fence. To get your dreams, I had to give up mine."

"It wasn't like that."

"You dredged up the most agonizing moment in my life—the one I can't stop replaying in my head—and you laid it at my feet. Of all the ways you could have gotten what you wanted . . ."

"I'm trying to protect you."

"I don't need protection," Evelyn said. "I need the truth."

The look on Nick's face was anguished. He warred with himself, knowing that he was on the verge of losing her forever. Yet, he also knew taking away her faith in her father would leave her homeless and adrift. He loved her too much to cause her that pain.

"Evie, please."

"I thought I knew you."

"You do," Nick insisted.

"I thought you would never hurt me. That what we had went beyond this war. I thought this was real."

"It is."

"Then be honest with me. How could you blame me for Matthew's death?"

Nick didn't answer.

"Give me something to hold on to," she pleaded.

"I love you," Nick said.

Her desire to believe Nick collapsed under the weight of his actions. She had trusted him with her heart and soul. In turn, he exposed her worst regret to indifferent eyes. The man standing in front of her was a stranger.

"Not enough," she replied. Then she turned and walked away, before he could see her cry.

Chapter 39

Los Angeles, 1948

As James drove her home, Evelyn was quiet.

"I'm sorry," he said, misreading her silence as anger. "I was harsh back there."

"You were right," she said. "It wasn't the time or place."

James pulled up to her house and put the car in park. He stepped out to open her door. Gently he took her hand in his, looking down at the beautiful ring sitting on the wrong finger.

"Have you thought any more about it?"

"It's the only thing I've been thinking of," she replied.

"Not the only thing."

"I can't help it. You know how I hate when something is unresolved. I need to find answers."

"Well, I suppose it'll keep me on my toes."

"You know I'm not giving this up, right? My work. It's important to me."

"I'd never ask you to stop, but, of course, things'll be different. We'll have our life at home. Maybe start a family and have two little buggers wonderfully underfoot. When we go out, we'll be the toast of society. We'll carry on your father's legacy. All you have to do is say yes."

"You have the next thirty years planned," Evelyn said.

"These are good things, Evie," James replied. "I know you want to change the world. We can find ways to do that together."

True adventures were so rarely a woman's prerogative. Especially after marriage. Since the moment he asked, deep down, she knew her answer. Didn't make it any easier to say.

"James, I've loved you since before I knew what love was," she began. "If I could design the perfect person, it would be you. You are the best of men . . . and you deserve the best of women."

"Which is what you are," James insisted.

"No. I'm not. I'm broken. I've been broken so long I don't remember what whole feels like."

"Then let me remind you."

"I wish you could. I wish we could go back to those days when it was you, me, and Matthew. When our worst nightmares were calculus tests and high school dances. We could be innocent again, not knowing anything more than this world right here. Back then, the years stretched out ahead of us, like some beautiful gift just waiting to be unwrapped. Life was so simple."

"It still is," he insisted.

"Not for me. Those days are gone, and so is the girl who lived them."

"Evie—" James began.

"During the war, I felt so alive. There was more joy and sorrow than I knew existed on the spectrum of human emotion. Looking back, maybe it was inevitable that I gave my heart away. Now in its place is . . . something else. Something shattered whose pieces no longer fit. I want to be the person you inspire me to be. You're offering me the most amazing future. I wish that could be enough, but it's not. Not anymore."

Gently Evelyn slid the ring off her finger and held it out to James. For a moment, it hovered there, catching the faint starlight, reflecting the crimson of her dress. Then James took it and slid it into his pocket, extinguishing its brilliance.

"I'll always love you," Evelyn said.

"That's what makes it so hard," James replied.

He stepped into his car and the engine roared to life. As he drove away, Evelyn watched the taillights fade into darkness.

Chapter 40

Nick was drunk. He left Sam Wilder's party at the observatory and found the nearest bar. He drank until the bartender kicked him out. Then he found a liquor store and bought reinforcements. When he finally hailed a taxi, he told the driver that he didn't want to be alone. They swung down a tree-lined street and stopped in front of a two-story apartment building. Nick didn't remember giving this address. It wasn't where he wanted to be—that house in Bel-Air was no longer an option—but Nick supposed it was better than nothing.

Light poured from the second-story window and the affront of his intrusion was lessened by the knowledge she was still awake. Nick staggered up the front walk. Pulling the door open, he concentrated on the sheer effort it took to keep the walls from spinning. Nick reached the stairway and sat down, closing his eyes against the bright lights of the hallway. He needed everything to stand still. Just for a moment.

Finding his feet, he took one stair at a time, gripping the banister as he hauled himself up to the second floor. Upon reaching the door, he fell heavily against the wood, his forehead knocking in slow rhythm. From inside, he heard the shuffle of papers, then footsteps approaching. It should have been enough time to steady himself, but, when the door swung inward, Nick fell across the threshold, landing in a crumpled heap at the feet of Katie Pierce.

Nick looked up from the ground.

"I was doing so well up to this exact moment."

"Sure you were," Katie said.

"I was standing," Nick replied. "Now I'm not."

"You're three sheets to the wind."

"Four."

Katie laughed in spite of herself, which Nick took as a good sign.

"Come on," she said, pulling him to his feet and ushering him inside. "Last thing I need is for the neighbors to talk."

"You'd think they'd had their fill of gossip already."

"Does anyone get their fill of gossip?"

They stumbled across the room until Nick was close enough to collapse on the couch in a position halfway between sitting and reclining. Katie shut the door and looked at this mess of a man.

"Nice apartment," Nick said.

"This place is a rathole," Katie replied. "But it's what I can afford."

"You're a rich woman now."

Katie pondered that statement.

"Guess it hasn't sunk in. Everything with George happened so fast. I barely got the chance to know him."

Her voice quavered. Tears sprang to her eyes and threatened to fall.

"Shit," Nick said. "I'm sorry. I didn't mean to . . ."

"How about we start over?"

"Yes! Let's do that! We should go dancing!"

Nick tried to get to his feet, but the floor kept moving.

"Maybe not dancing," he said.

"Normally, I'd offer you a drink, but I think you've had enough."

"I brought my own!" Nick cried triumphantly, pulling the bottle from his coat pocket. It was mostly empty. An inch of whisky rocked back and forth, temporarily mesmerizing him.

Gently Katie pried the bottle from his fingers.

"I'll get glasses."

She disappeared into the kitchen and Nick looked around the room. In place of the blood-splattered curtains was an old sheet, tacked up with penny nails. The ruined rug was gone, but the floor was stained, despite the obvious efforts to scrub it clean. It must have taken her all day to get the apartment into livable condition. Katie returned a moment later and followed Nick's gaze to where George's body recently lay.

"Yeah. Blood is impossible."

In one hand, she held a tumbler of whisky; in the other, a glass of water. She handed the latter to Nick.

"You're no fun," he grumbled.

"You'll thank me in the morning."

"I'm planning on sleeping until Friday," he replied.

"Gonna tell me what you're doing here at midnight?" she asked as she sipped her drink.

"I saw your light on," Nick said.

"Once you were already outside . . ."

"I can go," he said, starting to get up. He was not certain about the truth of that statement, but perhaps sheer force of will might allow him an iota of grace.

"Don't," Katie said. "You're always welcome. I'm sure we can find something to keep ourselves occupied."

"Monopoly?"

"Not Monopoly," she said with a smile.

Nick contemplated that notion.

"She threw me over."

"Evelyn?"

Nick nodded.

"She's done that before."

"This time felt real. There's that guy."

"James," Katie offered.

"She's gonna marry him," Nick said. "Who does a thing like that?"

"Plenty of people," Katie said. "He's handsome."

"Too handsome."

"Successful."

"If you like that sort of thing."

"Kind, funny . . ."

"Whose side are you on?" Nick asked.

"You're the one who stumbled into my apartment in the middle of the night to talk about another woman."

"Suppose that's not very nice of me."

"No, it's not."

"Okay. Let's talk about you. Why aren't you married?"

"That *is* a question," Katie said. "Maybe I'm waiting for the perfect guy."

"Doesn't exist."

"How about a good guy?"

"Boring."

"How about the wrong guy at the right moment?" Katie asked.

"Infinitely more interesting."

Katie set her glass of whisky down on the table and came over to Nick. Slowly she raised her skirt, inch by inch, until it revealed the tops of her stockings, attached with black garters. She set one knee beside Nick's leg and stepped forward to straddle him. Nick looked up at Katie, feeling both the need to stop what was about to happen and the inevitability of this outcome. She leaned in until he felt her lips against his.

"You kissed me," Nick said.

"If you like it, I'll do it again," Katie said.

This time, her kiss was longer—lingering and exploring. Through his alcoholic haze, Nick caught a waft of Katie's perfume. Vanilla mixed with something he couldn't quite identify. He sank into the moment, willing it to be enough. Pulling her closer, he felt her body pressed against his. It was no use. She felt strange and tasted wrong.

"She's jealous of you, you know," Nick said, breaking off. "Won't admit it, but she is."

"Then let's give her something to really be jealous of," Katie replied as she pulled off her blouse.

To Nick, this felt like a self-destructive kind of revenge he would regret in the morning. He kissed Katie, then tried to lay them both down on the couch. Instead, they crashed to the floor.

"Are you okay?" he asked.

"You're a mess," she laughed.

"Noooooo," Nick slurred. "Maybe."

She moved to be on top.

"A woman who wants to do all the work," he said. "I could get used to this."

She undid the buttons on his shirt, then dropped her head to trace the outline of his chest with the tip of her tongue. Nick relaxed his head back and looked above him. The ceiling was decorated in cracked plaster and water stains creating an abstract pattern. Then he looked behind him to the underside of the desk. There, just where Evelyn swore she'd seen it, was a hidden shelf with a copy of *The Iliad*.

"I need to catch my breath," Nick said.

"Am I too much for you?" Katie teased.

"Yes," Nick said, in all honesty. "Way too much."

"I'll get you another glass of water."

She went into the kitchen. Nick sat up to grab the book.

There was no inscription on the front cover. Katie returned to find him looking at the copyright page.

"What did you find?"

He held it up.

"A girl can enjoy an epic poem now and then, can't she?"

"Samuel Butler translation. Longmans and Green. Not many of these floating around."

"Don't tell me you want to spend the night reading?" Katie asked as she knelt down beside him.

"Words are swimming, anyway," Nick said. "Where'd you get this?"

"Dunno. Probably left over from high school?" she said. "I did have a little crush on my English teacher."

"This book is new," Nick said. "At least to you. Evelyn took your other copy."

"So that's where it went," Katie said quietly. "I thought it was the police."

She sat back on her heels. Even in Nick's drunken fog, he recognized the change in her. Gone was the flirtatious girl. In her place sat a woman with a flinty edge.

"Tell me you're not involved in this Wahlstatt mess."

"Wahlstatt?" she asked. "What do you know about them?"

"What do *you* know?"

Katie smiled ruefully.

"It's a shame. We could've had a lot of fun together."

She leaned in toward Nick and he thought she was going to kiss him again. Instead, she grabbed a paperweight from the desk and swung it hard. It connected with his temple. Everything went black.

Chapter 41

Evelyn slept fitfully. Her dreams were plagued by memories of Matthew's death. The stench of the hospital barracks filled her nose as she fought through broken men to reach him. The building kept extending outward and she had to push through more and more people. Sometimes they were not even whole bodies, but lost limbs clinging to her skirt and hair. When she finally got to Matthew, his pale face was ravaged by cold and hunger. He looked up at her with accusing eyes, asking why it took her so long to rescue him. The instant she touched him, a hole opened up in his chest. Blood seeped through her fingers as she tried to contain it. She begged him to hold on just a little longer. Tears rolled down her face as Matthew told Evelyn this was her fault.

It was a relief when the peal of the doorbell woke her from the endless loop of her nightmare. It took a moment to recognize she was safe in her own bed, no longer lost in Northern France. The doorbell rang again and she grabbed her robe off the chair next to her bed and made her way downstairs. Logan was already reaching for the knob when she entered the foyer. Since he was still wearing his business suit, she realized he had not yet been to sleep. His pale demeanor spoke of nights as anxious as hers.

Logan opened the door to reveal Carl, with his LAPD badge clipped prominently to the breast pocket of his coat. This wasn't a social call.

"What's wrong?" Evelyn asked. Tragedy was the only reason for him to be on her doorstep in the middle of the night.

"Evie, I need you to come with me," Carl said. "Captain wants a word."

"What's the meaning of this?" Logan said. "You can't drag my daughter out in the middle of the night without an explanation."

"Sam Wilder is dead," Carl said.

Logan slumped visibly and Evelyn hastened to his side.

"Daddy, are you okay?"

Logan managed to nod.

"It's just . . . I've known him a long time."

Unspoken between them was the fact this was the second person Logan had lost recently. Both were business contacts from the war. Evelyn studied her father and realized he was afraid.

"Carl, would you give us a minute?" Evelyn said.

He nodded and she led her father into the living room.

"What's going on?"

"It's . . . It's nothing."

"Stop lying to me. Are you in trouble?" Evelyn asked.

Logan spent his life trying to be a hero to his daughter. After Evelyn's mother died, he swore she would never want for anything. Not an iota of his attention. Not an ounce of love. Everything he did was for his children. However, his devotion cost him in ways he never anticipated and the bill was finally being presented.

"Let me help you," Evelyn insisted.

"I'm your father. I should be taking care of you."

"We look after each other."

"I promise," Logan said, "I'll make everything right."

Evelyn wanted to argue, but her entire family had a stubborn streak. Logan was intractable once he got an idea in his mind.

"You do things your way," she said. "I'll do them mine."

Carl drove Evelyn through the winding, mist-shrouded curves of Laurel Canyon. The car's headlights only illuminated a few feet in front of them. The hills felt ominous and claustrophobic.

"What's this about?" Evelyn asked.

"Nick," Carl replied.

"Is he okay?"

"He hasn't been okay for a long time," Carl said. "We won the war, but he came home utterly defeated. Sometimes we'd be out on patrol, when he was still with the LAPD, and it felt like old times. For a moment, Nick was back. He had a purpose and a mission. He was helping people. Then he'd remember you were gone. Next morning, he was in pieces all over again.

"We saw you one night. It was outside the Egyptian Theatre for some movie premiere. You looked the same as during the war. Tall, confident, as if you could take on the world. Nick sometimes said that you were invincible— your strength and self-assurance. You never knew how he saw you."

"I knew," Evelyn whispered.

"Nick stopped the car in front of the theater. I don't think he realized it until that instant, but he'd spent the past year and a half searching for you. Ever since he returned to LA, he expected to find you around the next corner. When it finally happened, he lit up. Then you turned and smiled at your new boyfriend. It wasn't the same as when you looked at Nick, but it was enough. I've never seen a man deflate so thoroughly. Less than a month later, he was slung out of the force. I tried to help him, but . . ."

"He's never been good at accepting it," Evelyn replied. "Why didn't you tell me he was in Los Angeles?"

"Would it have made a difference?"

Evelyn didn't know the answer to that question.

"When he told me he ran into you, a few weeks back, I worried he'd spiral further downward," Carl said. "Then I realized this might be his only shot at redemption."

"That's not fair," Evelyn said. "I don't know how to save him."

"I know. It's just sometimes I wish . . ." he trailed off.

"That things could be the way they once were," Evelyn finished.

Carl nodded.

In the distance, the flashing lights of police cars colored the fog red and blue. A lonely ambulance stood near the center of the hubbub. Its white paneling and red cross seemed a beacon in the night. Wearing his rain slicker and plastic hat cover, a uniformed policeman turned away cars and sent them back down the hill. At this time of night, his responsibilities were minimal. Carl parked behind the scrum. Evelyn saw several officers hovering around a curve in the road. Their hunched backs blocked her line of sight.

"What happened?" Evelyn asked.

"Sam Wilder ended up at the bottom of the canyon," Carl replied.

He led her to Captain Wharton, who stood in front of a broken, twisted guardrail. Evelyn followed Wharton's gaze to the bottom of the canyon, where a black Packard lay in a crumpled heap.

"Miss Bishop," Wharton said, turning to Evelyn, "thank you for coming."

"Thank you for making it seem like I had a choice."

"Heard you saw Sam Wilder earlier tonight."

"Along with half of Los Angeles. He had a fundraiser at Griffith Observatory."

"Exactly what was that entry fee?"

"It's no secret my father supports Sam Wilder's campaign," Evelyn replied. "Although, I suppose it's over now. He should know better than to tangle with these roads after a couple of drinks."

"It wasn't the booze that did him in," Wharton said. "It was the three bullets in his chest."

Evelyn stepped back in shock. A car accident was suspicious enough, but whoever did this wasn't trying to hide their tracks.

"Rumor has it you had words with Mr. Wilder."

"Yes. We discussed business."

"Exactly what business did you have with him?"

"That's what I'm trying to figure out," Evelyn said.

"Young lady, if you don't give me a straight answer, I'll haul your ass down to the station and lock you in a box for the next twelve hours."

"Let's dispense with the threats, shall we? We both know I had nothing to do with Sam Wilder's death. There's a reason you brought me here and it isn't to ask about a fundraiser."

"Where can we find Nick Gallagher?"

"Nick? What does he have to do with this?"

Wharton held up a wallet and a gun.

"Both of these belong to Gallagher. We found them in the car. I'm betting the gun will match the holes in Mr. Wilder's chest."

"You can't honestly think Nick killed him," Evelyn said.

"That's where the evidence points."

"A bit too strongly," Evelyn replied. "Despite his many,

many faults, Nick isn't a stupid man. Nor is he careless. He would've broken Wilder's neck before pushing the car into the ravine. To anyone investigating, it'd look like an accident. And you can be damned sure he wouldn't leave his wallet at the scene."

"So what you're saying is that if Nick Gallagher was behind this, he'd do it better."

"Yes," Evelyn said. "More than that, in all the years I've known Nick, I've never seen him kill a man without reason. Whoever murdered Sam Wilder is doing a poor job of framing him."

"Which is all the more reason to find him," Carl said.

"Where have you looked so far?" Evelyn asked.

"His office, his apartment, and every shithole bar between the two," Wharton replied.

Evelyn thought for a moment, then laughed humorlessly.

"He's just stupid enough to go there," she said. "You should pay a visit to Katie Pierce."

"We'd appreciate your company," Wharton said as he escorted Evelyn to a police car and held the back door open.

"I'm going to think of this more as a chauffeured ride than you arresting me."

"We'll see how the night goes," Wharton said as he slammed the door.

Captain Wharton, Carl, and Evelyn pulled up in front of Katie Pierce's apartment. The windows were dark. Evelyn looked down the street, but saw no sign of Nick's car. She led Wharton and Carl into the apartment building and up the stairs to Katie's door. She knocked twice, but there was no answer.

"Any other suggestions?" Wharton asked.

Evelyn reached into her handbag and pulled out her set of lockpick tools. Carl raised his eyebrow.

"Never leave home without them," Evelyn explained.

"I can't let you do that," Wharton said.

"Then turn around. Once I open this door, you have probable cause to follow me inside."

Wharton sighed, then faced the opposite wall.

"Is she always like this?" he asked Carl.

"For as long as I can remember," Carl replied.

Within seconds, Evelyn undid the dead bolt and popped the bottom lock. She swung the door open.

"Hello?" she called.

There was no answer.

Evelyn walked inside and flipped on the light. Carl and Wharton trailed her into the living room. There, beside the sofa, was a fresh bloodstain on the floor. A whisky glass sat on the table. Carl went into the kitchen and found the nearly empty bottle. He held it up for inspection.

"So Gallagher was here," Wharton said.

"Judging by the blood, I'd say he opened his mouth one too many times," Evelyn replied.

"You seem to know a lot more than you're saying, Miss Bishop."

"How I wish that was true," Evelyn said. "Mind giving me a ride to the station? Assuming you're not tossing me in a cell, that is."

"What's at the station?"

"Colette Palmer."

Chapter 42

Evelyn looked around the interrogation room. A single table stood in the middle with two metal chairs on each side. Above, fluorescent lights hummed quietly, their light creating harsh shadows. One wall had a two-way mirror whose other side bordered the observation room. The door opened and Colette Palmer entered. Dressed in a faded prison uniform, she looked exhausted. Her once-shiny hair now hung limp and dull and her wrists chafed under the handcuffs. She looked at Evelyn with surprise as she sat down across from her.

"Please take those off," Evelyn said to the policeman, nodding at the handcuffs.

He glanced toward the mirror uncertainly. Colette followed his gaze with a rueful smile.

"Where can she possibly go?" Evelyn asked.

The officer sighed and removed the restraints. Colette rubbed her wrists to temporarily erase the memory of the cold steel.

"Do you want anything?" Evelyn asked. "Coffee? Tea? Water?"

"No, thank you."

"That will be all, then," Evelyn said to the police officer.

He wasn't used to being dismissed like a waiter, but Evelyn took over this interrogation room as thoroughly as if it had been the dining room in her father's house. Not knowing what else to do, the policeman left. Evelyn and Colette heard the click of the lock sealing them inside this room.

"I didn't kill George," Colette said.

"I know," Evelyn replied.

"You do?" she asked, the first ray of hope entering her eyes. "But . . ."

"I helped bring you in?"

Colette nodded.

"It was never my intention. We just wanted to talk. Running made you seem guilty."

"I was scared. I—" Colette broke off, realizing Evelyn would not have pulled her out of her cell this early without reason. "What happened? Why are you here?"

"Sam Wilder is dead. He was shot three times."

Colette sucked in a breath of surprise. There was fear behind it.

"You need to tell me about Wahlstatt," Evelyn said.

"They'll kill me," Colette whispered. "And I have a sister, Marie."

"It can be our secret," Evelyn said, switching to French, as she glanced at the two-way mirror. Captain Wharton would not be pleased with an interrogation he did not understand.

"I love my sister like you loved your brother," Colette began in French.

"Her best protection is putting an end to this," Evelyn said.

Colette looked down at her hands. The remains of her careful manicure were chipped and peeling.

"I've done some terrible things," Colette began. *"None of it was intentional, but that doesn't matter. The consequences were real. I deserve to be in prison for my actions, and for all that George sacrificed to save me."*

"*You loved him,*" Evelyn said.

"*With every fiber of my being. He was the kindest man I've ever known. He's dead because of me, but I didn't hold the gun. Nor did I arrange for someone to kill him.*"

Evelyn reached out and took Colette's hand. She looked up, startled by this simple act of kindness.

"*You met George during the war,*" Evelyn prompted.

"*Yes, but my story starts before then. My father was a German soldier on the Western Front during the First World War. In the middle of a retreat, he was wounded and left to die by the rest of his battalion. My mother hid him on her family's farm, nursing him back to health. It wasn't a political act, she just couldn't stand to see anyone in pain. They grew closer, sharing stories and eventually planning for the future. On his last night, they made love. Two years later, my father arrived to find both of us living under the harsh rule of my grandfather, who never forgave my mother for bringing shame upon his family. Even after they married, Grandfather was unrelenting in his anger.*

"*My father took us back to Berlin. He thought being a veteran would ensure him a job. Instead, he looked for work every day, and every day, he came home with nothing. Though they loved each other, it wasn't enough. Especially after my sister was born. Simply to feed us, my mother took to loitering outside bakeries and cafés to fight for scraps at the end of the day. When Father discovered the level to which we'd sunk, he swallowed his pride and we returned, shame-faced, to my grandfather's house. My father worked the fields, biting his tongue at my grandfather's constant criticism. In private, he told me of the former glory of the German Empire and his pride in his homeland. When I was seventeen, he died in an auto accident. I tell you all this not for sympathy, but to explain what came next.*

"*In the following years, supporting the rise of the Third*

Reich felt like the only way to stay true to my father. I had no idea what the Nazis would become. One day, a German officer arrived in the village. Surprised to hear a French farm girl speak both languages fluently, he offered me the chance to serve the Fatherland. It started with small things. Writing letters in code about the town and places nearby. I gossiped about my neighbors and their sensibilities. It all seemed like an adventure. I was too young and stupid to understand the consequences.

"I was in Paris at university when I met George. One afternoon, I was at a café, and George asked if he might buy me a coffee. I was used to French men and their aggressive confidence. Yet, here stood this man in his finely tailored suit asking nothing more than to share a drink. After coffee came dinner. Then he walked me back to my flat, kissed my hand, and asked if he might see me again. I had never been courted before. During the two weeks he was in Paris, we spent all our time together. He took me to the opera and we got lost in the Louvre. Other days, we whiled away the afternoon watching the rain streak down a bistro's windows. When he returned to America, I thought I'd never see him again. But he kept his promise, writing every day. He made me feel safe and loved. Six months later, he asked me to marry him, and, of course, I said yes.

"It was 1939 and he wanted us to leave immediately, have the ceremony in London, then return to his home in Los Angeles. But I couldn't do that to my mother. Not after her shame in my being born out of wedlock. I insisted on a proper church wedding after I finished my degree. I was a fool."

"Germany invaded," Evelyn said.

"I still believed in the German cause. I even cheered when they came rumbling into town. Then people began disappearing. Their names were on the list I gave the Ger-

*man officer. Jews, Communists, and anyone who was dif-
ferent. My ignorance is no excuse for the harm I caused. I
wanted to flee, but . . ."*

"By then, you needed exit visas," Evelyn offered.

Colette nodded. Tears spilled over her cheeks.

*"George went through the American Embassy in Lon-
don. Through the Vichy government. Hell, he even applied
to Berlin, but someone kept blocking the paperwork. He
hired people to smuggle me over the border, but every time
I tried to leave, soldiers were waiting to escort me home.
In time, I discovered it was the German officer continually
denying my exit. He threatened to send me to the camps,
so George made a devil's bargain. In exchange for aerial
bombs, my family would be safe. I'd be protected and
eventually granted my visa. I had corrupted the most hon-
orable man I'd ever met.*

*"When I was released in '43, America was at war with
Germany. George's actions were treason. The officer blackmailed him to continue the supply. To keep me quiet, he
threatened my family."*

"Wahlstatt?" Evelyn asked.

Colette nodded.

"How was Sam Wilder involved?"

*"He was always a greedy man. Sam saw a way to make
a fortune and thought he could control the situation."*

"You think they backed his mayoral run?"

*"Most likely. The open shipping lanes aren't just for
people like your father. They'd allow Los Angeles to become one of the most unregulated ports in the country."*

"Wahlstatt is still operating?" Evelyn asked. "The war's
over."

*"They used to be Nazis. Now they're apolitical. There's
a lot of money to be made every time people find a new
reason to kill one another."*

"Who else is involved?"

Colette looked back down at her hands, unable to meet Evelyn's eyes.

"I don't know everyone."

"You know some."

"Be careful of the questions you ask. You might not like the answers."

"Answers are better than uncertainty."

Colette took a deep breath and looked to Evelyn. Her eyes carried something akin to pity.

"Wahlstatt was brutal," she said. *"They found someone's weak spot and exploited it. They blackmailed politicians, kidnapped soldiers' wives, and murdered children. Once, they captured a man's son as a POW and held him hostage in Northern France. They used his life as leverage to gain an essential navigation tool for aviation."*

It took Evelyn a moment to understand what she meant. Her brain refused to process this information. Her father would never betray his country.

"They'd been after Logan since the mid-1930s," Colette continued. *"But he wanted nothing to do with them. Earlier than most, he understood Hitler's true goals. After Kristallnacht, your father began petitioning the American government to approve Jewish visas. He offered to sponsor them and give them jobs in his factory. But at that time, the country refused most refugees."*

"I didn't know that," Evelyn said.

"Your father's a good man. He would have emerged from the war a hero, except for Wahlstatt. When Matthew's plane was shot down, his value as a hostage was immediately recognized."

"My father traded thousands of lives to get my brother back."

"It was his son. Everything he did was to keep Matthew safe."

"But he didn't *keep Matthew safe,"* Evelyn said.

She thought back to holding her brother in her arms as the life drained from his eyes. She remembered those final cryptic words, to tell their father he wasn't worth it. For so long, Evelyn believed that she alone was responsible for Matthew's death. Now every conversation between her and her father felt like a lie.

"*Logan was caught between two impossible choices. Betray his country. Or betray his family,*" Colette said. "*What would you have had him do?*"

"I don't know," Evelyn said.

"*We thought once the war ended, we'd finally be free,*" Colette said. "*Six months ago, the German showed up on our doorstep. He told George it wasn't over. It would never be over.*"

"*You made plans to leave?*"

"*George would have turned himself in, but I couldn't stand the thought of him paying for my mistakes,*" she said. "*I couldn't stand losing him. So, instead, we made plans to leave.*"

"Then Katie Pierce arrived," Evelyn said.

"*The timing was suspicious, to say the least. George bought her story—hook, line, and sinker. They had done their research, knew George had business in that town twenty years ago. Even knew he'd had a short dalliance. How they found these things out is beyond me. He truly believed she was his daughter. That's why I hired you to spy on her.*"

"*Did you ever think she was his mistress?*"

"*Of course not. George and I didn't have secrets. Not after everything we'd been through. It was easier to accuse him of adultery than to explain the whole situation.*"

"*I'm sorry I couldn't save his life . . . or Sam Wilder's.*"

"*Sam got what he deserved. George confided our plans to him and he betrayed us,*" Colette said. "*I know this is a lot and it might take time to process. But will you con-*"

tinue to investigate, now that you know about your father?"

Evelyn thought for a long moment. She wanted desperately to wind the clocks back an hour and keep herself from walking into this station and walking into this room. For once in her life, she did not want to know everything. Instead, she wanted to go home, give her father a hug, and pretend that the world made sense. This was all too much. Then she thought of the ghost who haunted her dreams.

"I owe it to Matthew," Evelyn said eventually.

"Thank you," Colette said, switching back to English. Tears sprang from her eyes as she stood to embrace Evelyn. "Bring those bastards down."

"Stay strong," Evelyn whispered.

"It helps to know I'm not alone."

Evelyn released her, then knocked on the door. The young officer opened it and ushered her into the hallway.

Captain Wharton caught up with Evelyn on the way out.

"What'd she say?" Wharton demanded.

"She didn't do it," Evelyn replied.

Then she turned toward the door and headed out to the street.

Chapter 43

Evelyn walked up the dingy stairs to Nick's apartment and knocked on the door. There was no answer. Quickly she picked the lock and slipped inside. Her brief glance the other night did not do the place justice. Carl was right to be concerned. Everything about the place spoke of a resigned hopelessness. There was no decoration other than the same photo that Evelyn had of herself, Carl, and Nick, tacked to the wall. A few dime-store paperbacks with broken spines were scattered around. Searching the entire place did not take long. Finding nothing, Evelyn locked the door and repeated the same task at Nick's office.

Then Evelyn returned to Wahlstatt's office. The small sign outside its door was missing. She turned the handle to find the door unlocked and the room empty. The desk, chair, and filing cabinets were gone, as was the ledger under the floorboard. Had she not stood in this room yesterday morning, she would have never known it existed. On the landing outside the office, she saw a woman cleaning the floors.

"Hello," Evelyn said as she approached. "I'm hoping you can help me. Do you know anything about the people who used to rent this office?"

The woman shrugged.

"They were here, now they're not."

"Did you ever see anyone coming in or out?"

"I guess," she said.

Evelyn reached into her purse and pulled out her card. She slid a five-dollar bill behind it and handed it to the woman.

"I'm a private investigator," Evelyn said.

"Really? Never woulda guessed."

"I get that a lot."

Now it was Evelyn's turn to wait. The woman turned the money over in her hand, then tucked the bill into her pocket.

"Always thought there was something shady about those people," the woman said. "Lights on at weird times. Never talked to anyone. Never seemed to stay long. One was a young girl. Pretty. Seemed a little fast, if you know what I mean."

Katie Pierce.

"Another was a handsome fella. Looked almost like a former soldier. Don't think he was with the girl, though. Sometimes she tried to be a bit too familiar, but he wasn't having it."

"Anyone else?"

"Middle-aged fella. Mighta been German," she said, dropping her voice to a whisper.

"Thanks," Evelyn said. "You remember any more details, or if you see them again, please give me a call."

"Lady detective," the woman said, shaking her head. "Something new every day."

Evelyn tipped her hat at the woman and stepped into the atrium, at a loss for where to go next. Searching for clues about Nick's whereabouts helped her avoid her father. She had no idea what to say to him about Matthew's death. Part of her was furious with him for making the deal with Wahlstatt. Another part understood his actions perfectly. She didn't know how to forgive him. Nor did she know how to stay angry.

Evelyn drove back to Bel-Air. Glancing at her watch, she realized it was already late afternoon. Evelyn entered the house to find the lights off and the rooms silent. There was no sign of life.

"Daddy?" she called out.

"Not exactly."

Evelyn turned at the sound of a voice she would never forget. Drexler, the Nazi commandant from Matthew's prison camp, stood in front of her. As before, he had a gun pointed at her. For a moment, she stared in surprise. Then all the pieces fell into place. This was the man who had gotten to Colette before the war. He was the same one blackmailing George and her father.

"You killed my brother," she said.

"He had served his purpose," Drexler replied. "It was no great loss."

Her rage rendered her temporarily mute.

"If I'd known who you were back in France, I never would've let you walk out of my office," Drexler said.

"And if I'd known who you were, I never would have let you live."

"Don't think you have cold-blooded murder in you," he replied.

"There's a first for everything."

"I should have given you more credit," Drexler said.

"People often make that mistake," Evelyn replied.

"It's one I won't repeat."

"Where's my father?"

"We'll take you to him."

" 'We'?"

From behind, Evelyn heard girlish laughter. It grated on her nerves as much as ever, but this time it had an edge.

She turned to see Katie Pierce holding one of her mother's silver candlesticks.

"I've been wanting to do this for a while," Katie said, swinging the candlestick.

Evelyn ducked out of the way and drove her shoulder into Katie's side, tackling her to the floor. Katie struggled to throw Evelyn off, but Evelyn punched her hard.

"And I've been wanting to do that for a while."

From behind, Evelyn heard Drexler's footsteps. She rolled to the side, just as he reached for her. From her back, she drove her foot into Drexler's knee. He moved just in time and she only landed a glancing blow.

"Shows more fight than the rest of them," Drexler said.

Katie rubbed her eye, which was already beginning to swell.

Evelyn sprang to her feet, ready to take on both of them. She never saw the third person, who grabbed her around the waist, slid a needle into her neck, and pressed the plunger.

Chapter 44

Evelyn woke, groggy and tied to a chair. It took her eyes a moment to focus and when they did, she saw Nick tied up across from her.

"Hey there, sleeping beauty."

"You're a popular man," she said. "Everyone's looking for you."

"Congratulations! You're the lucky winner."

"Bully for me."

Evelyn glanced around. They were on the main floor of Bishop Aeronautics. Other than the emergency lights, the factory was dark. A few mechanic's carts were scattered about, with stray tools lying on top. In the distance stood planes in every stage of completion. Their hulls formed ghostly shapes in the darkness.

"Should I ask how you got here?" Evelyn started. "No. Wait. Never mind. I saw evidence of you all over Katie Pierce's apartment."

"Is this where you say, 'I told you so'?"

"Do I need to?"

"How about for the sake of tradition?"

"How about you 'tradition' us out of here?"

"I would, if I could," Nick replied. "Turns out Miss Pierce has a way with knots."

"Such a shame things didn't work out between you two."

"For Chrissakes. Do you ever shut up?" Katie Pierce asked, coming down the stairs from Logan's office.

Evelyn and Nick glanced at each other.

"No."

This felt so much like the old days, it was impossible not to fall back into the same patterns.

"I'm guessing George Palmer wasn't actually your father?" Evelyn asked.

"That old fool?" Katie laughed. "He was gullible to his last breath. Do you know, when Dan O'Brien walked in, George actually tried to protect me? It was so nice to stop pretending I cared about him."

Evelyn looked to Nick.

"Okay, I can't help it," Evelyn said. "I told you so."

"You did."

"She's just terrible," Evelyn said. "I mean a really awful person."

"You're right."

"Wait, what was that? Can you say it again?"

"You. Are. Right. Happy now?"

"Hello!" Katie snapped, drawing their attention back to her. "What the hell is wrong with you two?"

"Wait, were we supposed to be scared?" Evelyn said. "Shit. Nick, be scared. You're more convincing than I am."

"Oh, no! I'm terrified," Nick deadpanned.

"Don't you take any of this seriously?" Katie huffed.

"We do . . ." Evelyn began.

"It's just that we've been here before," Nick continued.

"You threaten us."

"Drop the word 'torture.' "

"Guns come out."

"It's exhausting."

"We should just skip to the end," Evelyn said. "Where they end up in prison."

"Works for me," Nick said.

"Well, it doesn't work for me!" Katie stomped her feet.

"Now, now, dear," Drexler said as he descended the stairs. "No need for hysterics."

"You have no idea how frustrating they are," Katie said as she threw herself at him and nuzzled into his chest. Drexler looked uncomfortable with the public display of affection and extracted himself from her arms.

"Girl gets around," Evelyn said.

"She was never my first choice," Nick replied. "Kinda like the difference between steak and bologna. Sometimes you just need a sandwich late at night."

"You can get a nasty stomachache doing a thing like that."

"How do you think I ended up here?"

Katie looked beyond Evelyn and said, "Told you they were in love."

Evelyn glanced over her shoulder into the shadows. James stepped out slowly, reluctantly. For a moment, she stopped breathing as she stared in shocked disbelief. It took her several seconds to trust her eyes.

"I'm so sorry, Evie," he said.

"No," she said. "It's not possible."

"Oh, but it is," Katie taunted. "You think you know everything. That you've got it all figured out."

"How? Why?" Evelyn demanded.

"When they got Matthew, I was working for army supply. They told me if I helped them, they'd make sure he was safe. They promised once they had what they needed, they'd release him so he could go home to you and Logan," James said, pleading for understanding. "He was my best friend, but it was more than that. I was so in love with you that I'd do anything to keep you from pain."

"Yet, here we are," Evelyn said, motioning to the ties binding her hands behind her back. "What did they make you do?"

"At first, it was small things, like letting a few boxes of ammunition go missing. Then they kept asking for more, and by that point, it was too late. I was a traitor."

"What did they make you do?" Evelyn asked again.

James stared down at his hands, unable to meet her eyes.

"I gave them schedules for our supply boats, submarine routes, and the schedule for . . ." James trailed off. "I didn't know you were up there!"

"The bombing raids."

"If you'd told me you were working with the OSS, that you were on those planes, I never would have . . ."

"The soldiers on those planes were sons, husbands, and fathers. They had people who loved them just as much as we loved Matthew. You and Dad." Evelyn stopped and shook her head. "Neither of you realized this was the last thing he would have wanted."

"I wish I could take it all back and start over," he pleaded. "Maybe things would be different."

"Maybe," Evelyn said. "But time only moves in one direction."

James closed his eyes for a moment, processing Evelyn's anger and his own guilt. Then he turned to Drexler.

"You promised to keep her out of this."

"That was before she turned down your proposal. Now . . . ?" Drexler trailed off. He called up to the office. Dan O'Brien, the thug Evelyn disarmed in the alley, came down the stairs, prodding Logan with the muzzle of his gun.

"Daddy!" Evelyn cried out.

She had never seen him look so tired and utterly defeated—a boxer at the end of the match, knowing he'd lost the bout, and was just hoping to get out alive. His hands were tied and he stumbled with exhaustion.

"It'll be okay, honey."

His words did nothing to calm her fear. Then he saw James. His surprise mirrored Evelyn's.

"You were family," Logan said. "I trusted you like a son and hoped you'd become one through marriage."

"Logan, I'm—"

"I'm in no position to speak," Logan interrupted. "We both committed the same sin. Thank God my daughter was wiser than me."

"Let them go," James said to Drexler, still fighting for Evelyn. "Please. Logan will sign everything over and then we won't need them anymore. They can return to their lives."

"You were always shortsighted. Logan is my insurance so Evelyn behaves. And vice versa," Drexler said, turning to Evelyn. "You already got Sam Wilder killed. Would you have the same thing happen to your father?"

Evelyn glanced at James.

"I didn't know they'd hurt Sam," James said. "I swear."

"Was any of this real? Us? The future?" Evelyn asked.

"Of course, it was real," James replied. "I've loved you my whole life. Going to war just clarified things. Thinking of you helped me survive those long nights hidden in a bomb shelter. When I sat in the cold, rainy London weather, dreaming of Los Angeles, it was you I pictured. I swore when I got home, we'd finally be together. That I'd put all of this behind me and spend the rest of my life making up for everything I'd done wrong. But Drexler followed me here and blackmailed me to keep working for him. You were the one pure thing in my life, and I couldn't lose you."

"He wanted to gain control of Bishop Aeronautics through our marriage."

"It wouldn't have been like that," James said. "You'd never have known."

"And that makes it better? This is my father's company. His legacy," Evelyn said. "He built this place from the ground up and you'd hand it over to the man who killed his son."

"Evelyn," Logan said. "Please. Just walk away. We're trying to keep you safe."

Evelyn glanced between her father and James. Then she looked to Nick and followed his gaze to where a sharp piece of metal lay on the floor, near his chair. She nodded almost imperceptibly, then looked at Drexler.

"Safe," Evelyn said derisively. "Do we get to go back to our lives, or are we locked away in some basement and trotted out on ceremonial occasions? Is James my keeper? Am I meant to marry him as a guarantee on my inheritance?"

"No," Drexler said. "I only keep what's useful. You've made it clear he's not."

Drexler shot James in the chest. For a moment, the world stopped spinning. The smell of cordite hung in the air. James's shock mingled with the first pricks of pain. His eyes sought Evelyn's as his final sight. Blood stained his shirt as his knees collapsed and he fell to the floor.

Evelyn cried out, struggling hopelessly against the ropes that bound her to the chair. She fought to go to him. He needed to know that all their good memories could not be replaced by his betrayal. She pictured them playing as children; remembered him as a teenager, standing on the edge of their pool; and saw his anguished face when he told them about Matthew's capture. She cherished his gentleness after the war and thought about the house where he had planned their lives so meticulously. If she could have been that kind of wife for anyone, it would have been for him.

"James, please," she whispered. "Please don't go."

The last breath escaped his lips and his chest fell still. Logan stared in numb disbelief. Drexler raised the gun and pointed it at Evelyn.

"Is she still useful?" Drexler asked Logan.

"Yes," Logan said. "I'll do whatever you want."

"So that's how that works," Nick said. "You come in, ruin people, and walk away with the spoils. Probably includes that little tart beside you. Wouldn't have been my first choice, but I suppose beggars can't be choosers."

Drexler turned toward Nick, incredulous.

"I don't think she's as virtuous as you think she is," Nick continued. "God, did she throw herself at me! Sad and desperate isn't really my thing, but I suppose after you, anything's a nice change."

"Watch it," Drexler growled.

"It's adorable that you think she actually likes you. I don't know if she's capable of caring about anyone but herself."

Katie stepped over to Nick and slapped him hard across the face. He just laughed, not slowing his tirade.

"Personally, I gotta respect a girl who takes advantage of *all* her attributes. Don't let society get in the way of sleeping your way to the bottom. I mean, you come across as a bit dirty and disease ridden, but I'm sure that appeals to some people."

Katie slapped him again.

"Come on, sweetheart. Is that the best you've got?" Nick asked.

Katie punched him and his chair tipped over. He fell to the ground and his fingers closed around the sharp piece of metal lying on the floor.

"Let me be the one to kill him," Katie said to Drexler.

"Be quick. The boat leaves in fifteen minutes."

Drexler grabbed Logan by the arm and propelled him up the stairs to his office.

"Evelyn!" Logan called out, struggling to her.

"We'll keep her alive," Drexler said. "For now."

Logan struggled to get free and Drexler drove his gun into his side.

"Don't make me change my mind." Drexler nodded at Dan O'Brien. "Bring Evelyn."

"With pleasure," O'Brien said. He had a score to settle.

It became a race between how quickly Nick could saw through the ropes, before Katie found her gun, or O'Brien reached Evelyn. Nick's fingers kept getting caught on the metal and his blood stained the fraying ropes. Katie located Evelyn's purse and pulled out the small Beretta. She checked the magazine, then turned toward Nick.

"Seems fitting that you're killed with her gun," Katie said as she took aim.

"I really hate women like you," Evelyn said to buy Nick more time.

"Because you're jealous," Katie replied.

"Of what? Your crippling insecurity? Your constant need for a man? Your inability to think for yourself? The war taught us that women can do anything men can. Often better. How pathetic that you'd spend your life trying to impress someone like Drexler."

"Drexler still needs you," Katie said. "Doesn't have to be in one piece."

"I mean, you're good enough for now, but the moment he finds someone younger or prettier . . ."

Katie glanced at James's body.

"Shut up!"

"I don't blame you for wanting something on the side," Evelyn said, glancing at Nick's progress on the rope. Only a few strands left. She raised her voice so it would carry across the factory floor. "Dan O'Brien's not that bad if you like thuggish and bland. Does Drexler know about you two?"

O'Brien slid a sideways glance toward Katie, confirming Evelyn's suspicions. Drexler paused on the stairs as Katie whipped around.

"It's not true. You know it's not true."

"We'll discuss it later," Drexler said.

"You bitch," Katie said, raising the gun again.

"Go ahead," Evelyn dared. "Oh, that's right. You can't do anything without his permission."

Katie turned to Nick as he snapped the last of his ropes, freeing himself from the chair. He lunged at Katie, knocking the gun from her grip. It skirted under a mechanic's cart. Dan O'Brien fired two shots at Nick, who grabbed Evelyn and dragged her behind a row of airplane seats. Quickly he untied her hands.

"My father," she said.

"On it," Nick replied.

He shoved the heavy mechanic's cart in O'Brien's direction and grabbed the gun from underneath. Nick pointed it toward Drexler, who held Logan close. Not sure of his aim, Nick shot wide. Logan took advantage of the distraction to break loose. While Nick kept Katie back with the few bullets left in the gun, O'Brien grabbed Evelyn around the waist. He picked her up, reducing her leverage to almost nothing. She fought fiercely, bending his thumb back and kicking futilely at his legs. He tossed her about like a rag doll. Logan snuck up from behind, his hands still tied, and grabbed an industrial wrench. Swinging it like an axe, he brought it down on O'Brien's shoulder. It knocked him to his knees. Evelyn fought free; then she and Logan swept back into the darkness. Nick joined them a moment later, while Evelyn cut the ropes around Logan's wrists. They were well hidden, crouched among a few of the plane's massive wheels.

"Find them!" Drexler roared.

Katie and O'Brien spread out through the factory.

"Daddy, you have to go," Evelyn said.

"Not without you," he replied.

"We can hold them off," Nick said. "Once they have you, it's over. They don't care about hostages anymore. They'll do whatever it takes to get your signature, and then they'll kill us all."

"I can withstand torture," Logan replied.

"It's not you they'll torture," Nick said, looking toward Evelyn. Logan went pale. "And I wouldn't blame you for cracking."

"You need to get out of here," Evelyn said. Logan opened his mouth to protest. "You have to trust me."

Reluctantly Logan nodded.

"Do they know about the house in Big Bear?" Evelyn asked.

"Not unless James told them."

Evelyn swore quietly under her breath. The betrayal and loss were too complicated to sort out at the moment.

"Do you remember the ice-cream shop in Oxnard? The one Mom loved?" Evelyn asked. Logan thought for a moment, then nodded. "We'll meet you there by morning."

"Promise you'll be safe."

"I promise," Evelyn said. "Now *go*."

Footsteps approached from behind.

"We'll lead them away," Nick said.

Evelyn offered her father a brief smile as he set out into the darkness of the factory that had been his life's work.

Chapter 45

Evelyn and Nick headed deeper into the factory to lead Katie and O'Brien away from Logan's escape route. The darkness was Evelyn's friend as they wove through the massive, unfinished hulls of airplanes, skeletal and haunting in the dim emergency lights. They instinctively fell into their old patrol pattern. Nick slightly behind Evelyn, reassuring in her peripheral vision. She liked the familiar feeling of him having her back.

"Nick," she whispered. "In London . . ."

It was a hard conversation to begin. She still remembered the anguished look on his face. His plea to leave before the meeting with General Gibson. The questions surrounding that horrible moment kept her up at night and broke her heart over and over again until she trained herself not to ask them anymore. In the days since Nick returned to her life, they came unbidden to her mind.

"Why did you blame me for Matthew's death?"

"It was never my intention," Nick said. "I found crates from Bishop Aeronautics when we blew the munitions dump. Gibson was on the hunt for traitors."

"All the signs made me look like one."

"The safest place was outside the OSS."

"We have a lot to discuss, don't we?" Evelyn said.

"God, I hope so," Nick replied.

Evelyn reached her hand back and Nick took her fingers, squeezing them briefly. They turned, hearing the creak of the unfinished floorboards in the hull of a nearby airplane. Evelyn motioned to the open side door over the wing. Quietly Nick climbed the grated rung of a rolling ladder, stepping tentatively onto the wing. Unlike Evelyn, he wasn't used to its gentle curve, nor the aerodynamic polished metal that gave little purchase. Evelyn climbed the stairs at the front door just behind the cockpit. Stepping into the hull, she found herself looking at the back of Katie Pierce, who peered out the front window. She had sought higher ground to search for them. Evelyn raised the butt of her gun to knock her out, but Katie ducked just in time. She wheeled around to face Evelyn.

"Shoulda just shot me," Katie said.

"Where's the fun in that?" Evelyn replied. "I'd much rather see you in prison."

"Or maybe you're out of bullets. Either way, it works out well. I'd rather not have you damage the merchandise."

"The day you and Drexler call this factory your own is the day I burn it to the ground."

"That's what I appreciate about you," Katie said. "Your optimism. The idea that Drexler is going to let you live is adorable."

"Those who live in glass houses shouldn't throw stones," Evelyn replied. "Drexler doesn't seem the sentimental type and I'm guessing you know a bit too much."

"You never did like me."

"Damn. And I tried so hard to hide it."

Katie lunged at Evelyn, who sidestepped the charge, grabbed Katie's arm and swung her back toward the cockpit. There was a quiet thud as Katie hit her head on the aeronautics console. Evelyn wrested the gun from Katie's grip, towering over the dazed girl.

"Stand up," Evelyn said, motioning with Katie's gun.

Slowly the girl found her feet, looking murderously at Evelyn.

"So, what next?" Katie asked.

"Something tells me the police might like a word."

"You take me in, I tell them everything about your father."

It gave Evelyn pause.

"Or have you changed your mind? Are you going to kill me now?"

"Tempting as that is," Evelyn said, "I'm not you."

From behind, she heard Nick enter the plane from the door over the wing.

"Didn't need me, after all," he said.

"Could use someone who's good with knots," Evelyn replied.

"You're never going to let me live that down, are you?" he asked.

"Probably not."

Nick approached them, but was tackled from behind. He struggled against his attacker, managing to break free. When he turned around, he found himself face to face with Dan O'Brien. Katie took advantage of the moment to shove Evelyn, bouncing her skull against the curved wall. Katie knocked her feet out from under her and kicked her in the ribs.

Nick landed a solid punch in the larger man's stomach. O'Brien gasped for breath and Nick countered with a left jab. Unfortunately, O'Brien was ready for it and hit Nick with a vicious blow that snapped his head back. The only good thing about O'Brien's size was that he telegraphed his punches. Nick managed to dodge the next one and O'Brien's fist collided with the unfinished hull. There was a dull ring and Nick hazarded a glance at Evelyn, who was still on the floor.

Katie leaned back to deliver another kick, but her ambitions were greater than her abilities. Evelyn grabbed Katie's foot and stood up. The momentum tipped Katie out the open door of the plane. Evelyn heard a crunch as Katie toppled down the hard aluminum stairs. Shakily Evelyn followed her, but when she looked, Katie was gone.

Evelyn hurried toward the middle of the plane as O'Brien threw Nick onto the wing. Their fighting left them intertwined, and though Evelyn had a gun, she couldn't be certain of hitting her intended target. Finally O'Brien broke free, sending Nick skidding across the wing. He landed hard on his shoulder and there was a low moan of pain. O'Brien advanced so he was standing over Nick, a brutal smile on his face.

"Stop!" Evelyn said, her gun pointing at O'Brien.

He turned at her words and Nick drove his heel into O'Brien's knee. With the sound of a branch snapping, his leg bent in the wrong direction and the big man fell. Nick scrambled over and wrapped his arm around O'Brien's throat, cutting off his air. He grabbed at Nick's arm, then tried for his face. Finally Nick found purchase and twisted O'Brien's head sharply to the left. There was a sickening crunch as Nick broke his neck. Nick released the body and it slid off the wing, falling in a heap on the floor below.

Nick looked up to see Evelyn watching him from the open door. She made her way over and sat down beside him. He wrapped his arms around her, holding her tightly.

"Damage report?" he asked.

Evelyn moved her hand over her ribs.

"Bruised. Hopefully, not broken."

Gently she touched his face, which had suffered the worst of O'Brien's aggression.

"Probably won't be pretty in the morning," Nick said.

"So . . . par for the course?"

Nick smiled, seeing through her teasing bravado.

"How are you really?"

Evelyn shook her head.

"It's all too much. My father. James. I can't process it yet."

"There'll be time later," Nick said. "Let's find Drexler and finish this."

They descended from the plane and swept the factory floor. They were about to leave when they heard Logan's voice cry out in the darkness.

"Let me go, you son of a bitch!"

Evelyn and Nick rushed toward the sound. They hurried outside just in time to see Drexler drag Logan up the gangplank of a cargo ship. Katie was close behind, giving orders to set off. Nick and Evelyn ran to the docks, but they were too late. The ship was already chugging out to sea.

"Once they're in international waters, it's all over," Evelyn said.

Nick looked around, but there were no other boats.

"We can call the coast guard," Nick said.

"They'll take too long," Evelyn replied.

"You have an idea, don't you?" Nick asked warily.

Evelyn nodded.

"I'm not going to like it, am I?"

Evelyn looked at him with a slight smile he knew too well.

"Do you ever?"

Chapter 46

Running the length of the factory was a private runway, where Evelyn learned to fly. At one end, a massive hangar lodged most of Logan's personal planes. There were over a dozen, many of which were collector items. Others were prototypes that Logan flew around the country when meeting with prospective clients. As a point of pride, he kept all of them airworthy. Evelyn selected one with a front propeller and a small cabin containing two seats. Nick looked at the tiny plane with skepticism.

"This is insane," Nick said.

"I've had worse plans."

"None that I can think of."

"We're still here, right?"

"Only by the grace of God."

As Evelyn made a quick preflight check, Nick called the coast guard to report a ship carrying contraband goods and war criminals. He gave the general direction and the location from which they left. The man on the other end of the line promised to check on it, but Nick wasn't convinced he had the proper impetus. International water was only twelve nautical miles from the dock and the ship had a sizeable head start. Hanging up, he dialed Carl at the police station.

"Where the hell have you been?" Carl demanded. "Wharton's looking everywhere for you and now Evelyn's disappeared, too."

"She's with me," Nick said, filling him in briefly on what transpired the past twenty-four hours.

"Jesus," Carl swore softly under his breath. "How much does Evelyn know?"

"Not everything. Not yet."

"At least now you can explain why . . ." Carl trailed off.

"I will, once we survive this. Right now, we need you to stop that ship before they reach international waters," Nick said.

"I know the commander out of Long Beach," Carl replied. "I'll light a fire under his ass. But it might be too late . . ."

"We're going to slow them down," Nick said.

"Should I even ask?"

"It's one of Evelyn's plans."

"Well, shit," Carl said. "Try to stay alive."

Nick hung up and turned to Evelyn, who handed him a parachute.

"Haven't seen one of these since the war," Nick said.

"I know how much you missed them."

Nick slid into the right-hand side of the cockpit. Evelyn ran her hand over the smooth exterior of the plane, bestowing upon it whatever magic she possessed. Then she climbed inside, secured the door, and took the pilot's seat. Checking the controls again, she pressed the shotgun starter. The first one didn't catch and she slid in another cartridge.

"Maybe it's a sign," Nick said.

Evelyn pressed the starter again and this time the engine rumbled to life as the front propeller began to turn.

"Last chance to turn back," Evelyn said. "I wouldn't blame you. In all honesty, this plan has almost no chance of working. We probably won't make it onto the boat, and if we do, the likelihood is that we're going to end up as fish food at the bottom of the ocean."

"There's nowhere I'd rather be than on a suicide mission with you."

Evelyn returned his smile and set the plane in motion. They taxied to the end of the runway. It was illuminated only by the lights from the hangar and the stars above, but Evelyn could take off with her eyes closed. In the same way she knew every inch of the factory and every piece in an engine, so, too, did she know this airfield. She opened the throttle and the plane gathered speed as it hurled down the runway. The wheels bounced against every crack in the pavement.

Nick's hands tightened on the edge of his seat.

"Don't worry," Evelyn said, watching him from the corner of her eye. "I learned to fly before I could drive."

"Yeah," Nick replied. "But I've seen you drive."

They picked up speed until the ground dropped out from under them. Evelyn kept the lights of the plane off, not wanting to announce their presence. Once she cleared the top of the factory, she banked left, rising over the dark water of the Pacific Ocean. The moon illuminated her path, its light reflecting unevenly over the choppy water.

"The boat was heading southwest," Evelyn said.

Nick scanned the water, looking for the ship. It was already several miles out when Nick caught sight. Evelyn climbed to 2,500 feet as Nick shrugged into his parachute.

"This is a much lower jump than we ever did during the war," Evelyn warned. "You'll have to pull the rip cord as soon as we're clear."

Nick nodded. Evelyn locked the controls and moved out of her seat. She stepped into the harness, securing the

parachute across her chest. They both checked the magazines of their guns to ensure they were loaded, then tucked
them securely into their pockets.

"Just like old times," Nick said.

Gently Evelyn rested her hand on his face, feeling its familiar contours. Then she opened the hatch of the plane.
The cold night air rushed inside. Usually, they had jump-
suits, goggles, and a helmet. Their civilian clothes were little protection against the elements.

"You ready?" Nick asked.

"In three. Two . . ."

Nick grabbed her hand and they jumped together.

The moment they cleared the plane's draft, they pulled
their chutes. Evelyn and Nick drifted quietly until the boat
lay just below them. The ripple of the parachute silk was
masked by the roar of the ship's engines. They managed to
drop onto the deck unnoticed. Quickly they gathered their
chutes and stowed them under the tarp of a nearby life-
boat.

"Engine room is belowdecks, toward the rear," Evelyn
said.

Chapter 47

Nick and Evelyn prowled through the ship. The deck was filled with crewmen securing their cargo. The atmosphere spoke of a hasty departure. Evelyn opened a door that led down a whitewashed hall. It lacked any decoration, but beneath the paint was the faint outline of a bald eagle sitting atop an anchor. Many of the navy ships were decommissioned or sold off after the end of the war. Drexler must have picked this one up for a song. Evelyn had the advantage over Nick. When she returned from Europe in 1946, she caught a ride on a Liberty ship headed stateside for the last time. Bored, restless, and unable to sleep, she roamed around at all hours, learning every inch of it.

They quickly located the engine room. A three-man crew sweltered as they pushed the boilers to full steam. The chief looked at Evelyn with confusion.

"You can't be down here, miss."

"Really sorry, fellas, but we need you to stop the ship."

The chief looked to the other men incredulously. They weren't sure if it was a joke. Then Nick and Evelyn drew their guns.

"I wish there was a nicer way to do this," Evelyn said.

"Way I see it, you either stop the ship for us, or we shoot you and stop it ourselves," Nick added.

The crew appeared to be former navy, right down to the tattoos on their biceps. However, this work wasn't for God and country. It was for a strange businessman who spoke with a German accent.

"Is it really worth it?" Evelyn asked.

"Not for the shit they're paying," the chief finally admitted.

He reached over and pulled the lever to FULL STOP. The motor shut down as the turbines ground to a halt.

"No way Drexler didn't feel that," Evelyn said.

"We've got three minutes, tops."

"How do we disable this thing without killing anyone?"

The chief looked pained at the question.

"We'll be dead in the water."

"Coast guard's on the way," Nick replied.

The chief shook his head. Shutting down was one thing. Damaging his precious ship was a whole other. Evelyn looked over the dials. There were wires running from behind the control wheel.

"Do these go to the propeller?"

Reluctantly the chief nodded. Nick grabbed them and gave them a hefty yank. They were well bolted into the ship. They only had another minute or so before someone arrived to investigate their sudden stop. Evelyn pulled her gun, intending to shoot the wires.

"Don't!" the chief cried. "You could break a hole in the turbine and send us all to Hell."

Reluctantly he fished out a pair of bolt cutters and handed them to Nick. He turned away as the connection was irrevocably severed. The chief looked to Nick.

"Will you at least make it look like a struggle?"

"You sure?"

The chief nodded. Nick hit him with a hard right cross.

"Should give you a nice shiner."

Evelyn quickly tied up the crew, securing the ropes against a pillar.

"I know it doesn't seem like it, but we're the good guys," she said. "There was an older man brought on board by Drexler. Dressed in shirtsleeves. Probably handcuffed. Do you know where they're keeping him?"

"Haven't seen anyone, but best guess is the captain's quarters in the forecastle or down in the cargo hold."

"Thank you."

Evelyn and Nick hurried out of the engine room as footsteps approached. They reached the stairs at the front of the boat and climbed toward the crew quarters. Small cabins occupied both port and starboard side.

"Let's split up. It'll go faster," Evelyn said. Opening doors, they found empty cabins, supply closets, and a mess hall. Nick continued on, testing each handle until he reached one that was locked. Having finished her search, Evelyn found Nick looking for some way to break into the room. Evelyn pulled two bobby pins from the bedraggled mess of her hair and handed them to Nick.

"You're better at it," he admitted.

"Wow," Evelyn replied. "That's a first."

She slid the pins into the lock. It was unfamiliar and took several tries before the tumblers fell into place. They opened the door to reveal the captain's quarters. There was no sign of Logan, but they searched for anything that might prove useful. Opening the desk drawer, Evelyn discovered two copies of the ship's manifest. The first was the official one stamped by U.S. Customs. The other revealed the true contents. Evelyn handed them to Nick, who tucked them into his jacket.

Heavy footsteps rushed down the hall outside. They waited until the coast was clear; then they headed to the front stairwell. Descending three levels, they found a large door leading into the cavernous cargo hold. It was filled with a maze of crates stamped BISHOP AERONAUTICS, PALMER MUNITIONS, and WILDER ARTILLERY. Drexler had twisted these men's life work into treason. In the center, casting a long shadow under the only light, sat Logan, his hands bound behind the back of the chair, his mouth gagged with a filthy rag.

"Daddy!" Evelyn cried. She rushed to her father, pulling the cloth from his mouth.

"What are you doing here, Evie?" he asked, his voice anguished. "I thought you were safe."

"We will be," she said as she jimmied open the lock on the handcuffs. "As soon as we get off this ship."

Nick helped Logan to his feet. They turned toward the doorway to see Drexler and Katie Pierce blocking their path.

Chapter 48

"I'm a huge fan of persistence," Drexler said to Evelyn. "But yours borders on insanity."

Drexler and Katie raised their guns. Evelyn grabbed her father and ducked behind a row of crates. Nick was close on their heels.

"We should split up," Nick said. "I'll take Drexler. You two handle Katie Pierce."

"No," Logan said. "Drexler is mine."

Evelyn glanced at her father. There was an intensity on his face that worried her, but she did not have time to dwell on it.

"Don't get dead," Evelyn said to Nick.

"Back at ya," he replied, pulling the gun from his pocket.

As Nick made his way deeper into the cargo hold, the shadows blended together into complete darkness. He heard the subtle sound of a woman in heels trying to step quietly. Nick flattened himself against the side of a shipping container and waited, his gun raised. Her perfume told him this was Katie. He didn't know her scent particularly well, he just knew it wasn't Evelyn's. She came closer and closer, until he could hear her breath; then he fired his gun. In the darkness, he was acting on instinct alone. It was impossible to tell her exact location. The splinter of wood told him his aim was off. She fired two shots at him. One pinged off the steel behind him. The other found its mark, lodging deep in his shoulder. He stifled a moan of pain, but it was enough. She fired again. This one he ducked, lunging at her and grabbing her around her waist. She struggled to get away, but he held fast, despite the agony in his shoulder. They were fighting blind, but she managed to find the hole of the bullet wound and drove her fingers into it. The pain caused white flashes to pass through his brain as he fought to remain conscious. She used her advantage to break free and disappear down another row. Nick didn't need to beat Katie, he only had to give Evelyn enough time to find Drexler.

Across the cargo hold, Evelyn heard the sound of gunshots and felt a rush of panic. This could take all night.

"We need to draw Drexler out," Evelyn said to her father. "I'll get him talking while you circle around behind."

She stepped out into the center of the cavernous cargo hold.

"Drexler," she called out, her voice echoing through the maze.

She was exposed, gambling on his arrogance. Plus, until he had Logan's signature, he still needed her alive. Theoretically. These were not odds Evelyn preferred to play, but sometimes going all in on a crappy hand was the only option.

"Miss Bishop," he began, his voice silky, assured and shrouded in darkness. "Do be a dear and drop your weapon."

Evelyn held up her hands to show she had none.

"That's awfully brave, stupid, and not at all like you. Empty your pockets, raise your shirt, and turn around."

Evelyn withdrew the gun from her waistband. Drexler was still hidden and she could not get a fix on his location.

"Toss it under the crates."

Reluctantly she did.

"You're not going to shoot me," Evelyn said.

"You said that to me once before."

"And it was true then, too. I still have something you need."

"I admire your confidence."

"We can find a solution to our situation. You want my father's company. All I care about is returning home, safe, with you out of our lives."

"Then have him sign the papers," Drexler said. "This will all be over."

"Unfortunately, I'm not the most trusting of people. When you say it will be over, I feel like that means we'll end up at the bottom of the ocean. An outcome I'd prefer to avoid. Plus, there's the issue of money."

A laugh came from the darkness.

"You can be bought?"

"A comfortable retirement for my father and enough not to raise questions among those who monitor the transfer of ownership."

"Perhaps we could come to an arrangement," Drexler said.

"We'd need a guarantee," Evelyn said. "Some form of mutually assured destruction."

Finally Evelyn saw the outline of Drexler. Behind him was Logan, crowbar in hand.

"This is a good plan," he said. "Especially the part where you get me to talk this long."

Drexler spun around toward Logan and fired his gun. Logan dropped beneath the arc of the bullet and swung the crowbar at Drexler. It connected with a glancing blow. On the second swing, Drexler grabbed the descending iron and wrestled it from Logan's grasp. He brought the crowbar down on Logan's back with brutal force. Evelyn ran at Drexler from the side, grabbing his arm and breaking his hold on the iron and sending it clattering to the floor. He struck Evelyn with an elbow to her temple. Logan, utterly relentless, charged Drexler again, but this time Drexler was ready for him. He stepped sideways, catching Logan with a fist to his kidneys. Logan paused momentarily to fight the pain. Drexler used it to his advantage, flattening Logan with a series of punches. Evelyn picked herself up and returned to the fray, her nails scratching Drexler's face. Her other arm wrapped around his throat. Drexler attempted to shake her off, but Evelyn held tight. He backed into a crate, knocking the breath from her chest. Still, she held on. Drexler slammed her backward again. The third time, he cracked her head against the corner of a box. Pain radiated through her skull, blurring her vision. Evelyn's grip loosened and she slid to the floor, fighting for consciousness.

"Stay the fuck away from my daughter!" Logan roared, having found the discarded crowbar.

This time, it connected with the side of Drexler's head, knocking him to his knees. Logan hit him again as he fell. Drexler raised his gun, but Logan swung the crowbar again, smashing Drexler's hand. Logan continued hitting him, hearing nothing, seeing nothing, but his own blind rage. Drexler's blood spilled across the steel floor of the cargo hold. Evelyn heard the soft crunch of his ribs fracturing as he fell to his side, barely breathing.

"Daddy, stop!" Evelyn cried. "It's enough."

Logan looked down at the bloody mess. Then he called out into the darkness.

"Miss Pierce, if you wish to see Drexler alive, come out now!"

There was a long pause.

"I'm only asking once," Logan said.

He picked up Drexler's discarded gun and pulled back the hammer. The sound echoed in the silence.

"Don't hurt him," Katie said, appearing from the maze of shipping crates.

Evelyn stepped in front of her, blocking her view of Drexler.

"Gun. Now," Evelyn said.

Reluctantly Katie slid it across the floor. Evelyn picked it up, then motioned to the chair that once held Logan. As Katie walked, she looked down to see Drexler's bloody, broken form.

"What did you do to him?" she asked, tears in her voice.

"What he would have done to us," Evelyn said.

Quickly she tied Katie's hands and legs. Nick stumbled from the darkness, his face pale and drawn. The bullet wound in his left shoulder bled through his shirt and jacket, staining them so dark it was almost black.

"Nick!" Evelyn exclaimed, rushing to him.

"Just a scratch," he said.

"Awful lot of blood for a scratch," Evelyn said, gently pulling off his jacket, then peeling the fabric of his shirt back from the wound. He grimaced.

"How bad?"

"You'll be fine," she said, her voice shaking.

"I know I'm in trouble when you start lying."

She reached for Nick's good sleeve and ripped it off. Twisting it, she made a tourniquet and wrapped it around the wound.

"Ow," Nick said as she tightened it. Already the blood stained crimson flowers across it.

"Do you want me to be nice, or do you want to keep the arm?" Evelyn asked as the blood slowed to a trickle, and she helped him to his feet.

"Evie," Nick said, a warning in his voice.

Evelyn followed his gaze, to see her father standing over Drexler, the gun still in his hand. He hadn't moved during the time she tied up Katie Pierce and tended to Nick.

"Daddy?"

Logan glared down, as though he hadn't heard Evelyn. He wasn't aware of anything but the man at his feet. Drexler looked up at Logan and managed a smug smile.

"So, now what?" he asked. "You turn me in? Expose Wahlstatt and admit to being a traitor."

Logan's expression didn't change. Evelyn, who knew her father better than anyone in the world, saw a stranger. His eyes carried the warning signs of having been pushed too far, too long.

"Give me the gun," she said, reaching out her hand.

She was afraid to touch him and break the spell that held him in check. Unaware, Drexler continued speaking. It wasn't a plea for mercy. Like everything else in his life, he saw it as a negotiation. One whose terms could be altered at a later date. He thought he understood Logan as a man whose moral code would not allow him to kill someone.

"Let's put this behind us," Drexler said. "I'll up your percentage. Hell, you can be a full partner, now that we have Palmer's and Wilder's companies. You'll be a rich man."

"I'm already a rich man," Logan said.

"Daddy, please," Evelyn said.

"You ruined George Palmer, a man I respected," Logan said. "You corrupted James, a man I trusted. You threatened my daughter. And you killed my son."

Logan pulled the trigger. The bullet blew out the back of Drexler's head as Katie screamed. Drexler's body slumped to the floor. Evelyn stared in shock. Logan looked to Evelyn as he dropped the gun.

"I had to, Evie."

"I know."

Chapter 49

Leaving Katie tied up in the cargo hold, Evelyn, Nick, and Logan slowly and painfully made their way up the stairs. Logan was quiet. This was the first time he had killed a man. He did not regret his action, yet he also did not feel any relief at avenging his son. Instead, there was a deep numbness he didn't know how to process. The reality of Drexler's death would hit him at some point, but for now, his mind existed in limbo, unable to move forward or back.

Beside Evelyn, Nick had his left arm tied to his chest in a makeshift sling. Each step jolted his wound and he gritted his teeth against crying out. He had lost a lot of blood and staying upright was a challenge. Their climb might as well have been Everest.

"We're almost there," Evelyn said as they rounded the last flight.

On the main deck, the crew milled about, uncertain what to do with the ship dead in the water. Evelyn, Nick, and Logan sat down, awaiting rescue. It was almost an hour before the first of the LAPD and coast guard climbed over the side. Carl spotted them immediately.

"Can you get us off this thing?" Evelyn asked.

"What am I going to find belowdecks?"

"Oh, your basic disaster," Nick said.

"Why am I not surprised?" Carl replied.

Carl glanced toward Logan, who still hadn't said a word. Then he looked toward the other members of the LAPD.

"These guys are gonna want to talk to you," he said.

Evelyn pulled the dual shipping manifests from Nick's jacket. They were stained with blood, but the writing was still legible.

"This should keep them busy for a while. Nick needs a hospital."

Carl's LAPD boat was anchored below, but Nick was in no shape to climb down the ladder. A life raft hung near the edge. They got into it and lowered it to the water. Evelyn released the cables tying it to the ship, rowed to Carl's boat, and helped Nick on board. He lay across the back bench with his head cushioned in her lap. Logan sat beside them, an unreadable expression on his face. Carl turned the key and the engine rumbled to life. Pulling away, they sped across the dark waves toward land.

"What happens next?" Logan asked finally.

Evelyn glanced at Carl, who turned at the question.

"Can you put us in at Bishop Aeronautics?" Evelyn asked Carl.

"Evie," Carl said, "he's a traitor."

"I know," she replied. "But he's also my father."

Carl thought for a long moment. After all the suffering they saw during the war, he hated everyone who would sacrifice others for his own needs. He believed in punishment as a deterrent, yet he also knew Logan Bishop would never be in a place to harm his country again. If it was anyone other than Evelyn, he would have made a different decision. Turning the boat slightly, Carl headed to the factory. When they reached the docks, Evelyn hugged him.

"Thank you," she said.

"I still have questions," Carl replied.

"What hospital are you taking Nick to?" she asked.

"The one in San Pedro."

"I'll meet you there. And you . . ." she said to Nick. "Don't you get into any trouble while I'm gone."

"No promises."

Logan knelt down beside Nick.

"I'd ask you to take care of Evie, but it's pretty clear she can take care of herself," Logan said.

"That, she can."

"Then make her happy," Logan said. "It's all I've ever wanted."

"I will," Nick promised.

Logan followed Evelyn onto the dock. Carl put the boat in reverse and headed toward Terminal Island, where an ambulance awaited Nick. Evelyn turned to her father.

"How much money do you have in the safe?"

"A couple thousand dollars."

"It's not a lot, but it should get you started. I'll get you more when I can . . . assuming they don't freeze my accounts."

"Where am I going?"

"Wherever you want. Cuba? Switzerland? Australia? Take a plane and disappear."

"Evie, I betrayed my country. I *should* go to jail," Logan said.

"What would that serve?" Evelyn asked. "It won't bring Matthew back, nor any of the other soldiers who were killed."

"Can you forgive me?"

Evelyn did not know the answer to that question. Logan's actions caused the deaths of innocent people. Her heart ached for their families in the same way that it ached every time she thought of Matthew. Logan's treason was a fact she would never be able to forget, yet she also did not have the energy to carry so much anger. Her father was still the man who raised her with enough love to carry her through the darkest days. He was still the only family she had left.

"I wish we had more time," Evelyn said. "We should've been honest with each other from the beginning."

"I wish I'd been braver. I wish I'd been more like you."

Their relationship would never be the same. Logan was no longer an untouchable paragon of strength and honor. Instead, he was human, subject to the same fear and uncertainty as everyone else. For the first time, Evelyn saw her father as an equal, rather than the man who would always protect her. It made her unbearably lonely. She put her arm around him and led him inside.

On the main floor, James's body lay where it had fallen. Gently she touched his face, then covered him with a canvas tarp.

"I never suspected," Logan said. "He was such a good friend to you and Matthew. Maybe that blinded me to his true intentions."

"He was caught up in the same web," Evelyn said.

There would be an inquiry later, but for now, she had to keep moving before grief consumed her. They headed upstairs and Evelyn was startled to realize that her father was no longer young. She wasn't sure if it had been a gradual progression, or if it had happened all at once over the past week. In his office, Logan opened the safe and pulled out several stacks of cash. He put it into his navigator's bag, then grabbed his old leather bomber jacket off the coatrack. Though he always dressed in a suit to come to the office, his jacket was a remnant from his barnstorming days. Putting it on made him feel like anything was possible. Life had gone so terribly wrong. Maybe now, from a distance, he could find a way to make amends.

"I'm leaving you a mess," Logan said.

"I've had worse."

"If you need me, I'll be back in an instant. If I hear of any blame coming down on you, I'll return to set them straight."

"I know, Daddy."

"I'm gonna miss the hell out of you," he said.

Then he reached into the safe and handed her an envelope. She tore open the seal and scanned the pages. It was a transfer of ownership of Bishop Aeronautics, dated the day after George Palmer's death.

"You were right. You were never meant to be a socialite. You were meant to change the world," Logan said. "I always dreamed of Matthew taking over. After he was gone, I couldn't quite let go of that image. George's death woke me up to the fact that I needed to make a plan. You're the obvious choice. I know you think I only see you as my little girl, but the truth is, I'm in awe of your strength and humbled by your brilliance. The company's in good hands."

Evelyn walked into Logan's arms and he held her for a long moment. Realizing this was goodbye made it almost impossible to let go. When they stepped apart, both had tears glimmering in their eyes. Evelyn set the ownership papers back in the safe and closed the door. She and Logan headed out to the hangars. At the threshold of the factory, Logan turned and looked back into the dark, cavernous space. He had built all of this from scratch. Every girder, every tool, every single part within these four walls, he selected. Letting go was harder than he ever imagined. Then he looked to Evelyn. She, even more than this place, was the culmination of his life's purpose.

"It's yours now," Logan said.

"I'll take care of it," she promised.

With that, he turned his back on all he had built and headed out to involuntary exile. They walked to the airplane in silence. Logan set his bag inside and began his pre-flight check. Evelyn watched, realizing her father had the same habit of running his hand along the body of the plane and talking softly to it. They both treated the machines like they were more than just metal and wires. To them, they were living, breathing creatures that would hold them safe. When he finished, Logan looked to Evelyn.

"Love you, Daddy."

"I love you, too."

He gave her one final hug, her face pressed against his shoulder. Then Logan climbed the stairs into the cockpit. He closed the door behind him and the plane roared to life. Slowly it taxied onto the runway. The engines revved, building power, before barreling down the long asphalt strip. Evelyn raised her arm in a final salute as the wheels left the ground. It climbed higher and higher into the night sky, until finally its lights disappeared into the darkness.

Chapter 50

The taxi dropped Evelyn off in front of the hospital in San Pedro. The sky was turning from black to the deep indigo that precedes dawn. Evelyn was utterly exhausted. The weight of the past two days pressed down upon her. By now, she should be familiar with the numbness that came from shock, but it always felt unique. She wanted to surrender to tears, but those would come later. Instead, she put one foot in front of the other and propelled herself inside.

Carl dozed in a wooden chair in the waiting room. An empty cup of coffee sat forgotten on a nearby table. Gently Evelyn shook his shoulder and his eyes popped open, suddenly alert. It was a leftover reflex from the war and Evelyn felt strangely reassured to know she was not the only one still affected. Carl looked around, confused, but then he recognized the pale green walls of reception.

"How is he?" Evelyn asked.

"Lost a lot of blood, but they're giving him a transfusion and patching up the shoulder."

Carl twisted his watch and looked down at it.

"He's probably in a room by now."

"Thanks for coming tonight," Evelyn said.

"You know I always will."

Evelyn nodded.

"At some point, we need to talk about your father, George Palmer, Sam Wilder . . ." Carl said. "And we'll have to do it with Captain Wharton."

"Can it wait until after I've slept?"

"Yes," Carl replied. "When you're asked, which you will be, you and your father were long gone by the time the coast guard got to the ship."

"You're a good man, Carl Santos."

"I try," he replied, giving her a hug.

Then Carl gathered his coat and headed out the front door. Evelyn went to the registration desk and asked for Nick's room number.

"Are you family?" the woman asked.

"Yes."

The room was mostly dark, other than a small call light on the wall. Nick's shoulder was bandaged in clean white gauze and strapped to his chest. In his other arm, an IV trickled saline into his veins. Careful not to dislodge any wires, Evelyn kicked off her shoes and crawled into bed beside him. Without waking, he moved slightly to make room, and she fell asleep instantly.

A few hours later, a nurse threw open the curtains, flooding the room with California sunshine. Evelyn groaned as her eyes blinked open. She found herself wrapped around Nick. The places where he ended and she began were indistinguishable.

"Morning," he said with a smile.

"Morning."

"This is highly irregular," the nurse said brusquely. "These aren't even visiting hours. How did you get in here?"

"Magic," Evelyn said as she climbed out of Nick's bed.

"Well, you have to go," she said.

Evelyn turned to face the nurse. Even with her hair in knots and her makeup long gone, Evelyn was a commanding presence. To Nick, the fact that she was standing there felt nothing short of a miracle.

"No," Evelyn replied.

That one simple word threw the nurse into confusion. She was used to having her authority obeyed without question.

"This is highly irregular," she mumbled again.

Evelyn stood by the window, gazing out at the city while the nurse changed Nick's bandages. Young women in swaying skirts and high heels strode to work. Their sunglasses fought the glare and their purses perched across their forearms. Sharing the sidewalk were businessmen in suits, hats shading their faces. Some lumbered out of Packards. Some were thin and spry, filled with enthusiasm. The normalcy of the day felt surreal.

Evelyn looked back to Nick as the nurse hung a new saline bag, gave him a shot of morphine, and promised to return with breakfast. One breakfast, she clarified for Evelyn's benefit. Then she huffed out of the room, leaving them alone.

"How are you feeling?" Evelyn asked as she pulled a chair up beside Nick's bed.

"Better, now that you're here."

She took his hand and entwined her fingers with his.

"You promised me answers," she said. "No more secrets between us."

"No more secrets," Nick said, tightening his fingers around hers. "It was the mission in Northern France."

"The one with Matthew . . . ?"

"You were in the office with Drexler while Jean and I rigged the munitions dump with explosives," Nick said. "There were several crates from Bishop Aeronautics. I didn't know what to think. Maybe they were hijacked. Maybe a midlevel soldier was purposefully misrouting them. Maybe your father was involved. All I knew was that I couldn't let you find out."

"Matthew must have known," Evelyn said. "His last words were to tell Dad he wasn't worth it."

"After you lost your brother, I didn't want you to lose your father," Nick said. "I had no idea about the extent of Logan's involvement, but I couldn't take that chance. It would have broken you."

Evelyn tilted her head, acknowledging the truth of that statement.

"At the time, I thought you'd never need to know. But when the war ended, you wanted to stay in the OSS."

"You didn't."

"Berlin or Russia wouldn't be my first choice of places to live, but for me, it was always enough just to be with you."

"So, what happened?"

"General Gibson," Nick said. "He wasn't going to send us to any of those places. Instead, he wanted us to root out black-market profiteers. Traitors."

"People like my father . . ."

"I was afraid. During the war, we had so much access. We were behind the lines, we could get to enemy commanders, even to the upper levels in our own government. If it turned out your father was guilty, I worried they'd see you as a collaborator. You'd be executed for treason."

"So you chose the one thing that would make me leave," Evelyn said. "Being blamed for Matthew's death."

"I wanted you to come away with me. If only we'd never walked into that meeting."

"You were trying to protect me," she said. "And I didn't believe you."

"No. You didn't."

Nick's statement hung between them.

"You must have hated me," Evelyn said.

"Sometimes," Nick admitted. "Sometimes I was so angry I couldn't see straight. Sometimes I wanted to tell you the truth and defend myself. Sometimes it just felt so unfair. When I saw you again, whole, seemingly happy, I knew I'd made the right decision."

"I don't think I was ever whole without you," she said. "I still love you."

"And I never stopped loving you."

Evelyn leaned over Nick's bed and kissed him. Despite everything that happened, despite all she had to face on the horizon, she knew, for the first time in three years, it would be all right.

Chapter 51

James's funeral took place on a warm, sunny day that felt incongruous with such a solemn occasion. The church was half-filled, with James's sobbing parents in the front pew. His mother clung to Evelyn's hand like a life raft, just barely staying afloat. His father, a stoic man, ducked his head so no one would see him cry. Nick sat near the back, reassuring in his presence, but not close enough to flaunt their relationship in front of two people who once believed they would call Evelyn their daughter.

James was laid to rest on a grassy hill overlooking the dry basin of the Los Angeles River. The cemetery was lush and green, with flowers dotting many of the headstones. The mahogany coffin was lowered into the earth as the priest read from Scriptures. Afterward, James's parents made their way to the waiting car. Evelyn stood by the grave, trying to figure out how to say goodbye. Even though she didn't want to marry James, she did love him. He brought her back to life after the heartbreak of war and she would be forever grateful to him. With James and Matthew dead, and her father beyond her reach, Evelyn felt like her childhood memories were fading into shadows.

*   *   *

Several weeks later, Carl walked into the president's office at Bishop Aeronautics to find Evelyn sitting behind her father's desk. She wore a blouse, with the sleeves rolled above her elbows. Her suit jacket was tossed carelessly over the back of a chair. She smiled at him before turning back to the contracts in front of her. Carefully she read each one, then signed in triplicate. She handed them to Ruth, Logan's longtime secretary.

"Tell Robert Six at Continental we'll have their first shipment two weeks ahead of schedule. Get me a meeting with LaMotte Cohu at TWA as soon as possible. Also, one with Juan Trippe over at Pan Am," she said to Ruth, who took notes on her steno pad. "They're expanding at an exponential rate and I want to remind them that we're their best choice."

"Anything else?" Ruth asked.

"While I'm on the East Coast, I want to meet with Benjamin Franklin Fairless at U.S. Steel. We're paying too much. Hell, get me a meeting with all my father's suppliers . . . and their competitors," Evelyn said.

"You really are Logan's daughter," Ruth replied.

"Not everyone thinks that's a good thing," Evelyn said wryly to Carl. "A few of the men didn't like answering to a . . . What was the word they used, Ruth?"

"Oh, no," she demurred. "I don't think that needs to be repeated."

"I've been called worse." Evelyn shrugged. "I fired them. The women who worked here during the war already knew the job. No training necessary."

"How'd that go over?" Carl asked.

"We pay better than anywhere else. If they don't want to be here, that's fine. I've had no trouble finding skilled workers. Plus, productivity's up fifteen percent."

"Your father would be proud," Ruth said as she swept up the signed papers and left.

"This office suits you," Carl said.

"I'm exhausted," Evelyn confessed. "I know it's going to get easier, but it's a steep learning curve."

"Never known you to fail, once you put your mind to a thing."

"Tell me you come with good news," Evelyn said.

"Good enough," Carl replied. "They're not pressing charges. After my testimony, yours, Nick's, and General Gibson's, they determined you had no idea of your father's actions during the war."

Evelyn let out a sigh. She hadn't realized how worried she was until that exact moment. Since her father's disappearance, she grew to love running Bishop Aeronautics. All that time she and Matthew spent playing in her father's office or hiding among the half-built planes, she learned more than she realized. She inherently understood how the factory worked, each part in harmony with the other. This place was her childhood and her future. More than anything, it was home.

"What did they decide about my father?" Evelyn asked.

"It's no longer his business. With him out of the country, he doesn't threaten the safety and stability of the United States, so they're not going to pursue him. I think their exact words were 'It wasn't worth the allocation of resources.'"

"Plus the scandal," Evelyn said. The military did not want it known that three of their largest suppliers had been traitors.

"That too," Carl conceded.

"Did you hear what Colette is doing with Palmer Munitions?" Evelyn asked.

Carl shook his head no.

"Said she didn't want to keep profiting off other people's misery. So she and Sean Macintyre are retrofitting the factory to make kitchen appliances. According to her, weapons have no place in this new world."

"How I wish that were true," Carl replied.

"Maybe this time will be different," Evelyn said without much hope in her voice.

"Well, I'm going to be in the thick of it," Carl said as he opened his jacket and pulled out a shiny new badge. "FBI made me an offer."

"In DC?" Evelyn asked, her heart sinking.

"Give up the sunshine? Are you kidding? They put me in their Southern California office. Plus, you know Nick would get into too much trouble without me."

"That goes without saying," she laughed. "You should come over for dinner soon."

Carl looked less than enthusiastic. "I've had your cooking."

"If you can believe it, Nick Gallagher is actually kind of domestic."

"Now that is something I have to see," Carl replied, promising he would stop by soon. He gave her a warm hug, then headed down the stairs. Evelyn watched him go. Across the factory floor, the hum of the machines was reassuring and ever present.

Evelyn worked until long after dark. She returned home to find Nick in the kitchen.

"Something smells good," she said, giving him a kiss.

After he got out of the hospital, Nick planned to stay at Evelyn's house, recovering, for a few days. Those days had turned into weeks, then a month, and then more. At first, Evelyn's neighbors were scandalized by a man living there, especially with Logan gone. She couldn't care less for the judgment of those who spied from their front windows. Nick, however, thought about her reputation, believing it was something she might need one day. He intentionally ran into the gossiping women while they walked their dogs and hinted that he was Evelyn's new security guard. After Logan's disappearance, she couldn't be too careful. The news quickly spread among the ladies who lunched and Evelyn remained welcome in their circles.

At a certain point, Nick stopped by his apartment to pick up the rest of his clothes and his meager possessions. The place looked even smaller and shabbier than he remembered and he was happy to give up his lease. He soon found work calling to him again. After his and Evelyn's success with Wahlstatt, he suddenly had more clients than he could handle. He took over Evelyn's office on Rodeo Drive, and for the first time, he chose only the cases he wanted.

Nick opened the oven and pulled out a perfectly roasted chicken, basted with rosemary and lemons. Crackling garlic potatoes came next.

"Wow," Evelyn said. "It's like magic."

"Says the woman who thinks cheese and crackers are a perfectly acceptable dinner."

"They're not?" she asked.

"No."

"Even if I pair them with wine?"

"Still no."

"Well, I have other skills."

"That, you do," Nick said with a smile.

As they ate, Evelyn told him about work and Carl's visit. Nick, in turn, told her about his new case. He liked getting her opinion on things. It helped him see beyond the surface. She asked questions he would not have considered and analyzed people's motivations on a deep level. Nick watched her, a smile curving his lips. Everything he ever wanted was sitting across the table from him. He took Evelyn's hand and led her into the living room. Turning on the record player, there was a moment of soft static before music poured from the speakers. It was their song. Nick held his hand out to Evelyn.

"Dance with me?"

She stepped into his arms, leaning her head against his shoulder.

"Once upon a time, I had a plan," he said.

"Gotta love a good plan."

"Drinks at the Savoy, a hotel room upstairs, with champagne chilling," Nick said. "It got all kinds of messed up."

"That does happen."

"Maybe simple is better."

Nick pulled out a small velvet box.

"I've been carrying this around with me for the past four years."

He opened it to reveal a slender gold band with a tiny diamond.

"You gonna say the words?" Evelyn asked.

"Do I have to?"

"Yes, Nick Gallagher. You have to."

He took Evelyn's hand and got down on one knee.

"You are the best part of my life. The thing that makes it worth living. God knows I'm not perfect. Or easy to live with. I expect we'll have some epic quarrels. The one thing I know is that I don't ever want to lose you. So, Evelyn Bishop, in the name of making it official, will you marry me?"

This time, there was no hesitation.

"Yes."

He slid the ring onto her hand and kissed her. They stood in her living room, dancing slowly. The ghosts that haunted them both were temporarily vanquished. They had a fresh start and the rest of their lives to spend together. The future stretched out, filled with possibility.

Author's Note

This story started with a simple question: Who would my grandmother have been if she was allowed to choose her own path in life?

I was very close with my grandmother. She was well read, taught me to play cards, and had a wicked sense of humor. However, she could also be a challenging person. Gram was born in 1917 and grew up wanting to be a nurse. Unfortunately, she came from a very strict family who believed a woman's place was in the home. Her parents insisted her only option was to become a wife and mother.

I believe my grandparents loved each other, but that does not mean Gram loved her life. She did everything that was expected of her, from raising six children, to baking bread and washing clothes, to hosting elaborate parties and furthering her husband's career. Yet, whenever she spoke of her past, it was with regret and disappointment for her unrealized dreams.

With Evelyn, I imagined something wildly different for my grandmother. Evelyn faces the same societal expectations; however, she has the freedom, family support, and financial stability my grandmother did not.

I set the story in Los Angeles because it is my home. I moved from New York in my early twenties, expecting to stay three months for an internship, then leave what I thought would be a shallow, soulless city. I've now lived here over twenty years.

Despite coming to the West Coast to work in the entertainment industry, I had not seen many old movies. That changed at a cemetery. During the summer, I would picnic with friends while watching classic films projected against the wall of a mausoleum. It was there that I first saw *The Big Sleep*, *Chinatown*, and *Rear Window*, among others. I loved that the suspense was not necessarily built around car chases or things exploding. The mystery drove the story, and in several of these films, Los Angeles played a starring role.

Many of the settings in this book are places I love, especially the Griffith Observatory, the Bradbury Building, and the Central Library downtown. With each, I felt a sense of magic the first time I set foot there. I also chose more mundane sites from my own experience. For example, Katie's apartment is based on where a friend lived for several years. Writing about these locations gave me a chance to explore them again with fresh eyes.

My grandmother was a huge inspiration to me. I've done my best to set her free and allow her to start over in Los Angeles. Hopefully, by reimagining Gram into Evelyn Bishop, she can also be inspiring to others.

Acknowledgments

A huge thank-you to my agent, Kathy Green. I'm grateful to you for taking a chance on me and your wonderful advice along the way. To John Scognamiglio and the incredible team at Kensington, thank you for making my words better and turning them into something the world can read.

Ezra Siegel, Dave Ihlenfeld, Jessica Stebbins Bina, and CeCe Pleasants Adams: You are amazing and gave me brilliant, thoughtful notes during the many, many drafts. Thank you for your time and your honesty. April Flores Gibbons, I appreciate all your help with the music. Alex Duben, thank you for holding my hand through this process.

Missy Stamler, Neda Laiteerapong, Tucker Hughes, Danielle Lindemann, and Sarah Rath: Thank you for keeping me sane. It was not an easy task. Leif Lillehaugen, your faith and encouragement kept me writing long after everyone, including myself, thought I should quit. I am indebted to you.

To my son's teachers, my work is only possible because of the kindness, intelligence, understanding, and patience you show every day with Akiva. He is in great hands and I am in awe of you.

To my mother, Lynn Steinberg, thank you for your endless love and support. To my father, Michael Steinberg, thank you for making me believe this was something I could do. I wouldn't be here without both of you . . . literally and figuratively.

And to Jason and Akiva, you are my home and my heart. I love you.

UNDER THE PAPER MOON

ABOUT THIS GUIDE

The suggested questions are included to enhance your
group's reading of Shaina Steinberg's
Under the Paper Moon!

1. What made you decide to read this book and has it met your expectations? Why or why not?

2. At the end of the war, Nick made a difficult decision that cost him his relationship with Evelyn. Do you think he made the right choice? At the end, when Evelyn fully understands Nick's reasons, do you think she believes he made the right choice? What would you have done in this situation?

3. During the story, Nick asks Evelyn to believe in him, even though he would not explain his actions. Despite loving him, it's something she finds difficult. Do you think she should have been able to believe Nick when he said he had her best interests at heart? Do you think Nick is justified in being angry at her lack of faith? When is it acceptable to keep the truth from someone?

4. In the story, Evelyn is in love with both Nick and James. They are two very different men, representing two very different parts of her life, her personality, and her potential future. Throughout the story, who were you rooting for her to choose and why? Have you ever been faced with this type of romantic choice? How did you make your decision?

5. Even before the war, Evelyn was a tomboy who never felt like she fit in among society. Who or what do you think was the largest influence on her choosing a path that was different from most women in the 1940s? What challenges do you think she faced in forging a new path? Have you ever felt confined by what was expected of you?

6. Evelyn uproots her life and goes to war to save her brother. How far would you go for someone you love? Have you ever been faced with having to go to an extreme for someone?

7. Sometimes the people Evelyn investigates are people she knows socially. Would you be comfortable looking into the personal lives of your friends and family? Why or why not? What line would you refuse to cross?

8. Evelyn came from a very close, loving family. Nick's family was terrible. How do you think this influenced their personalities and their relationships? How have you been shaped by your family of origin?

9. Everyone in this book is affected by the war in one way or another. How do the characters deal with everything they've gone through? Do you think it's possible to compartmentalize traumatic events?

10. Two characters made horrible trade-offs to save the people they love. Do you think their actions are justified? If not, what do you think they should have done, instead? Do you think they should be punished?

11. Evelyn ends the book by taking on a very large task. Do you think she will be successful at it? What in her life has prepared her for this new challenge? Have you ever faced something that felt overwhelming and how did you deal with it?

12. Film noir, especially detective stories set in the late 1940s, is a popular genre. How does this book pay homage to those movies and how is it different? How does Evelyn compare to the private investigators and how does she compare to other female leads?

13. The title of the book, *Under the Paper Moon*, refers to the song "It's Only a Paper Moon," which was popular in the 1930s, '40s, and '50s. In what ways

does the title have meaning beyond just being Nick and Evelyn's song?

14. How much do you think the cover of this book represents the story?

15. Where do you think Nick and Evelyn go from here?